ANTHOLOGY
YEAR TWO

INNER
DEMONS
OUT

Edited by JOhnny Morse

THE FOUR HORSEMEN PRESENT ...

ANTHOLOGY

YEAR TWO

INNER DEMONS OUT

First Edition

Copyright © 2013 The Four Horsemen
All Stories and Artwork © their Respective Creators
All Rights Reserved

ISBN 978-0-9858925-1-7

Editor: jOhnny Morse
Book design and Layout by Danny Evarts
Line Editors: Tim Deal, Mark Wholley, and jOhnny Morse

Cover based on a photograph by jOhnny Morse

www.anthocon.com

This volume is dedicated to Rick Hautala,
a generous soul who left us too soon but will live on forever
through his incredible body of work.

Rick and his wife Holly gave an amazing amount
of love and support to our little venture.

We are blessed.

Contents

INDEX OF ILLUSTRATIONS

ABOUT THE ARTISTS

DANNY EVARTS is a designer, illustrator, and editor of books and magazines. He lives with his partner in the Maine woods, mostly to avoid unruly mobs with pitchforks. Find more at *gallery.dannyevarts.net*.

SUSAN SCOFIELD is an artist currently based in York, PA. She studied Visual Arts at the University of California San Diego, earning a Bachelor of Arts Degree with an emphasis in photography.

CANDACE YOST is the Uber-Volunteer of Anthocon, avid cat lady, Falcor rider, and fiend of the written word.

IN YOUR HANDS YOU ARE HOLDING the Four Horesmen's second Anthology. If you are not already familiar with us, welcome. And for those of you that are familiar, welcome back. We really do appreciate your support, and without you we never would have been able to get this far.

As of this writing the four of us are busy preparing for AnthoCon 2013. It's hard to believe that AnthoCon is entering its "junior" year.

2013 was challenging to say the least, filled with highs and lows. One of the lows? Rick Hautala, to whom this tome is dedicated.

If anyone could be considered the patron saint of AnthoCon, it would be Rick. He was there from year one and very supportive of this whole undertaking. Sadly, Rick passed in March of this year and his loss is still being felt by the literary community. If you haven't yet had the enjoyment of reading one of Rick's stories, I would suggest taking some time to pick up one of his books. Rick was not just a talented author ,he was also one heck of a nice guy.

Rick, you will be missed.

Since many of you are aware of who we are, we'll refrain from going into detail of what AnthoCon is all about, or about the origin of the Four Horsemen—you heard all about that in the first anthology (and if you can't recall, read the foreword from our first volume). But for the uninitiated, we'll be brief.

AnthoCon is an annual three-day event which draws an exceptional crowd of authors, artists, and fans of all genres from all over the world. We get to say that since we had an attendee come all the way from New Delhi, India to attend in 2012. And many Canadians keep returning, as well. That makes us international, right?

This current offering is comprised of stories from some (but not all) of the amazingly talented individuals that attend our event. If you're not familiar with the festivities, stop by anthocon.com to learn more on future events.

This anthology is a little bit bigger than the first, a testament to the fact that our community is growing. From the contributors, to the editing and design, the efforts of many are represented within this volume. It is our sincere hope that you enjoy Inner Demons Out.

Excelsior!!

—*The Four Hoursemen*
jOhnny, Tim, Danny & Mark

ANTHOLOGY
YEAR TWO

INNER
DEMONS
OUT

BRACKEN MACLEOD

MINE, NOT YOURS

SOME OF THE KIDS NEXT TO ME LAUGH as the girl on the hospital bed screams about killing her baby. Fake blood coats the inside of her thighs and the bedspread between them. A couple of kids dressed as a doctor and nurse say something I can't hear because the hyperventilating girl behind me keeps repeating "ohmygodohmygodohmygod" and sobbing. She's been like that since the second room on the tour of The Hallows House. Peter Stott—"Pastor Pete" to the kids—pops up again from behind the bed wearing a ridiculous rubber devil mask and begins preaching. "You thought that you were going to find love in cyberspace, but instead you were raped! And now you've killed! Your! Baby!" He's shouting much louder than he needs to in the enclosed space. Maybe he thinks we can't hear him through the mask. He steps around the bed with a flourishing gesture to redirect our attention between the teenager's legs, just in case any of us thought there was anything more interesting to look at than a young girl's thighs. The boy playing the doctor continues the morality play.

"Nurse. This bleeding isn't normal. I don't think we can stop it."

"Oh my God, Doctor. What do we do?"

"It's too late; this one's gone. Come on. We have other abortions to perform."

Pete laughs again from behind the mask and shouts at the bleeding girl. "You're going to Hell! But it's okay because it was your choice!" The girl on the bed pretends to die while the doctor shrugs like that sort of thing happens to him all the time and walks out of the room.

Not one of them has ever actually been in this situation and it plays like a politician talking about hard work. Even though this is my third time through the house, I still haven't gotten over my urge to howl for these kids to stop pretending they know what pain is.

I unclench my fists and stuff them back in my jacket. I have to consciously fight to keep from wrapping my fingers around the butt of the gun in my right pocket.

The girl behind me sobs again. Her friends are dragging her through the house despite the fact that she's clearly wanted to leave since the drunk-driving skit in the first room. The girls on either side of her whisper reassuringly, "It's okay," and "It's not real," in between giggles and groans of excited disgust.

The Devil laughs again, sounding like a Bela Lugosi impression done by someone who's never actually seen Dracula. "We'll be seeing her again real soon," he shouts, hinting at the penultimate room in which we're treated to the pleasure of watching the sinners from all the previous skits suffering in Hell.

The teenager dressed up like an angel who has been our guide apologizes again for the sights she must subject us to. Her smug look belies any real regret. She loves every minute of trying to send us running in a panic into the arms of her lord. She motions for everyone to proceed. Awaiting us in the next room is a semi-racist gangbanger party that'll devolve into an argument over a "ho" and a shooting. While everyone else files past, I lag behind, slipping into the shadow of black plastic stapled to the wall. The last of the kids leave and the angel shuts the plywood door behind her. I hear the latch of the slide bolt on the other side.

No one gets to backtrack; no one escapes Hell.

I step out of the darkness and over the cheap rope separating the performance area from the spectator path. Walking up to the Devil, I say, "Pastor? Excuse me, Pastor Stott." He lifts up his mask to reveal black-ringed raccoon eyes and a confused expression.

"I'm sorry sir, but you need to stay with the group."

I know he recognizes me. He pretends not to and gives me that Cheshire smile he wore the first day I saw him. He was standing up in a pulpit and my daughter sitting next to me on the pew was on the edge of her seat like she was at a rock concert. He kept looking down at her from that perch of his and I remember thinking at the time, *Damn, this guy knows how to work a room.* Even my wife seemed moved and she grew up around Evangelicals and Charismatics.

"I'm Andrew Matheson," I say, like we haven't met after sermons, church barbecues, bake sales, Easter passion plays. My wife and daughter were always the vanguard at those events. I was the quiet guy who hung back trying to give my daughter the room to be herself without her old man intruding and embarrassing her. How I wish I had ever stepped forward. "I'm Mattie Matheson's father."

"Mattie? Oh, *Amanda*."

She hated being called Amanda. She was christened "Amanda Hugginkiss" in the fourth grade and was mortified. We told her she could be called anything she liked and my wife suggested Mattie. I hated it. I sounded to me like some blue-haired Indian Bingo player down by my mom's place in Florida, but for her it was like being born again. Taking control of her name had allowed her to take control of her life. She took the name and wore it like armor.

"We haven't seen Amanda in a long time," he said. I want to pistol whip him for his feigned ignorance. "I'm sure you haven't," I say instead. My hands are shaking and I'm afraid the gun might slip out of my pocket. I grab hold of it and a soothing calm like morphine flows through my body. It's cool grip pressing into my palm, warming, taking my heat and becoming a part of me.

"You tell her we miss her at Loving Heart. She should come back to service on Sunday. In the meantime, you should head on into the next room. You're missing the show." He points toward the locked door. "I'll radio and get Sheila to let you through."

I grab his pudgy arm and pull him closer. "I've *seen* the show. I want you to know that I'm Mattie Matheson's father." I look into his eyes searching for a hint of guilt. If there is any, either the black grease paint hides it or he's a much better actor without the mask.

"Got it," he says, shaking me off. I get the first real glimpse at the devil beneath the disguise. He's got a moon-shaped face with bright blue eyes that peer through that greasepaint like pools of ice. I can see that he knows me but won't admit it. Not given what else he knows.

"Pastor Pete?" The girl from the bed appears out of the gloom at the back of the stage. Fuck! I was too anxious to corner my target and I didn't make sure the room was clear first. The other two times I cased the show I was paying attention to the live act, not looking behind the scenes. I take a step back. Not with a witness. Not with a child in the room.

She approaches us timidly, her hospital gown fallen back down covering the red Karo syrup staining her thighs. Her hands are bright red from pawing at the gore. She and the other kids were supposed to be moving on to take their places under the Lexan glass in the floor of the "Hell Room" where the teenagers who "died in their sins" throughout the house will writhe in eternal agony.

"Laylah. Would you please take Mr. Matheson to meet his friends in Hell?" He looks at me with the Sunday morning smile. "Or maybe you'd just rather go right to the prayer room, since you've already been through it."

"It's funny you'd put it like that."

"Pastor Pete?" the girl repeats. She looks afraid to come near me. I can't tell if it's how I look or who I am. Either way, her instincts are good.

"What is it, Laylah?" Pete asks.

"Amanda Matheson … Mattie … she …"

"My daughter killed herself last month," I finish for her. My wife says she "passed away" or "she left us." But that's bullshit. Our only child killed herself. No euphemism exists that can soften the truth of it.

Pastor Pete stands quietly, trying to look shocked to hear the news. It must not be a look he tries on often, because I can see the muscles in his face twitching at the unfamiliarity of this expression. He knows what she did as well as why she did it. He took everything we built up and broke it down, taking everything from her—even her name—until all she had to lean on was him. "Mr. Matheson," he says, "I am sorry to hear we've lost Amanda, but—"

"*We* haven't lost shit."

"I understand you must be upset, but—"

I slap him. The Devil mask pushed back up on his head goes flying and he steps back a couple of feet, holding his face. *That* expression is real. Laylah gives a shocked squeak. I close the distance, hitting him again this time with a closed fist. He drops the walkie talkie. It chirps as it clatters away. Laylah shrieks. I really wish she wasn't here to see this, but she is and I won't get another opportunity to be alone with Pete again. Not after this. I hold a finger up to my mouth encouraging her to be quiet. With all the shouting coming from the next room, there's really no need. She could start screaming her head off and it'd all sound like part of the act. It's why I want to do this here. Gunshots and screams are what you get for the price of admission. Still, I want Pete to hear me without having to shout. I don't like raised voices.

"What do you want?" he slurs. Blood dribbles out of his mouth as he paws at the floor looking for the radio in the dark.

"Mattie's dead because of you."

"You said she killed herself. If she chose to sin, I only ever tried to keep her on the right—" I'm not even close to getting tired of hitting Pete, but we don't have all night so I pull the gun and shove it in his face as encouragement to be judicious with his words. I really want him to be conscious when I pull the trigger but everything he says makes me want to beat him to death instead of shoot him.

He opens his mouth to say something. I slip my finger inside the trigger guard and he thinks better of verbalizing whatever it was that occurred to him. Instead, he paws at his split lip and stands back up to face me.

"She left a note." I say. "Do you want to know what she wrote?"

"I don't think it's anything I want to hear, Andy."

No one calls me Andy. The way he's making me feel, I can barely keep to the plan. He took Mattie's name and now he's messing with mine, trying to use it against me.

"Before you do anything you'll regret," he continues, "why don't you just hand me the pistol?" He holds out his hand. It's soft and white and I imagine it touching my girl. I want to break his fucking fingers.

Laylah hesitantly moves closer. I watch his eyes tracking her, trying to give her subtle directions with them. I don't know what she can see through the dim light and his makeup, but I pay attention to her in my peripheral vision anyway. Despite the gloom, she's easy to see in the white gown. She's almost glowing.

"Mattie wrote that she hoped that her baby in Heaven would never be able to look down and see its mother burning in Hell. She hoped it wasn't really like The Hallows House." Saying the words is harder than I thought it would be. I don't want to utter them. I hid the note from the police so they wouldn't see her final confession. I didn't want them to know what he had done to my little girl. But then the medical examiner found the fetus and I had to give the police my DNA to prove it wasn't my baby. That's when my wife moved out. I was cleared, but she's stayed away anyway.

Pete's caring preacher look falls away and his expression goes blank. He saw it then. Laylah being in the room wasn't going to stop me. "I d-don't know what this has to do with me," he stammers, lying. "Can we pray together?" The tremor in his voice getting worse. "Matthew 6:14 says—"

"She mentioned you by name in her note. Her last words were that she hoped you would forgive her for killing your baby when she died. Your baby."

His stupid round face is covered in sweat despite the chill in the house. I can see in his eyes he's thinking hard about how to get out of this. He's making a plan and playing it out in his head. Struggle with me for the gun? Run for the door? Call out for help? But I've been planning longer. I'm stronger than he is. The doors are locked and we're alone. The overacted fight in the room next door will soon erupt in hysterics and shooting. And that's all I'm waiting for. He's running out of time.

I check my watch. The tour is staggered every twenty minutes. I've kept Pastor Pete for five, maybe seven. I don't know; I lost count. The first time I saw his face the only thing that occurred to me was blowing a hole in it. I can't wait much longer. If I do, they'll notice the Lord of Hell is missing. "Pray," I say.

"What?"

My hand is shaking, but I'm pretty sure at this range I won't miss. Pastor Pete has to see that as well. "Pray! Pray that I'll let you live. Get on your fucking knees and ask *Him* to move me."

Pete drops to the floor, blank look in place, and begins performing like it's a Sunday morning tent revival. "Dear Lord, Jesus Christ, I pray in your name that you deliver us from the influence of the … of the Devil and that you move dear brother Andrew's heart—"

I clock him in the forehead with the butt of the gun. The dull thud of metal on bone sounds like a hosanna to me. "Don't pray for deliverance. Pray for *forgiveness*," I say.

Struggling to get back up to his knees he says, "I have nothing to ask forg—"

"I dare you to say that again. Say it again with a straight face so I can feel even better about killing you."

Slowly, so I don't startle and accidentally pull the trigger, Laylah places her hand on my forearm. Her skin is sticky from the fake blood, but her touch is still tender and soft, like the down of her white wings. I don't remember her having angel's wings in the scene. I guess she was getting ready for her next part in the play when I interrupted her.

I try to remember whether at the end she's saved or one of the damned, but all I can think of is Pastor Pete. His eyes narrow as he judges whether her distraction would be enough for him to make a dash for it. It isn't. I'm focused on him kneeling there looking like a dog that doesn't know whether to jump or roll over.

"Can I have the gun, Mr. Matheson?" she asks.

"Sorry, kid. I need it. I need it until I feel the hand of God move me. Do you think we've got his attention?" My anger is turning into sorrow as I try to keep the hitch out of my voice. Everything has gone wrong and the plan doesn't make sense to me anymore. I know that this won't bring my Mattie back. Nothing will. Not prayer, not faith, not hope—all things I've given up. The girl is sapping my resolve. She's not part of the plan. I don't want to hurt her.

She looks so much like my daughter.

"Our Father, who art in Heaven, Hallowed be thy name," Pete says.

"Not feeling it." I bluff, holding back my tears. "Try harder."

"Forgive us our trespasses as we forgive those who trespass against us."

"You're running out of time."

Laylah's hand slides down my arm, lightly squeezing my wrist. She's gentle, but there's something else there: the strength I'm losing. She whispers to me, "You don't have to do this. It's not your fault."

"You're right. It's his," I insist.

"What does your heart tell you?" She places her other hand flat on my chest—those slender hands like Mattie's.

"... and the glory. Forever and ever."

I lower the gun.

"God has touched your heart," he says. "Amen."

"Laylah changed my mind. *She* touched me."

"Forgiveness is the first—"

"I don't forgive you!" For a moment the look on his face turns from satisfaction to fear as he expects me to raise the gun again and fire. Without the girl there, I might have done just that. Instead, I feel calmness wash over me. Someone cares about me even though I don't. Feeling clean for the first time since I put the flesh of my flesh in the earth I let the girl in the angel costume take the gun from me. I shouldn't let her have it—it's irresponsible—but I can't stand the weight of it in my hand any more.

I'll make sure she gives it to the police when they get here. She lets her other hand linger on my chest. The coldness of her fingers pierces through my coat.

"I'm sorry, Mr. Matheson," she says.

"Don't be."

With a voice that sounds like a velvet bow pulling gently across cello strings, she says, "Vengeance is *mine*, not yours." The sound of the shot makes my ears pop and ring. Pete falls forward choking and grasping at his guts as his life splashes out through his fingers.

"What did you do?" My words are muted and far away, like I'm standing at the far end of a tunnel shouting at myself. If Laylah answers me, I can't hear it. She fires again into the top of his head and he crumples. The second shot is just a dull thud. Smoke drifts into my eyes. Pete chokes his bloody last breath onto the plywood floor.

The girl with the terrible, shining face turns around. She's a horrifying vision that fills me with despair. All light and no warmth. And she looks like my daughter. She extends her great wings and beats them once, buffeting me with a frigid wind that stings my eyes. Embracing me, she holds me tightly and whispers in that sonorous string quartet voice, "Blessed are those who mourn, for they shall be comforted." Her body leeches my heat and I'm not comforted.

I feel cheated.

I push back and try to look in her face. "Where were you when Mattie needed comforting?"

She looks at me with blank, all-black eyes. "I was with her. She was heavy laden and I gave her rest." Her face is an expressionless nightmare of frigid detachment and brilliant light like reflecting silver. Tears sting my eyes. I try not to see my daughter staring at me, cold and dead, a vicious shining thing with wings and no soul. I try not to see Pete behind her, on his knees bowing down like a supplicant.

Her voice grows louder and thicker and painful. "Come. Take comfort in your faith. Let me give you rest."

"Like you gave it to Pete? To my daughter?"

It steps back. "Who are you to question me?" it asks, raising the gun to my face. I lurch forward grabbing for the pistol. The angel resists. "Where were you when the foundations of the Earth were laid?" The thickness of its voice is pounding in my head like a hangover or a concussion. I try to twist the gun out of its hand, but it's stronger than I am. I shove with the last bit of force I can muster and its howls deaden the shot. The gleaming white thing falls in a sudden heap to the floor. I look down at the angel as it blows away like smoke on a breezy hilltop leaving behind only Laylah in her stained hospital gown. The right side of her skull is a ruin of torn tissue and black wetness under the red lights. Kneeling down, I pull the wingless corpse up onto my lap. She's warm.

But getting colder.

A kid in a shitty silver lamé angel costume peeks in the door looking for Pete, ready to lead the next group in. He looks at us, silent and mouth agape, trying to contextualize this fresh Hell out of place among all of the other scenes. I look up at him, imagining what he sees: a sobbing man embracing a girl with half a face and his church leader crumpled and ruined in front of us—a mockery of the *Pietà* or Caravaggio's *Entombment*. The boy sprints back out the door screaming for help.

His cries sound like part of the act. Just like I planned.

I think about the angel and pull Laylah closer. I think about faith. Without hope, what's that really worth? I put the gun to my temple. "This is mine, not yours."

BRACKEN MACLEOD is a former martial arts teacher, university philosophy instructor, and attorney. While spurning the law education, he values the fight training. Books of the Dead Press recently published his debut novel, *Mountain Home*.

CRAIG D. B. PATTON

UNKNOWN CALLER

I'VE AVOIDED TELLING THIS STORY. The *real* story, not the one I told the police. It scares me. But I've started having nightmares. Maybe it will help to write it down, to finally tell the truth.

For starters, it wasn't Jeremy's idea to go to that warehouse. It was mine. We had gotten into urban exploration a year earlier. Now that *was* his idea. He found a Tumblr account with all these beautiful, strange photos of crumbling hospitals and factories— even amusement parks. The people in the shots wore camo and dust masks. Or they were silhouetted or turned away from the camera. You couldn't identify anyone, because some of the places they went were illegal. He wanted to try it and I said yes.

See ... at that time we were both saying yes to everything. Maybe even for the same reason. We had been together for four years. I wasn't looking to get married. I wasn't sure I ever would, which disappointed the hell out of my mother. I like to think I was trying to figure out whether we were built for the long road. But I started this to tell the truth and the truth is I don't know. Maybe we had already run out of road and we just kept running, trying not to notice.

First it was adventure sports: skydiving, bungee jumping, zip lines. We got SCUBA certified and dove wrecks. We had great stories to tell friends and coworkers. People thought we were pretty damn cool and maybe that kept us going too. Everyone wants to be in the cool couple.

Our celebrations became more adventurous to match. We drank more. We got a few tattoos and piercings that no one else could see. The sex got rawer. We were wild. I loved the sense of abandonment, of being so utterly open. It felt like trust and maybe it was. But now I wonder if we were just addicted to the thrills, just playing, like kids.

We found a site with links to urban exploration spots near us in Connecticut. Newgate Prison in Granby looked like it might be cool except for the security guard. Neither of us was looking to get arrested. Our first expedition was to an abandoned army bunker near Bradley Airport. It was pretty lame. Just one of those steel huts that make you feel like you're inside a giant soup can lying on its side. There were rotting desks and other bits of furniture. Some strange wooden objects. That's it. But we had snuck onto state property, gone someplace we shouldn't be, so it was still a thrill.

Next we tried to go to this old hotel in Windsor, but it turned out to be demolished. We went a little further afield and checked out Powder Ridge, a defunct ski area in Middlefield. Now, *that* was cool. We got into a bunch of buildings. But my favorite part was the lifts. The chairs were still hanging on the cables, as if the place had been evacuated mid-season during an apocalypse. I took a lot of pictures of them. There was something beautiful about how lonely they looked—all those chairs waiting for people who never came. That's why the idea of finding a phone booth graveyard intrigued me.

It's not like I had a thing for phone booths. I just found this amazing picture taken at sunset of a field full of rusting phone booths in England (or, phone boxes, as the British call them). Ran a search and pretty soon I had a collection of images of phone booths and phone kiosks from all over the world. I also learned some history along the way. The first public phone in America had been practically down the street in a bank in Hartford. Didn't it make sense, I thought, that there might be a site nearby filled with old phone booths?

It took some digging, but I found documents about delivery of decommissioned phone booths to an address in the South Meadows neighborhood of Hartford. I checked and confirmed there was still a warehouse there. I'd scored our next urban exploration site.

Jeremy thought it was funny. He was still teasing me on the way there that night.

"Where's your costume?"

"What?"

"I figure you're going to change into Supergirl once we find the right phone booth."

"Ha ha. She doesn't need a phone booth. Neither does Superman."

"No?"

"No. That's just a pop culture myth."

"Weird."

"You want to hear something weird about a phone booth that's actually true?" I was enjoying being the expert.

"Sure."

So I told him about the Mojave phone booth. For 40 years there was a phone booth in the Mojave National Preserve in California. It was 8 miles from the nearest paved road. There were no buildings near it. In 1997 a guy spotted an icon for it on a map on the Internet and got curious.

Jeremy wasn't impressed. "So?"

"So he went out and camped next to it for a month."

"What? Why?"

"He was some religious nut. Said the Holy Spirit told him to do it. Wound up answering over 500 calls."

"Did God call?"

"Nope."

"That sucks."

"Yep. Bunch of calls from Sergeant Zero though."

"Who the hell's Sergeant Zero?"

"Some guy in the Pentagon."

"Says who?" Jeremy would question whether rain was wet.

"Says Sergeant Zero."

"Huh. Maybe Sergeant Zero was God."

"Probably thinks he is."

We found the warehouse easily enough, tucked behind the converted and newer structures closer to the road. It was Sunday afternoon, near dusk. We drove through empty parking lots and then off into the weeds and pulled up behind it.

After a little hunting, we got lucky and found a broken ground floor window. One whole side of the frame was popped out. We draped a doubled-up canvas tarp over the exposed part of the wall to cover anything sharp and climbed in. A short walk down a hallway led us to a bizarre wonderland.

"Okay. Yeah. Good call," was all Jeremy could say.

I didn't have any words at all.

Thick shafts of glorious golden light slanted down from the second floor windows on the opposite side. With only a narrow balcony ringing that story, the light poured down on the warehouse floor where we stood gaping at row after row of phone booths.

Now, most people in this country who even know what a phone booth is picture one of two styles. They think of the wall or pole mounted kiosk (the hopelessly dull end of phone booth evolution and not even a booth at all) or they think of the metal and glass freestanding ones (Superman's supposed changing stall). Or maybe they watch Doctor Who and think of the TARDIS.

The truth is that early phone booths were an art form, an architectural exclamation, sort of like old movie houses. Ten feet in front of us, covered in dust stood one made of polished wood. The glass was broken and the door was hanging off, but inside was a raggedy *upholstered seat*. In the row to our right, a few spots back, stood another wooden one with pilasters. Even the more ordinary ones looked grand in the light, the alchemy of sunset turning grimy metal and glass to unpolished gold and diamond.

I started taking pictures. Lots and lots of pictures. Close ups of details, wider shots down the rows. There was a stack of doors with bronze filigrees propped against a wall that looked like a massive set of playing cards. Jeremy found a staircase and I went up to take some shots while he poked around. The view from the balcony was amazing. There must have been a thousand phone booths in that warehouse. Time slipped away as I took shot after shot. The light started to fail, but we weren't ready to leave so we turned on our headlamps and wandered.

We found it back toward one of the far corners. The box was nothing special, just another metal and glass one. But it had a phone number spray painted in yellow vertically down the door. It looked oddly official to me. Made me think of photos from New Orleans after Katrina—all those symbols on roofs and doors to indicate a structure had been checked and whether there were bodies. There was a big dent in the frame to the right of the door, but it looked in good condition otherwise. I took a picture.

"Let's call it," Jeremy said. He pulled out his phone before I even answered. Just another impulse thrill. One more plunge into the unknown.

"Why?"

Jeremy smirked. "To see if Sergeant Zero answers." He started dialing.

I didn't know what he meant. "Wait. That's stupid. The phone's trashed. It's not conn—"

The phone started ringing. It was that old school ring you hear mostly in movies or on TV now. A familiar, innocent sound I'd heard hundreds of times, but it made my skin crawl. I stared through the glass at the receiver.

Jeremy started to laugh but it choked off. He looked ... not scared, but definitely anxious until he saw me watching and covered it with a joke. "What? You not taking my calls now?"

It was just a phone ringing. I'd figure out how later. I opened the door. The ringing stopped. Cut out right in mid-tone. I turned back to Jeremy to say something sarcastic about crank calling me.

"Hello?" he said into his cell.

Now I was pissed. How far did he think his stupid little joke could go? "Cut the crap."

"Yes, this is Jeremy. How did you know my name?"

Who the hell was he talking to? For a second I wondered if it really was Sergeant Zero, if there was some poor guy in the bowels of the Pentagon responsible for monitoring phone booths. I couldn't make out the voice at all.

Jeremy nodded. "Yes. I understand," he said, and then his eyes ... See, I loved Jeremy's eyes. They were these deep, dark pools of brown and if you watched closely, you were guaranteed to see a bit of mischief swim by. Clever eyes. Damn sexy eyes. Eyes that had gotten me to do all sorts of things. His eyes were always so alive and then they just went flat. All the life vanished.

He lowered the phone.

"Who was it?" My voice shook. I wanted to know what could be so awful to make him look like that. I didn't want to know at all. I wanted to just turn and run but I didn't. I just stood there, my heart racing as the shadows deepened.

"So are you having fun?" His voice was as expressionless as his eyes.

"What?"

"Your little field trip. Get what you wanted from this stupid idea?"

I felt more confused than annoyed. "You said you liked it too."

"Yeah, well, I've been saying a lot of things. Want to hear some more?"

I didn't answer.

He leaned toward me. Just a bit, but I took a step back. "I'm sick of you," he said, his voice filled with scorn. "You've just been tagging along for a long time now."

The words felt like a physical blow. They took my breath away. "What?" I said in a tiny gasp.

"You do what I do. You listen to what I do. You talk like I do. And why? Because you're so goddamn boring on your own. You're twenty-nine years old and you don't have any idea who you are."

"Why are you saying these things?"

He advanced and I stumbled back against the phone booth. "Because they're true and it's way past time someone told you the truth. You're nothing. Waitressing tables and driving your crap car and hanging with me because it's the only thing that makes you feel alive, the only thing that makes you believe you're worth anything at all."

I burst into tears. I'm ashamed of it, but I did. Because it was true and I had hidden that truth so well that I believed it wasn't there. Now he had yanked it up and out of me and thrown it in my face.

He started shouting. "You're nothing. Nothing but a damn slut. No one's gonna miss you." He raised his fist.

One of the things you have to have if you spend much time at adventure sports is quick reflexes. I ducked and stepped sideways under the blow. He swung wildly again and I backed away from him down the aisle. "Stop!"

Jeremy's hand smashed into the glass of the booth. When he yanked it back it was covered in blood. He didn't say anything. He didn't even look like he felt it. It was like he was drunk. But even drunk, Jeremy had never been violent or spoken to me like that. No, the Jeremy I knew was gone. He had disappeared right in front of me.

Whatever was wearing him came at me again and I turned and ran. But Jeremy was faster. There was no way I would make it to the window and out before he caught me. Even if I did, what the hell was I going to do next? Sprint across the empty parking lots screaming? Try to hide in the weeds? No way. I couldn't escape and there was no one around to help me.

Ahead of me one of the metal-framed doors was leaning against a booth. I skidded to a stop and yanked the door into Jeremy's path. No plan. Just did it. I guess I was hoping to slow him down a bit. But he was awkward, slower to react than my Jeremy had been. The door hit him in the side of the head as he tried to dodge. He fell. His phone tumbled to the floor and the door came down and smashed it.

I ran to the end of the aisle before I realized that I was alone. It ... Jeremy never got up.

In my headlamp beam I could still see his body—a dim lump on the floor. I waited for what felt like a long time before I took a few steps toward him and called his name. He didn't move, but no way in hell was I going to walk right up and check his breathing or something. I've seen too many movies. I'd stay safe, call 9-1-1, and wait for whoever came. I pulled out my cell.

The phone in the booth to my left started ringing. A shrill, staccato series of notes. Scared the crap out of me. I yelped and jumped probably a foot in the air. The phone was hanging off the inside of the booth by one screw, the receiver dangling to the floor. But it kept ringing anyway.

Another phone started up behind me and I whirled to shine the light on it. It was in one of the gorgeous wooden phone booths. I remember it had inlaid carvings of grapevines. The thing should have been in a museum someplace but there it was, ringing an impossible melody of notes in perfect pitch.

Several more began to ring and I finally fled. I ran as fast as I could, begging any god that cared to help me. More and more phones started ringing. Ahead of me. Off to the side. Dozens of long dead phones brought back to life by whatever Jeremy woke calling that number. The warehouse filled with the freakish jangle of them ringing.

I found the window, tumbled back out and didn't stop running until I was back in the car. I was so scared by then I might have even driven away but the keys were in Jeremy's pack.

Instead I called 9-1-1. I told them I'd left my phone in the car and had to come out to call since Jeremy's was smashed. I told them the door had fallen on him and that I wasn't sure if he was breathing and that I was too scared to go back in. The lies came easy. They came easy for a long time.

After what felt like an hour I heard sirens and then a fleet of emergency vehicles came tearing into the parking lot. The fire department broke open the doors and I showed them where I'd left Jeremy. Like an idiot, I was hoping he was alright. I wasn't worried about the phones anymore. Somehow I knew they'd keep quiet with such a large audience.

Jeremy was dead when we found him ...

Things get blurry for awhile after that. I remember crying. I remember being led stumbling out. I remember sitting on the bumper of one of the vehicles with a blanket over me. I remember it smelled like moth balls.

There were condolences and a lot of questions in the days that followed. Jeremy had *died* for God's sake. But the evidence supported my statement that the door had struck him. There was no motive for anything else, no indication of foul play, and the autopsy came back that he'd died from blunt force trauma. We had broken into private property, so there was a fine to pay, but that was it.

Jeremy's family took over on the memorial service. They did everything without really talking to me. I had met his parents a few times, but they lived in Cincinnati. His older brother and sister lived even further away. So it's not like we were close, but I started getting the idea that maybe Jeremy never really talked about me much. I was just the chick he ran around with doing the stupid stuff that got him killed.

My friends took care of me. Work was great. They gave me the time I needed. Everyone accepted the story I'd given the police. Things had just gone bad for us on one of our cool couple adventures ... which was true.

It started the day after the memorial. I was back in my apartment after spending a week at my friend Lisa's place. I was just home from work and trying to figure out if I was hungry enough to eat when my cell rang.

The screen read UNKNOWN CALLER with a number I didn't recognize. I ignored it. No message was left. A minute later my home phone rang. UNKNOWN CALLER again. Same number. But suddenly it looked familiar.

I stared at the number, my heart pounding. Three rings. Four. My answering machine picked up. "Hi! Sorry I'm not—"

The call disconnected. My cell started ringing again and I didn't even look at it. I shut my cell off and unplugged the land line.

The photos from the warehouse were still on my camera. When I turned it on the last shot I had taken appeared on screen. I stared at it, at that spray painted number running down the side of the booth. It was the same damned number. I opened a bottle of bourbon and drank until I stopped shaking.

But Sergeant Zero was patient. Yes, that's what I call whatever the hell it is. Anytime I plugged the phone back in or turned on my cell, Sergeant Zero called again within minutes. UNKNOWN CALLER and the phone number from the booth.

I changed my numbers. Sergeant Zero found me again.

I asked for the calls to be blocked and traced. But the number leads back to a PBX that has been out of service for a long, long time. No one at the phone company could explain it.

"Huh. That's really interesting," one perky rep said.

I swore at her for a good minute before I hung up. Because it's not. There's nothing interesting about being stalked. It's terrifying.

My friends told me to just ignore it, but the calls kept coming. Finally I realized I needed to do something drastic. So I moved here, to upstate Middle-of-Nowhere USA. I bought a three-room cabin at the end of ten miles of dirt road where it's just me and the wildlife. My closest neighbor is fifteen miles away. The center of town (if you can call a 2-pump gas station, a general store, a laundromat, and a bar the center of anything) is even further.

There's no phone service to the cabin. No cell coverage on any network. GPS shrugs and gives up. I have a generator for now but I'm sick of the noise and the smell. I'm saving to go solar. I barback. I knit. I have a shop on Etsy for my sweaters and scarves and stuff. (You'd be amazed what people will pay for mittens and booties for little kids.) I've gotten pretty good at guitar and I write a lot in these journals.

My family and friends worried about my decision to become "a hippy hermit" as my mother put it. But they went with it because I had "suffered a shock" (Mom again) and because I seemed happier.

I was. But all the peace and quiet gave me time to think. I've been thinking about Sergeant Zero. I've been wishing I went back to the warehouse and spray painted over that phone number. What if someone else goes there and calls it? What if Sergeant Zero—it, whatever—reaches someone else?

And what if it already did? See, I figure it got my numbers from Jeremy's phone ... so that means it could take all my contacts from mine ... and how many jumps are there between any of us these days?

In my nightmares countless phones are ringing.

I see the displays lit up: UNKNOWN CALLER.

I hope no one answers.

CRAIG D. B. PATTON's stories and poems have appeared in *Supernatural Tales*, *Illumen*, *Wily Writers*, *Shroud Magazine*, and other markets. You can learn more at *flawedcreations.wordpress.com* and follow him on Twitter at *@craigdbpatton*.

STACEY LONGO

OLD MAN'S WINTER

LIFE WAS NOT FAIR, THE OLD MAN KNEW. He'd known this ever since he was a child, when his world had been perfect and his parents had doted on him until his little sister came along. Then, all of a sudden, he'd had to share his cookies, his rocking horse, and worst of all, his parents' time.

The old man did not take unfairness well. He liked to restore balance as swiftly as possible. Which is why, at the tender age of six, he'd smashed his little sister's head against a rock until her skull caved in.

He'd blamed the incident on an accidental fall, and his parents had believed him—the truth would have been inconceivable to them—and once again, the old man's universe had fallen back in order, with his mother and father hugging him even tighter, their only remaining child.

The old man's father had been a chemist at Pfizer, working at the plant in Groton for forty-four years until he dropped dead of a heart attack in the laboratory, shattering the Petri dish he was holding. His father had been instrumental in developing the rabies vaccine, and when he'd died, he'd left his wife and son a healthy estate. But the old man had plans, and taking care of his mother as she moved in to her golden years was not in the cards. He smothered her with a pillow as she slept, and continued on with his life's path, finding himself a wife.

On the streets of Groton, his temper was well known, so he moved to a rural area of Connecticut, buying himself a hundred acres to guarantee himself privacy from nosy neighbors. He went to the Methodist church long enough to find a hardy local girl that swooned when he courted her. They married, and he never set foot in church again, much to Mary's chagrin. The first time she nagged at him to come back to the flock, he punched her hard enough to knock out a molar. She never asked again.

Mary bore him two sons, two years apart. The oldest was named Junior after him; the youngest, Jerry. Junior was brilliant and bold with dark, hard features like the old man. Jerry was quiet and watchful and as blonde and soft as his mother. The old man focused all of his attention on his oldest son, teaching him how to stand up for himself in the most concrete of terms. A note soon came home from school in Junior's book bag with threats from the teachers to not let Junior back the next day due to the brutal sucker punches he'd been doling out at recess. This would not do, and the old man now faced the problem of Junior's behavioral issues. He beat the problem out of his son with a heavy belt.

As Junior got older, his brother became his favorite target, and Jerry took to hiding in the dark corners of the neighbor's horse barn to avoid his brother's haymakers. The old man encouraged his sons to work out their problems with their fists; it would toughen then up as men. Jerry often sported a black eye or a makeshift cast on his wrist until his sophomore year of high school. That summer, he hit a growth spurt that left him four inches taller and sixty pounds heavier than his brother, and Jerry fought back. Mary had to rush Junior to the hospital with a broken jaw.

The old man was furious. He'd decided to run for Town Council that fall, and he couldn't have his idiot sons messing up his chances with gossip-inspiring breaks and bruises. He grabbed his youngest boy by the back of his neck and whipped him around to teach him a lesson about keeping up appearances. To his surprise, his son's fist met his nose in such an explosion of pain that the old man was on his knees before he knew what hit him.

There was no room in the old man's life for troublemakers. Even that infernal Bible that Mary kept on the living room table said to honor thy father. After he had his nose set, the old man kicked Jerry out of the house, disowning him. He forbade Mary from seeing her baby boy, the one that was so like her; she disobeyed him only once, walking four miles down the road to meet him at Bolton Lake and slip him a few dollars she'd stolen from the old man's wallet. The old man had broken her fingers, one by one, that night after dinner. He did not tolerate thieves. Then he crushed her toes so she could not walk such a distance to meet her son again. The old man was fairly sure he'd cured her of her ways, but for good measure, he waited until she was kneeling out in the vegetable garden one sunny morning, and then slammed the small of her back with a four by four. Mary was never able to stand completely upright again, which was, of course, what she deserved for crossing the old man. He was pretty sure her precious Bible said to honor thy husband, too.

When he'd moved to town, the old man had invested in an old quarry. He'd slowly leveled out the land and had started construction on a cheap housing development. Once Mary lost her looks and started stooping like an old woman, he took up with the girl that kept his books for the development. She had hair red as fire and a great set of gams; the old man would have killed Mary if she'd ever dared to dress in skirts that ended right below the knee, but Red was different. A mistress could get away with things that a wife could not, and Red was a real firecracker. Until he found her one evening crying in the dark shack she used as an office at the construction site. Red was pregnant; the old man would have to divorce Mary and wed her, or she would be ruined—ruined!—in their small town. The old man took her for a walk around the site, his arm over her shoulders, consoling her; he strangled her silently and laid her body out like a starfish in the bottom of a foundation that was set to be poured in the morning. The old man was not afraid of a little hard work, and he poured the foundation by himself that night, smoothing out the cement until it was perfectly even, just as dawn broke. When Red's father came by the site a few days later, the old man immediately began yelling at him, telling him to tell his irresponsible daughter that if she couldn't show up for work for three days in a row, he'd give the job to someone who would. He ranted and bellowed until the worried father was cowed in to leaving, never able to ask if anyone there had seen his little girl.

Junior had no interest in his father's business, and left home after high school to join the army. He was killed in Vietnam eight months later, and for a moment, the old man felt something akin to sadness. He chalked it up to heartburn and ordered a cheap pine coffin for his fool son who was too stupid to duck a sniper's bullet. Junior's grave lay unmarked for years, until the local veterans' services paid for a steel plate marker to honor the town's fallen son.

It was just the old man and Mary after that. Mary hobbled off to church three days a week, praying for salvation, or at the very least, escape. The good Lord was merciful, giving Mary cancer in her female parts. She refused to go to the doctor for surgery or radiation, which was fine with the old man. He thought all doctors were crooks, and although Mary was growing thinner and grayer every day, she had a quality about her the old man didn't ever remember her possessing. It seemed almost like … satisfaction.

Mary died in October, and the old man ran a short obituary in the paper, listing himself as her only living survivor. He settled in to his retirement, letting Mary's garden go to seed. He had his prescriptions for the arthritis in his knees delivered to his house along with his groceries, and he spent his days in front of the television, sipping a Pabst Blue Ribbon and watching the fights.

Until today. At this moment, the old man's youngest son was standing before him, blocking the view of his Zenith. Jerry looked good for sixty, though his hair was thinning, and his face was creased with the same lines that had been permanently furrowed in Mary's forehead.

"Hello, Pop," Jerry said lightly.

"Not your father," the old man mumbled, perturbed. The highlights from the Frazier fight were supposed to re-run in just a few minutes.

"Won't take but a moment of your time. The house," Jerry paused, looking around. "Wow. The house looks like shit. What happened to keeping up appearances?"

"Repairs cost money. Don't have a lot of money," the old man huffed, and Jerry laughed.

"You sly old liar. You've got more money than Rockefeller. You're just too stingy to spend a dime of it." Jerry grinned, a toothy, pained smile, and the old man scowled.

"What do you want, you little bastard? I'm busy."

"Sure you are, sure you are. I can see that. I just wanted to stop by and let you know how I've been, Pop. Got married, which I guess you would have known if you'd gone to Junior's funeral, seeing as Gail came with me. Anyway, no matter. She left me," he sighed, waving his weathered palms as if to push this news about his failed marriage aside. "She said I had issues. I suppose I do. Always have. I like to think I got them from you." Jerry stopped a moment to cough. The old man watched him with hooded, rheumy eyes.

"Always knew you'd be a failure, even at marriage. Your mother was with me 'til the day she died," the old man boasted.

"Yup. I know," Jerry said, nodding. "We kept in touch, you know. I went to church every Sunday just to see her. What a rotten life she had with you. You bullied the will to live right out of her. Hope you're happy." The old man was frowning, furious. How dare—his wife!—behind his back, after he'd *ordered* her—he struggled to stand, to face his disgraceful spawn. Jerry pushed him back down on the couch.

"She's dead; you can't punish her any more. But see, here's the thing, Pop. I've spent a lot of years struggling to get by and wishing for one thing—just one thing—my whole life. But here you are, still living, breathing, right as rain." Jerry shook his head. "Guess it's true what they say—evil never dies."

The old man clenched his fists. He refused to let this snot-nosed punk talk to him so disrespectfully. Why, he was a pillar in the community, with all he'd done, filling in the quarry and building new homes. Every year, he even donated twenty dollars to the Auxiliary Club when they had their fundraiser. He wasn't about to let Jerry *disrespect* him—

"Relax, Pop. I'm here to tell you something you'll probably enjoy," he continued, scratching his chin. "I've been diagnosed with terminal cancer. It's too far along and all over my pancreas and my liver. Got only a few months to live," Jerry said, and the old man couldn't help himself. He chuckled.

"Yeah, I thought that would cheer you up, you wretched bully. But here's the thing, Pop. I've got a few things on my bucket list I want to get to before I die. That's why I'm here." Jerry smiled, pulling out the gun that had been tucked in his back waistband, hidden from the old man's view. "Seeing you dead has been at the top of my list for years."

The old man blinked. His youngest boy was pointing a pistol right at his head, and for the briefest of moments, he was shocked. Then he broke out in a wide grin.

"Not so unlike me after all," the old man beamed, just as his son pulled the trigger.

STACEY LONGO is a writer, horror fan, comic book aficionado, and the author of *Pookie & the Lost and Found Friend*, a children's horror picture book. Learn more about how fabulous she is at *www.staceylongo.com.*

Richard Wright

Bulimia Daemonica

Jenny had been falling for a long time, almost a year by her reckoning, and when she finally hit the water it hurt. She tried to twist as she plummeted towards it, to smooth the impact by lining herself up for a dive, fingers first, head tucked down. By the time the thought was fully formed it was too late.

She slammed into the water on her back, and it was like crashing through a brick wall. Her splashdown sounded like something shattering. Air vanished from her lungs in a single rush as pain wrapped tight around her. Water closed over her face, and falling became sinking. Dazed, she realised that the oxygen slapped so brutally from her would not be replaced. Screwing her eyes closed, still reeling, she tried to make her muscles her own again. Her arms made vague waving motions. Her feeble legs tried to kick. With the pressure building in her chest, she struggled to remember something as elemental as how to swim. Co-ordination was beyond her. She was going to die.

Blood massed at her face as she sank deeper, as though trying to get as far from her desperate lungs as possible. She felt as though her cheeks would burst like ripe, juicy fruit. Her heart worked with superhuman fervour, ramming out a rhythm that would dance her to death.

She touched bottom, shoulders first, and the shock of that gentler landing startled her. Before she could call the reflex back she opened her mouth and took a shocked breath, then wondered what drowning was going to feel like.

She woke, her heart fluttering like a dying moth in her chest. In that first moment of panic she wondered if it was going to stop altogether, but the sensation of water in her lungs drained away as the world filled in the nonsense of her surroundings.

Sitting up, ignoring the playful black spots that danced over her vision, she massaged the small of her back. The green room of the Lyceum was not the most comfortable haunt at the best of times, and definitely wasn't built for sleep. Ironic, given that it was supposed to be a place set aside for actors to relax between scenes. Perhaps the designers had collaborated a little too closely with the directors of their era, working with them to create the perfect space to ensure that actors didn't get too comfortable before meeting their audiences.

From the speaker above the door she could hear swearing in the auditorium. It was Tommy, the stage manager. Somebody else giggled, then went silent. She winced as she imagined Tom shooting them a glare that could mummify human flesh. She didn't blame him. Technical rehearsals were a necessary evil, especially on a show as big as Joan, but they were incredibly tedious. Actors grew bored as they skipped to the lines and positions that surrounded each lighting change or sound cue. Every technical change needed to be ironed out to the last detail, and like most West End musicals Joan was a complex production. The Talent had an ungracious tendency to forget that the techies needed a rehearsal just as much as they did, and usually considered the technical run something of a lark, to be giggled and clowned through while the crew struggled to make hundreds of precise adjustments. Tommy must be close to losing his patience altogether. She wouldn't like to be the cause of that, but had nothing to fear on that front.

As usual, she had failed to bond with the rest of the cast, despite having the lead role. When she had been offered the part she had hoped that being so central to the production might make things easier, but it hadn't worked out that way. After weeks of intense rehearsal, she still exiled herself rather than lounge about with the rest of the cast in the stalls. Maybe it would be nice to joke about during the tech run with the others, but she simply wouldn't know how to do it.

She stood, trying to derail both her own train of thought and the tiny ball of fright and tension in her belly. Her back twinged hard, and she did some slow stretches to loosen up. Not easy, even though the chain mail she was wearing was custom made to be lightweight. It was deceptively comfortable, but she wouldn't be trying to sleep in it again.

When she finished, she ran her voice through some basic warm-ups. Just some consonants and vowels to stretch her mouth a little. She didn't have to sing during the tech run, just say the lines to time so the crew could judge the changes they were trying to orchestrate, but it never hurt to be ready. If she damaged her voice just two nights before the show opened, hopefully to a full house of musical lovers, she would make a disaster of a glorious opportunity.

Upstairs, Tommy grunted satisfaction with whatever change he was working on. "It'll do. What's next …? Joan's entrance. Jenny? Jenny, get up here." Feeling her neck redden, she made for the door to the backstage area, imagining Tommy peering out into the darkness of the stalls. "Jenny, get the hell up here! It's two in the morning for Christ's sake! I want to get home before dawn!"

Shaun watched from the darkness of the Dress Circle as Jenny scuttled on to the stage, red with embarrassment. There were times when he wondered why she was in this business. The mildest of rebukes or criticisms would cut her to the quick. Musical theatre, with its dramas and personalities, was hardly a profession for someone as sensitive as his leading lady.

Whenever he had such a thought though, he listened to her sing. Jenny had one of the most unique and moving voices he had ever heard. It was finely trained, yet somehow retained a startling rawness, as though her throat were bleeding song. Even if she hadn't been an astonishing singer, she would still be among the cream of the acting crop. When he was casting *Joan* he had visited several of the long-running musicals to get a feel for the scale of the production he was aiming for. On seeing *Les Mis* he had fallen most of the way in love with the actress playing the tragic Eponine, and wept unashamedly at the character's death. A few weeks later he heard that her contract was up for renewal, approached her agent, and secured her telephone number. *Don't renew*, he told her, *don't sing Eponine anymore. Join my cast. Sing Joan of Arc for me.* When she said yes, the tremor in her voice thrilled and afraid, he had known the production would be a success. Every successful long-running musical production that he could remember had gained its notoriety through the excellence of the original cast. What would *Phantom* have been without Michael Crawford and Sarah Brightman in the original roles? A disjointed shambles—a couple of good tunes, a deeply unsatisfying plot, and a flashy set. *Joan* was better than that: it was tight, moving, and dramatic. With Jenny in the lead, it was going to make history.

Yet beyond her gifts, she remained an enigma. Within a profession populated with eccentric socialites, she was like something sculpted from finely crafted glass, which might shatter if you passed too closely by. Shaun was beginning to worry that the only history the show was going to make was in the crushing of his lead actress. The pressures on her were enormous. He knew because he had put most of them there, hoping she would rise to the challenge of guiding the whole production. Instead he had watched as she shrank before his eyes. He was terrified that she was going to break down.

Leaning back in his seat, he frowned as Jenny make her stuttering apologies. Though she had shriveled as a person, nothing had yet touched her performance. When she sang, she lived. No, *Joan* came to life, smothering Jenny entirely, leaving no trace of the frightened actress. Joan was fiery, passionate, a warrior. Where were these qualities in Jenny, that she could fill Joan up with them? Buried so deep that she had forgotten they were a fundamental part of her. They surfaced only when she wore somebody else's name.

It wasn't the limelight or the acclaim of her peers that Jenny sought when she took to the stage. It was herself.

It was five o' clock in the morning when Jenny got home to her flat, and considering the scale of the production it could have been worse. It was testament to how good Tommy was at his job that, despite the delays caused by the cast's attitude, he had wrapped up in record time. Everyone had gone home happy, ready to sleep deeply before the dress rehearsal the next evening.

Jenny wasn't ready for bed yet. Her evening had been fraught— she had a particular loathing of dress and technical rehearsals. For the rest of the run she could get by without having to talk to many people. Most of the socialising was done in the bar afterwards, and after making excuses the first few times she would be left alone. When the curtain came down she would be straight out of costume and into a taxi. During these two special rehearsals though, there was more hanging about than she was comfortable with. More chance that somebody might notice her. More chance that they might stare.

Jenny liked people, that wasn't her problem. She just knew that they didn't like her.

Locking the door behind her, she took a deep, cleansing breath as she hung her coat up. Some of the tension left her shoulders, though the ball of jiggling anxiety in her stomach stayed fast where it was. She would deal with that later.

Flicking on the light, she walked quickly to the bedroom, the beginning of ritual bringing with it the first notions of comfort. Dragging her clothes off, she reached for a bathrobe, shivering at the touch of the night air. Her central heating had switched off automatically at midnight, and the flat was beginning to cool. Reaching down, she switched on the electric blanket hugging the mattress of her bed, then scuttled to the kitchen, her heart beginning to pound a little faster in anticipation.

Deep within her, the anxieties of the day still knotted and churned, but that was fine. She was dealing with it now.

Reaching up to the cupboard above the fridge, she swung the door open and took stock. Two large bags of chocolate chip cookies. She had purchased them that morning in preparation for coming home, but still found herself worrying that they somehow might not be there. Pulling them down, she swung the fridge open. Inside were a vast tub of vanilla ice cream and a bottle of diet cola. Tucking the cookies under one arm, she pulled these free, shivering even more now. Carefully balancing her treasures, she walked back to the bedroom.

As she clambered beneath the duvet, the warmth of the electric blanket welcomed her. Propping a pillow against the headrest, she drew the duvet close to her chin, her own body heat starting to pool around her, bringing further comfort.

Closing her eyes a moment, she enjoyed the heat and the softness. Still though, the deep anxieties danced, spoiling an otherwise gentle moment. She would never be able to sleep with them clinging there, so she pulled the bag of cookies closer and began to feast.

There was no true joy in the delicate mix of sweet tastes, but rather a robotic, monotonous consumption. Hand to mouth, hand to mouth, chew and swallow. Hand to mouth, hand to mouth, chew and swallow. As her body toiled to fulfil her needs, her eyes went their own way, darting around the posters on her walls. Though she was twenty-nine, a visitor would be forgiven for thinking they had stumbled into the bedroom of a teenager. Skinny female idols surrounded her, luminaries of Hollywood and the music industry. In places, the posters were three deep, and not an inch of the wall beneath the lip-glossed faces was showing. All around her, the beautiful people smiled. More important than beauty though, these were the popular people. Millions loved them.

Before long, the cookies were gone, and without looking down she prised open the ice cream tub. Some might have eaten the cookies and ice cream together, using the chocolate biscuits to scoop out frozen bliss. Had she been eating for pleasure, Jenny probably would have too.

She was not eating for the pleasure. This was just preparation.

Though her stomach was full now she could still feel the ball of anxiety spinning inside her. No smaller than before, if anything it was larger. She hated what she was doing, and that self-loathing made the ball stronger.

She took a long swig of cola, draining half of the litre bottle in one go, hardly tasting it as it flew down her throat. Then she started into the ice cream, gobbling it down as though she were starved. Her eyes saw only people more popular than she. Her mouth numbed, and she wished she could create the same sensation in her soul. Numbness. Peace.

The ice cream was gone. Blinking, she looked down at the empty tub, unable to reconcile the time she thought had passed with the amount she had devoured. A glance at the clock showed she had been eating for fifteen minutes, almost without pause. She felt bloated and sick. Carefully, she lowered the empty tub to the floor behind her and took up the cola. Tilting her head back, she drained the rest of the bottle. Her stomach was floating, but somewhere in there, her anxieties still spun.

Carefully, she peeled back the duvet and climbed from the bed, feeling heavy and unstable. Her bladder pressed its need on her, and she walked slowly, head down, to the bathroom. Pushing open the door, so ingrained in her routine that she hardly noticed yanking the cord to switch on the light and twisting the cold tap on the sink to full, she leaned slowly over the bath.

Then she opened her mouth and thrust her right index finger down her throat. After nearly a year she found she was losing her gag reflex, and she had to ram her finger back and forth against the soft flesh behind her tongue, wincing as her fingernail tore at delicate membranes still healing from the previous night. Finally, when she was nearly in tears from the frustration, her oesophagus contracted and her mouth watered with cold saliva. Yanking her hand free, noting only vaguely the blood staining the tip of her finger, she closed her eyes as the contraction reached her stomach and reversed, bringing the contents of her binge with it. Cookies and ice cream had been a deliberate choice, learned through experience, soft and sweet. There were no hard lumps in the mixture that rushed into her mouth, and the sweetness was still there in part, masking the acrid foulness of her digestive juices. She opened her eyes and groaned, then watched coffee brown vomit splatter indecorously from her to the white porcelain. Another groaning heave brought more, laden this time with cola so that the gas forced some of the mixture into her nose with a half-belch, and she clutched weakly at the side of the bath as the acids burned her nasal passages and her heart flutter-danced. Two more heaves and she was done.

Spitting a couple of times, she straightened up shakily, looking down at her own steaming mess with a sense of triumph. She half expected to see that little ball of anxiety buried within the mixture, an egg-like bag of pain and dread. Wherever it had gone, it no longer twisted within her, and she was proud that she had taken control of that one small part of her life, that she had acted and made things better.

Sometimes she thought that was all she would ever be able to control. The sink tap was still running, and she swiveled to turn it off. She didn't know her neighbours at all, but paranoia still made her drown out the noise of her voiding in case they heard. If they did they probably wouldn't care, but Jenny couldn't escape the feeling that what she was doing was wrong, that she must conceal her actions as much as possible. If she thought the elderly couple in the flat next door suspected, she would not be able to walk past them with her head raised, to smile her shy smile and move on.

A glance in the mirror above the sink caught her off-guard, and for a second she saw something that wasn't her, something that was scarcely human. Clammy white skin made the dark hollows beneath her eyes into caverns, and for the first time she saw how gaunt she was becoming. The harsh glare of the bathroom's single uncovered bulb made the sharpness of her cheekbones evident, and her hair was lank.

She swigged some mouthwash and swilled it about her teeth, a habit she had adhered to since reading that bulimics (for she suffered no illusions about being one of that shadowy tribe) eroded their tooth enamel through the constant re-exposure to stomach acid. She didn't know if mouthwash was solving that problem, but the action made her feel better.

Action. She was taking action.

She spat, noticing the threads of bright scarlet from where she had jabbed repeatedly at the soft meat of her throat. Not to worry, the cuts would be closed by the morning. Not to worry.

But worry she did, a tiny gush of chemical anxiety washing into her empty stomach. Every time she voided, the relief lasted for a briefer period. Jenny took a deep breath, trying to trap the stability she had begun to feel within her. Wanting to be asleep before the fear swamped her again, she rinsed the bath and sink clean, then hurried from the cold bathroom.

Diving beneath the duvet, grateful for the dry, prickly warmth of the electric blanket, she closed her eyes in desperation. Sleep resolutely failed to drown her waking troubles, and already she was tensing her gut as the fears grew stronger. If she had ice cream left, she would have repeated the voiding then, and that knowledge alone was enough to make her curl into a foetal ball of misery.

It had been a year since she had begun throwing up as a means of cleansing away her doubts and terrors. She remembered the day, but the actual train of thought that led her to ram her fingers down her throat remained frighteningly elusive. It was during her run as Eponine in *Les Miserables*, on a Monday. The show was closed that night, and she had taken up an old friend's offer of dinner. It had been a few years since she had since Jemima, not since shortly after drama school, where they had been close friends. Out of the blue, Jemima had called to ask her to dinner the next night. Jenny had been tired from the show, and had wanted very much to put the engagement back a week, but there had been a thinly masked edge to the invitation that made her decide to pull up her bootstraps and make the effort. She was glad she had, as she hadn't been back to visit since.

Dinner had been lovely. They had talked, though Jenny couldn't remember what about, and drank. Late in the evening, with Jemima half-asleep on the couch, Jenny had gone looking for the toilet. Full from the evening meal (Jemima had always been a remarkable and enthusiastic cook), wondering why her friend had only picked at her plate, Jenny had made her drunken way to the bathroom. The very next thing she remembered was her fingers pushing her tongue down, her gag reflex triggering straight away, then the gleeful release of vomit pouring from her.

She had never actually decided to do it, she was sure. Though shy back then, she was almost certain that her fear of the world had grown since she discovered the soothing release of the voiding. She had not done it again for a week, but when she had it had been wonderful and shameful, and a couple of days later she had done it again. Around about then the dreams of falling had begun, and recently ... recently ... she couldn't remember, though she knew that there was more now to those dreams. A sense of something approaching completion. It was at once her bane and salvation.

Release. It was her release. Other people had lovers and friends, hobbies and pleasures. Jenny had the voiding.

She was crying when sleep finally consented to take her.

She touched bottom, shoulders first, and the shock of that gentler landing startled her. Before she could call the reflex back she opened her mouth and took a shocked breath, then wondered what drowning was going to feel like.

Air flooded her lungs, and she opened her eyes.

Far above, she saw the surface of the water, a brilliant, turbulent blue. Between her and it, there was nothing at all. Struggling weakly to her feet, wondering where all her hurt had gone, she noticed that the back of her pink dress was damp while her front was perfectly dry. There was water beneath her feet. Not a thin layer above a firm surface, but a deep ocean descending as far as she could see, darkening until it was solid black many hundreds of metres down. She stood on it with ease, her feet leaving shallow depressions in the smooth surface, her pale reflection staring back at her. Behind her, the impression of her prone body on the water was slowly filling in.

Shaking her head, the wet hair hanging down to her neck heavy and uncomfortable, she threw off the sensation of vertigo and looked around. It was as though someone had hollowed out the sea, carving a mile-high space between the surface and the bulk of the water. There were no inhabitants in that strange half-world, only the water above and below.

As she wondered what to do next, her eye caught something in the far distance, a bright flash of light on the horizon. She tilted her head, and there it was again. A reflection, she surmised, visible only from a certain angle. Grateful to have a purpose, she decided to approach it and see what shared this world with her. Wary, she stretched her foot forward. Just because the laws of physics had been perverted to allow her to stand where she was on the water, she didn't trust that this was going to hold true for the whole journey. When she put her foot down (noticing as she did that she was still wearing her shoes—ridiculous pink creations that matched her short dress), she found the surface firm enough, though the slight sinking as she put her weight forward was disconcerting. Another step proved equally supportive, and slowly she began to cross the water.

Jenny woke up hot, realised she had not turned off the electric blanket, and rubbed her cried-out eyes. All at once, the fear flushed though her. Resisting the urge to curl into a tight ball, she glanced at the clock and saw that it was nearly midday. Time to add more waking hours to her pointless existence.

She ran her fingers down her body, and gasped as she traced her torso. Ribs stood out like a tiny mountain range on her chest, and she threw back the duvet in sudden fear. Climbing from bed, ignoring her bladder's need for a moment, she staggered to the full-length mirror beside her wardrobe and peeled her T-shirt off. Standing in just her knickers, she gazed in blank shock at what presented itself to her. It had been no illusion—her ribs were indeed jutting forth, the space between shadowed and hollow. Her thighs looked thinner than she remembered, and now that she was really seeing herself she noticed with a start that her breasts were smaller and looser than they had been. Her heart spasmed weakly beneath those skeletal ribs as she tried to convince herself that it was a trick of the cruel daylight.

She couldn't remember what she had looked like the previous day, but now that she saw it was no real surprise. She looked repulsive, and was it any surprise that people did not want to know her?

Fighting back more tears, wondering if it was possible to dehydrate through weeping alone, she opened the wardrobe and looked for something to hide herself beneath.

Shaun bit his nails as he paced at the back of the stalls. Before him, the dress rehearsal crawled agonisingly by. In the orchestra pit, the musicians were playing superbly, the conductor earning every penny of his extortionate price tag. The technical changes Tommy had worked so hard to perfect were ... well ... perfect.

Joan looked and sounded beautiful, but it had no heart. Most of the cast was battling valiantly to deliver, but there was little they could do. They weren't the problem. Jenny was the problem.

Technically perfect, her voice soared and dived, span and cut, but there was nothing behind it. It was an empty, soulless vessel, the very opposite of the passionate performances she had been giving throughout rehearsals. If he closed his eyes, Shaun could hear the shadow of what *Joan* could be. When he opened them, watched the lifeless puppet going through its practiced motions on stage, even that pale reflection was lost.

At that moment she was weaving limply through the second battle scene, not missing a beat of the elaborate and brutal dance. That was what she made it—a beautiful dance rather than the lustful, energetically choreographed chaos they had worked so hard to develop. While the rest of the cast hurled themselves with spectacular energy across the stage, trying to make up for Jenny's lack of lustre, she was performing a delicate ballet.

Something else bothered him too. When he had popped into the dressing room to wish her luck he had been shocked at the haggard, pallid waif he found there. Overnight she seemed to have shed a quarter of her body weight, and he wondered if she was sickening for something. At the heart of his suspicion was the fear that she might already have sickened, that she had followed so many of the theatrical profession into a battle with HIV. That was what it looked like to him, though he couldn't be sure.

His breath caught. As he had been thinking, he had been watching the battle on stage, staying a beat ahead of the dance and waiting for Jenny to follow. Suddenly, she wasn't there, and he backtracked to see her collapse in a dead faint. Everything stopped. The whole theatre caught a breath and watched her go down. Then one of the dancers, Bert, stepped forward to catch her.

Without preamble, the impossible happened. For the briefest of seconds it wasn't Jenny falling at all, but a yellowed skeleton, brittle and ancient. There was no flash of light to accompany the transformation, no sound effect to make it real. It was simply there, and then gone. Shaun blinked. Bert stepped back in shock. Jenny hit the floor with a cry.

At the sound of her voice, everyone moved towards her, crowding around as people always do when somebody faints, using up the oxygen that would right her again. Shaun ran down the aisle, already shouting people back. As he called, he told himself that he had not seen what he had seen. He had been thinking about how thin she looked, and he was very tired. Small wonder that his imagination was starting to rule over his eyes.

It didn't wash, because he was not alone. Something had made Bert recoil, and Shaun was willing to bet that if they compared notes things would become very strange indeed.

They wouldn't talk. They wouldn't exchange notes. Nobody would do anything at all, because it was not the sort of thing you spoke about. Already Shaun was shunting it to the back of his own mind as he walked onto the stage to see if his leading actress was hurt.

On the bus home, Jenny rubbed her bony shoulder, trying to massage away the bruise. She hoped it wouldn't stiffen up for the opening night. She was embarrassed and bitterly depressed. Bad enough to faint under the bright lights, though she should have expected it given how weak she felt, but she knew she had been dreadful. Performance had always offered salvation from the daily woes she wrapped herself up in, but that day she had been going through the motions and she knew it. Worse still, she couldn't remember how to fire the spark that took her out of herself and into her characters. Looking down at her slack belly, she was surprised that she didn't look pregnant, so large did the ball of anxiety inside her feel.

On the walk back to the flat she bought herself three large tubs of ice cream, knowing that there was one place she could still go for release.

When she put her foot down (noticing as she did that she was still wearing her shoes—ridiculous pink creations that matched her short dress), she found the surface firm enough, though the slight sinking as she put her weight forward was disconcerting. Another step proved equally supportive, and slowly she began to cross the water.

At first her own mistrust of the water that should not be holding her up made the going slow. She knew that she was dreaming. The laws of slumber were not to be trusted, were mutable and erratic. The difference between a dream and a nightmare was the space of a heartbeat. Though there seemed nowhere for her fears to hide in this vast world, that could change in a flash. Yet despite her worries, nothing sprang out to surprise her, nothing changed.

Soon, she was setting a healthy march towards the point where she thought she had seen the reflection. Until she saw its faint outline, she wouldn't be entirely sure that she was going the right way. With no point of reference to guide her, she could be walking in a huge circle without knowing it. Time passed, and she was more aware of it doing so than she would have thought possible. Weren't dreams supposed to be a blur of MTV edited images, fast-paced and indistinct? The monotony of her walk was almost a nightmare in itself.

Finally, she saw a vague distortion in front of her and to the left—she had wandered off course after all. Had the landscape not become so familiar she would have missed it entirely, for it reflected the choppy waves far above her perfectly. She thought she knew what see was approaching— a mirror. It was disappointing that so peculiar a dream should have for its conclusion such a cliché. Nevertheless, the mirror remained a point of focus in an otherwise featureless world, and she continued towards it. For the first time, she realised that she had the choice to do so or not. There was no compulsion to continue, no sense of the inevitable, of events happening beyond her control. What did they call that ... lucid dreaming? Yes, she was lucid. To test the theory, she stopped, just because she could. Turning round, she took a few steps in the opposite direction.

She had free will, for what little it was worth. Though she could sit and wait to wake up if she wanted to, the sensation of time passing was almost painful, like fingernails scraping a tender throat. She turned again for the mirror, picking up her pace, the quicker to end it.

It faced her full on, and she saw her own distant reflection closing on her. The shiny surface was crystal clear, and the illusion of another person in the vast sub-aqua landscape was almost reassuring, but the more she looked the more she realised that there was something not quite right about what she was seeing. There was no colour there ... was her reflection naked? She ran her hands down her body, finding her dress still hanging from her. Odd. She quickened her pace.

When she saw what was wrong, she shuddered. It didn't stop her walking though, until she was standing before a mirror very like the one *in her flat. She knew that the thing reflected was herself, but her jaw still worked in silent denial. It was a human skeleton, her skeleton, the bones reflecting a peaceful blue from the water around them. Was that what she was doing to herself? She wanted to cry, but instead reached out her hand to the glass. The skeleton raised a bony arm with her, the finger extended.*

There was no glass in the mirror. It was just an empty frame. She realised that only when her finger touched the dry, old bone of the skeleton's own

---

Jenny woke with a jump, and the dream vanished before she could capture it. She was left with a vague sense of horror, and a strange itch at the tip of her finger. She sank back into the duvet, as fear and exhaustion slammed into her.

She lay there for an hour, trying to summon the energy to move

---

Shaun sat in the bar, watching the audience make their slow way back to the auditorium after the customary interval drinks. They seemed happy enough, but not eager, not enthusiastic. The buzz of conversation was casual, not excited.

Joan had opened wonderfully, the cast putting on what could have been the performance of their lives. It died with Jenny's first entrance. From the moment the burden of the production left the ensemble to balance on her shoulders, the show became a pleasantry and nothing more. Shaun didn't want that. Shaun wanted to shake the audience's world, for the short time he had them. Jenny had the potential to do that, but he no longer knew how to make her. Act One had been a virtual repeat of the dress rehearsal. She was flawless, but hollow. There was nothing for the audience to engage with, to battle alongside. *Joan* was going to run a month and then close.

Downing his drink, fighting back tears of frustration, he made his way back to his traditional seat in the third row of the stalls to endure Act Two.

Jenny danced the second battle scene, wanting nothing but to curl up and die. Whatever gift she had possessed, it was gone. There was nothing coming from her but noise. The lassitude that infected her was unshakeable, even with the music buoying her up.

Her connection was lost. How could she identify with a woman who fought for her beliefs, when she couldn't even fight her way out of bed in the morning? She might as well be dead.

It was a human skeleton, her skeleton, the bones reflecting a peaceful blue from the water around them. Was that what she was doing to herself? She wanted to cry, but instead reached out her hand to the glass. The skeleton raised a bony arm with her, the finger extended.

There was no glass in the mirror. It was just an empty frame. She realised that only when her finger touched the dry, old bone of the skeleton's own. Her heart stuttered. The skeleton's jaw dropped open with laughter, while her own mouth remained rigidly closed.

When it reached forward and grabbed her wrist, yanking her toward it through the empty wooden frame, she was unable to offer even a token defense.

And she was still dancing, still singing. In a blink, the world of the theatre had become less than the dream. She was doing both, living both, and the dream was more real.

As the skeleton spun her round, pulling her against its chest, she had a moment of perfect recall from her meal at Jemima's flat. Not a pleasant night at all, and how could she ever have thought that it was? Jemima opening the door, white and stick-like, nothing but skin and bones. Her obvious fear and confusion. The way she moved vegetables weakly around her plate with a fork. Though she talked about old times, she seemed to be somewhere else, as though she were two places at once. Moving through to the living room afterwards, refusing to say what was wrong, yet so weak that Jenny had to support her on the way, had to lay her down on the couch.

Then Jemima had ... Jemima had ...

Shaun watched with rising horror. Something was terribly wrong. Jenny was getting weaker, and the audience sensed it. Not slower, not less perfect, but *weaker*, like a candle guttering out. Was she going to faint again? Should he end the charade there and then? Leaning forward in his seat, he dug his nails into his palms.

Jenny felt herself fading away, the last of her energy conserved for her voice. Even that was going to stop soon. It was all going to stop soon, and ...

Jemima had stopped. One moment she was breathing weakly, her eyes half-closed, then her lids drooped, and her chest stopped moving. Jenny had stopped too for a full minute, simply staring, not believing. Then she had dropped to her knees beside the couch, her eyes already searching for the telephone. Lifting her friend's wrist, shocked to find herself holding little more than bone wrapped in cold skin, she hunted for a pulse.

The thing in Jemima jumped.

Jenny fell back, the sensation in her hand vanishing, as something rewrote her mind. Unthinking, she reeled into the bathroom, bent low over the toilet, and thrust her fingers into her throat for the first time.

It felt good.

The thing inside her smiled as she collected her coat and left.

It had stolen her life away.

In the world of the theatre, there was nothing left of her but voice.

Shaun prayed for it to end. Jenny was tied at the stake, and the flame effects were starting in all their spectacular glory. She had one final song, which should have been the showstopper but wouldn't be, and then she would be off and he could call an ambulance. She sagged against her stage bindings, and he prayed that she would not put too much weight on them. His eyes were wide, and the moments dragged out. He hardly noticed that he was muttering under his breath, the same phrase over again.

"Finish it, finish it, Christ just finish it …"

Holding her close to its dry bony ribs with one arm around her waist, the skeleton lifted its other hand before her face. Paralysed, her eyes wide, she watched it grip her jaw and squeeze. She tried to clench her teeth together, to defy it in some small way, but had no power, no energy. Her mouth eased painfully open.

In one swift motion it thrust the hand into her mouth, down her throat. Jenny tried to scream, but could only choke as the fingers gouged, plunging deeper. She didn't gag at all.

Now that it was inside her, the skeleton released her waist, spinning her round to face it. She looked into hollow eyes as the arm shoved deeper into her, up to the elbow now, the hand rooting toward her belly. It was going to climb right into her. She knew with sudden certainty that when it had done so she would simply stop in the real world. Her hands came up to meet the skeletal arm, but she didn't have the strength to fight it. With a heave, the creature forced its way up to the shoulder, scraping painfully against her teeth as it went.

In the real world, the first chords of her final ballad sounded out. Jenny heard them with crystal clarity, felt them in her groin, in her stomach, in her chest.

She connected.

Taking a deep and measured breath, she raised her head.

Shaun was rising from his seat, about to rush to the wings and call an ambulance, when Jenny lifted her head.

No, not Jenny.

Joan lifted her head, and looked into the audience with a sudden calm. His skin chilled, and he sank into his seat with goose bumps rising across his body

---

The final ballad began, and Jenny felt the sudden, explosive connection, the tide of strength. The demon paused in its rooting, perhaps searching about for the ball of dread it knew it should find deep within her. Though in the dream she could not breathe, she knew that in the world of the theatre there was sudden power surging through her, and the two worlds were closer than they had ever been.

Her hands found new purchase on the creature's ribcage. The demon recoiled, aware that something was wrong, that the weakness it had worked so hard to breed had vanished. It tried to withdraw the arm from her throat, and she bit down hard on bone, holding it while her muscles flexed.

Shaun's heart wanted to burst as Joan sang her defiance from the flames, fierce and strong even as the world rid itself of her. Jenny's voice was in his veins, better than blood, making him forget his worry and doubt, making him forget himself. Nothing existed but the sweet emotional pounding of her song. He drowned in it, and loved the drowning, and wept. Around him, the audience lost themselves to her too. She had won them.

Gripping fast to its ribcage, she took the song deep into herself, filling herself up, and heaved. With an ear-splitting crack, the ribcage shattered. The demon howled its agony.

Yanking her head back, ignoring the knife pains in her throat as the arm came free, Jenny seized it in her hands and ripped it away at the shoulder. As the song climaxed, she took the demon apart one bone at a time, joyously aware that every one she broke brought the two worlds in which she existed a little closer together.

When the final bone was shattered the demon parasite was dead, and there was only the world of the theatre. Silence ruled. Jenny went limp in her stage bonds, feigning death at the moment of rebirth. At last, she was alive again.

Joan died. Shaun didn't dare to move, for fear the moment would shatter like glass. His cheeks were wet. His shirt was wet. He had not cried so since the traumas of childhood, and was crying still. With great effort, he turned to the woman beside him. She was white and stained, her own tears having ruined her make-up.

Along the row someone finally broke the perfect, dark stillness, leaping to his feet and applauding madly. The rest of the audience followed suit at once, with bliss and heartache on their faces.

RICHARD WRIGHT writes strange, dark fictions from his home in India. His scribblings include the novels *Cuckoo, Thy Fearful Symmetry, Craven Place,* and the novella *Hiram Grange and the Nymphs of Krakow.* Visit him on the web at *http://www.richardwright.org.*

JOHN GOODRICH

A POOR SINNER'S HANDS

ELI WAS WEEDING HIS CORN WHEN HE SAW THE PREACHER kicking up yellow plumes of dust on the road. A colored preacher must have been some kind of lost to have come near to Eli's farm.

"Greetings, brother!" The preacher's wave was cheery, despite the hot Louisiana sun. He wore a black jacket, and a grey vest over a white shirt. Steel pince-nez perched on his nose, and his bowler had seen a lot of travel. Cradled under one arm was a thick, leather bound book.

Eli was inclined to let the man pass by. But the familiar itching in his palms told him it wouldn't happen. Maybe if the preacher turned out to be a decent person, nothing bad would happen.

"You must have been walking for some time." Eli leaned on his hoe. The heat had a raw smell of dirt and dry, layered with the ever-present reek of pigs and wandering chickens.

"I bring words of hope and comfort, brother. Glad tidings and wondrous revelations for you to hear." The preacher wore his best smile, which didn't give Eli much hope. Just another wandering sermonizer looking to unload his enormous words. Still, the sun was hot, and Eli wouldn't mind wasting some talking time in the shade.

"I am Brother Pomfret." They shook. Pomfret's hand was nut-brown, and soft. Eli's was black as charcoal from years of farm work in the pitiless sun, rough as tree bark.

"Eli Taff. Would you like some sweet tea, brother?"

They retired to Eli's porch. The ancient one-room farmhouse was more a shack than anything else. Eli's tools hung on the porch wall, protected from the rain. With no neighbors within half an hour's walk, Eli did not fear thieves. They sat on rickety chairs at the wobbly table, each with a chipped glass, a pitcher of sweet tea between them.

"How are your crops?" Pomfret was more than willing to fill the silence.

"Slow since we haven't had much rain. Where are you from?"

Pomfret smiled.

"I have come from New Orleans with some good news that could not only help you, but alter your life forever." Brother Pomfret placed his weighty book on the table, and touched it as he spoke. "It is not difficult to discern than you are not a church-going man, brother Eli. And I do not blame you. Many men see the Baptists and Pentecostals as extensions of the unfair way of things, keeping the poor man down, letting the rich man feel virtuous as he gives out scraps of charity."

Well, the man talked a good game. Eli nodded. The letters on the book's thick spine spelled out *Cthaat Aquadingen*. He expected the itinerant preacher would be carrying a Bible, but Eli didn't let his surprise show. Not long ago, a colored man could have an unpleasant encounter with the night riders if he let on that he could read. Old habits died hard.

"The pious wait for their reward in the next life." Brother Pomfret put on his preaching voice. "But there are those who hunger for justice in this one."

Eli snorted. "Ain't no justice."

"What if there could be? Forces exist beyond those we see every day. Power beyond what small-minded white men think they have."

Eli sat back in his chair. This was dangerous talk, even between two colored men in the middle of nowhere. He rubbed his hands together, hoping to relieve their tension.

"Ten years ago," Eli said. "I was fighting the Nips on Okinawa while that cracker James Pray sat on his ass because of his flat feet. Jackie Robinson and Newk helped the Dodgers trounce the Yankees in last year's World Series, and I still get called 'boy' when I go into town. I suspect you get the same treatment, so why don't you stop pussy-footing around and tell me what you are about. You talk around your meaning long enough, my hogs'll get hungry."

"A revolution is coming," Brother Pomfret said in a conspiratorial whisper. "Those who have power will be crushed, and those who have helped will reap rich rewards."

"I've heard this before. What are you, a Wobblie come to build us a union? You always come with big promises, but when you leave, your fellows men are out a glass of sweet tea and whatever else we gave you. You prey on hope, take what you can, and move on. If I talk to the right person, you'll dangle under a tree before nightfall."

Pomfret removed his steel-rimmed pince-nez and cleaned them on his jacket sleeve.

"I'm not talking about anything as small or impermanent as a union, brother Eli. I'm speaking of a universal brotherhood of man, of ancient ways that are greater and more terrifying than anything else on this earth."

"So you're a Voodoo doctor, come to tell me about Legba and Erzulie? I may not be a good Baptist, but I don't put a broom across my door at night, either."

Pomfret put the tips of his fingers together.

"The soul of man is older than this country, more ancient even than Africa. Some dreams are so deep and powerful than we will never understand them. Only some have the courage to reach out to what is greater than us all, to find the strength to free ourselves. Only some can be free of the hypocritical morality that the powerful use to keep the rest of us down."

Eli refilled his tea. "But how? You could worship head lice for all I care, but what do you do? Charity, good works, and lemonade? Dynamite and bloody murder? What kind of revolution you talking about?"

Pomfret's hands began to tremble as passion overcame him.

"There shall come a time, brother Eli, when the earth shall shake, the sea boil, the sky turn strange when the stars become–"

"The last shall be first and the first last and the meek shall receive the Earth?" Eli stood as he spit the platitudes, but the preacher would not be put off.

"Nothing so simple. All shall be overthrown. The world we know shall be ruined, and only those who have prepared, those who have given proper worship to the Great Old Ones shall receive their favor." Eli walked behind Pomfret, but the preacher stared glassy-eyed at something Eli couldn't see. "All shall fall before them, whether strong, meek, black or white. Antiquated morality shall fail. Sinners and saints will share the same fate, all who are unprepared will be meat for the grinder."

Eli took a hammer from the wall. He stood over Pomfret, who was bug-eyed, staring at a private vision.

"Saints and sinners will share the same fate? That's a relief, brother." He smashed the hammer down.

The preacher's skull splintered from the force of the blow, making a dent the size of a teacup. Pomfret's hands flew up as his legs kicked at the table. A wordless gabble poured out of his mouth as his limbs spasmed. Eli brought the hammer up, but the body went limp. Eli caught the corpse's collar before it could slump forward and bleed on the table.

Shouldering the body, Eli brought it to the barn. There, he hung it by the ankles with the chains he used when slaughtering hogs. With the sharp butchering knife, he cut the clothes off, piling them under Pomfret's head so they would soak up the blood. With practiced motions, he hacked through the shoulders, severing the arms. The hip joints required some back and forth with the blade, but the weight of the torso pulled on the sinews, making them easier to cut.

In less than twenty minutes, Eli had stacked the arms and legs, and laid the torso a little to the side. He looked at the head, eyes rolled up and already attracting flies, the skin ashen grey, before gathering it all up and dumping it in the pigpen. He would come back for the larger bones in the morning.

The clothes he burned; the blood made reeking clouds of smoke as it sizzled, but it was better than leaving anything a bloodhound could track. Eli looked at his shaking, evil hands. Why did they make him do such things?

He clenched them into fists, and surveyed his clean-up. All seemed right, until he walked back to the house and saw the thick, leather-bound book still sitting on his table. He wouldn't be able to sell it. A book this size would attract attention. He had to get rid of it. If anyone found it, they would know he had killed the wandering preacher.

Still, he couldn't bring himself to burn it. Books were rare in his world, and precious. He would have to keep it out of sight.

He ran a hand over the old leather binding, savoring the smooth, comfortable feel. It felt worn, but cared-for. *Cthaat Aquadingen.* He muttered the name to feel it in his mouth. It tasted of dry stones, the dust of ages, and rotten fruit.

Curiosity pushed his hand to open the front cover, forced him to leaf through the book. The pages were old and rough against his fingers, uneven at the edges. What kind of book was this? It looked older on the inside than the cover suggested. The letters were strange, deformed. Had they all been hand written?

Fascinated now, he turned the pages with reverent care. Long lines of words marched across the page's white expanse, the musty smell of old books reminded him of long-ago school, and a glimmer of fondness followed.

He laid a finger on a line of text, and began to read.

For mankind is but a blink in the eye of the Great Old Ones, now growing, now waning, irrelevant and changeable as the winds. They wait, for while Their time is not now, it shall be. When the stars align and all things are right, They shall be as gods again, powerful, eternal, the new pole around which the universe shall turn.

Eli's lips formed silent words as his finger slid under them. He wasn't sure he understood the passage. It didn't sound like the Bible to him. He closed the book; that was enough distraction for one day. The sun was a blazing red ball on a black horizon, and he hadn't gotten all his corn weeded. More work tomorrow.

Assuming the preacher didn't have friends who would try to find him. A shiver ran through Eli's frame. Why did his hands need to kill?

Before he went to sleep, he knelt next to his bed, clasped his evildoer's hands together in supplication.

"Forgive a poor sinner, Lord. My hands are covered in the blood of many, and I have again sinned against You. Help make me Your tool, Lord. Help Your wayward son find a way to serve You."

Eli was a long time falling asleep.

The week went by slowly, and Eli couldn't get the book out of his mind. What were the Great Old Ones Pomfret had talked about? What was *Cthaat Aquadingen* supposed to mean? Maybe he should have listened to the preacher a little longer. The things he'd said about the coming revolution, of saints and sinners sharing the same fate, they stuck in Eli's head.

He unpiled some of the stove wood and pulled out the box he'd hidden the book in. He didn't open it. He looked at it, then put his hand on the smooth leather cover. It reminded him of a well-worn saddle, something rubbed constantly, dark with age.

He closed the box. He should get rid of it. Burn it in his stove, and he'd at least get a hot meal out of it. But then he wouldn't have any answers.

Eli was a sinner. What if he could share the same fate as someone good, someone virtuous, someone who didn't murder? Someone whose palms didn't itch? What sort of religion taught that?

A nonsense one. Eli lay down and tried to sleep.

An hour later, he was at the wood pile, tearing it down until he had again uncovered the box. He brought it back to his shack, and lit a candle. *Cthaat Aquadingen*'s weight threatened to collapse his table. Despite this, he opened the book, and began to read.

Eli walked to town that Saturday. He passed by the lunch counter and its "We only cater to white patrons" sign. Further down the road was the nameless general store. Eli took off his hat to show proper deference to Old Simon, who sat in a rocking chair on the verandah.

Inside, paddle fans turned slow circles in the listless air. James Pray sat behind the counter, fanning himself, twin half-moons of perspiration above his belt-restrained belly. He looked up when Eli came in, but didn't bother to get to his feet.

Ten minutes later, Eli placed a small handful of candles and a dictionary next to the cash register.

"Dictionary?" Pray's surprise would not be contained. "What d'you want a dictionary for, boy?"

Eli's palms itched. The image of Pray in a spreading pool of his own blood flashed through his mind. He forced the thought aside. He didn't want to end up dangling from a tree. Anyway, the thought of dragging Pray's fat carcass all the way back to his farm was tiring.

"I've been reading my Bible, Mr. Pray. But some words I don't know. Like 'asunder.'"

The fat man relaxed. A doughy hand pressed the keys on his cash register.

"Well, the dictionary says three dollars and ninety-five cents, so I'm going to have to charge you five. Another dollar for the candles makes six." Colored customers always paid more at Pray's.

Eli counted out six dollars, and laid them on the counter. Pray put the money in the register, then placed Eli's purchases in a paper sack.

Eli had never been much of a reader. Even with the dictionary open next to *Cthaat Aquadingen*, his progress was slow. Only when he was reading the book, one finger beneath each word, did his mind and his hands work in unison. During the day, he hoed the weeds out of his corn, fed his pigs, killed his chickens. His hands did the work as his mind turned over the strange phrases he had read. As the days passed, the words grew in his mind like weeds, choking out other thoughts.

Unable to sleep in the dark hours before dawn, he would return to the book. He no longer bothered to hide it. It lay open, on his rickety table, next to the dictionary. His mornings began with reading a few pages as he delayed work. The book waited while the chores got done, he studied into the lonely night.

His need to finish the book grew, his thirst for knowledge concerning the Great Old Ones. They were described as mighty, beyond the understanding of mortals. Godlike entities who insinuated themselves into the affairs of men. Their power sapped the life from humanity. Right now, they were imprisoned, constrained. But the Great Old Ones would rise in power to destroy all who opposed them.

The book's allure was powerful. Entities with strange names such as Mordiggian, Zhar, and Dagon promised their followers a liberation from constricting morality. Gangs, or cults prepared the way, on the promise of power, glory and freedom once the eldritch powers had returned. Eli imagined what life would be like under those victors, the pettiness, the viciousness of humanity unfettered.

Once these inhuman *things* were free to raven and destroy, would they feel gratitude? Eli had heard a lot of promises in his life. When people got what they wanted, they often forgot those promises. He'd made and broken a few himself. If he helped to free them, Eli would be free to kill with impunity, even authority. The thought rocked him. He could be the one with power. His killing hammer would never stop, rising and falling, smashing the skulls of men, women, even children, and face no reprisals. To spatter the whole world with blood, to swim, to drown in a bloody ocean that he shed. This, the Great Old Ones swore would happen.

He looked at his hands. He knew what they wanted. They'd killed six men and two women since he had returned from the war. Eli remembered the slaughter on Okinawa, the men who had been butchered, the ground littered with the mutilated and dying. He remembered the mad rush of Jap soldiers who died screaming on Eli's bayonet. The relief that had rushed through him when it was over, that he was alive when so many around him were not.

Eli shoved the book away, breathing fast. He shook his head to get rid of the images of gore and splintered skulls. He wanted it. He longed for the satisfaction, the release, of indiscriminate murder.

His sins, he knew were too great to be dismissed. God judged him, but the Great Old Ones would not. He longed for the peace that would bring, to no longer be torn apart by the acts he could not control. To take cover from the wrathful eye of the forbidding Lord who would punish his actions with anger and suffering. More than anything, he longed to be whole again.

October had eased the summer's heat when Eli came to the last page of Cthaat Aquadingen. When he looked at himself in his wash basin, the face reflected was hard to recognize. He was gaunt, his skin ashen grey, eyes rheumy from late nights and early wakefulness.

He was not certain of everything that *Cthaat Aquadingen* said. He did not understand how the Great Old Ones could be so powerful, and yet need humans to bring about their return. Nor did he truly understand what they were, or what the book described as "their extra-terrene matter with lapses of materiality." But he knew they desired their freedom. And the book was clear that only human worship would bring about their return.

A few days later, he was again leaning on the thick pine counter top of James Pray's store.

"I've sold my farm, Mr. Pray. I'm headed out."

"You headed up North?" Pray said it with the pinched distaste he had for anyone who left his tiny domain.

"New Orleans."

"Whatever for?"

Eli hefted his new two pound hammer. One last time, he imagined the feel of Pray's splintered skull, the sight of the fat man's blood and brains spattered across the floor.

"I met a man named Brother Pomfret who said he came from New Orleans. I aim to meet the people he worked with, and show them the ways of the Lord."

JOHN GOODRICH has produced weird and warped stories for *Arkham Tales*, *Cthulhu Unbound*, *Dead but Dreaming 2*, *Cthulhu's Dark Cults*, *Urban Cthulhu*, and the NEHW's *Epitaphs*. Sample his madness and comic-book obsession at *qusoor.com*.

B. E. SCULLY

THE DYING HOUSE

CROSS THE BRIDGE AND WALK TOWARD THE EAST EDGE OF TOWN
until you reach the overgrown railroad tracks. Nothing but weeds
and creeper vines travel along those rails now, but sometimes they
still get the chance to take folks where they need to go—at least
folks headed for the Dying House, that is.

Follow the tracks past the abandoned mine and you'll notice
the houses getting leaner. Not run-down, exactly, but forced to
prioritize. You might see a place with broken rain spouting or
boards nailed over the windows and yet there won't be a single weed
growing in the immaculate patch of grass out front. You see that
little trailer down by the toppled billboard sign? The green moss and
mildew stains are about the only paint job left to speak of, yet just
last summer the owner added on a brand new redwood porch with
hand carved railings and everything. You'd be mistaken to think
the residents of River Town don't take pride in their neighborhood.
They've just got to handle that pride a little more carefully than
most folks.

There's always lots of dogs lying around in the dust or chasing each
other through the backwoods—no shortage of cats, either, though
you see less of them. You sure do hear them, though, wailing in the
lonesome moonlight for some demon accomplice that may or may
not ever show up. If you cross in at night you might see open fires
burning on the road. Sometimes men and women gather around
them in haphazard clusters, sometimes they just burn alone.

Probably wiser to go during the day, though. It's not that the
folks of River Town aren't friendly—they'd be the first to invite

you in for a cold drink on a hot day, or take a look under the hood of your car to see where that smoke may be coming from, or direct you back toward the highway if you strayed a little too far off your tourist map. But they don't like strangers coming around concerning themselves with things that don't concern them, especially when it comes to the Dying House.

About a year or so ago some sharp-eyed reporter took notice of the numbers—suicides, murders, some combination thereof— you name it, the Dying House has seen it. Some say it started back in 1853 when old Boaz Fabry went mine-mad. They say it used to happen a lot back then, when men would go underground before first light and not come up again until dark had set back in. They say some of them got to be like subterranean creatures that forget how to live in the light; they could be eating breakfast or smoking an evening cigarette as normal as can be and then just up and go crazy. They say it's because they got to longing too hard for the dark, and had to go back to it for keeps. Whether you believe those old tales or not, what no one can argue with is that one day old Boaz Fabry came home from the mines and took an axe to the heads of his wife and six children before blowing his own to smithereens with the business end of a shot-gun. Even though it was little more than a clapboard shack at the time, ever since then the place has been known as the Dying House. The original went down to the termites years ago, of course. Its replacement burned down to the foundation in the 1912 fire that took every last member of the Nettles family, but it always gets rebuilt again one way or the other. It's not really about what kind of structure sits there, anyway; it's the place itself. Who knows—maybe it goes back even farther than Boaz Fabry to when there wasn't even a proper house there at all, just a mud hut or some sticks put together for shelter.

Places like that, where Death comes to live, go back way before folks think to give names to them. Places like that go all the way back to the very beginning.

"Why would anyone want to live in a house like that?" the sharp-eyed reporter kept asking around. "I'm guessing with its history it sells cheap, but still ..."

It's true that the Dying House never sells for much more than the price of the land it sits on. But the folks that come here aren't looking for a real estate bargain. They come to the Dying House because they *have* to. Maybe they're just driving around one afternoon or sitting on their front porch watching the sky go by and think, "Well, it's time." They pack up their pots and pans and bed sheets and set out on what seems like one-last-chance at whatever it is they've been looking for and failing to find. And that kind of path always leads to places like the Dying House. Maybe some of them already realize they've reached the end of the road before they even unpack their coffee cups; maybe some of them keep hope alive a little while longer. But it doesn't really matter one way or the other if they care or even know about those who came before them in the Dying House. It's their house now.

The local newspaper takes care to include what happens at the Dying House in the Crime Blotter. Nobody here is trying to hide anything, after all, and you can go straight to the local library and read all you want about the place until Mrs. Jeffries closes up for the night. But the town understands that there are things in this world that defy any words you try to put to them. Even those who never cross the river or go anywhere near the east edge of town know to leave the Dying House alone.

It's easy enough to find, though, if you know where you're going. Just take a sharp left at the end of the lane by the refrigerator graveyard and then another sharp left at the first gravel driveway and you're there. Nothing remarkable about it—just an ordinary prefab with faded-to-grey vinyl siding and a roof in need of repair. To look at it you'd never guess at all the lives that left this earth inside its walls.

Maybe that's why the sharp-eyed reporter was a little disappointed when he first saw the place.

"*Something's* got to be off about that house," he kept telling himself and anybody else who would listen. "There's no way this one house would have so many death associated with it for no reason. That would be one hell of a coincidence, and I don't believe in coincidences."

He was an eager kind of fellow, this reporter. He knew all the dates and details by memory, and he liked to reel them off like he was giving a news report: the Clayton family in 2010, where the mother strangled both her children with a piece of retractable laundry line before hanging herself from the big oak beam across the entryway; the old Skeene couple in '98 who shut up all the windows and turned on the gas tap before sitting down at the kitchen table with a copy of *The 101 Most Beloved Poems* opened up in front of them—on and on he'd go, that reporter, until he reached all the way back to old Boaz Fabry in 1853.

It was clear enough that the young fellow wasn't storing up all this information just to write some ordinary old newspaper article. No, this was going to be something much bigger than that; maybe a whole book or a made-for-TV movie all about the Dying House. And everyone in River Town agreed that just couldn't happen.

As luck would have it, at the time the reporter was doing his poking around the Dying House was in the process of being continued. Its last resident had been a piano player named Charlie Jones with long ebony fingers and midnight secret eyes. Long into the night you could hear him and that piano locked in tortured, tangled embrace. Chopin, Bach, Gershwin, Joplin, Sibelius, Ellington— you name it, Charlie could play it. He could have been one of the greats, all right—should have been, in a better world. But in this one that alchemy of luck and timing and whatever else that's needed besides talent and hard work never came Charlie's way. He'd made a decent enough living from his music, but a living isn't enough for those with the taste of greatness in their mouths.

One moonless night the folks of River Town were sitting at the water's edge listening to Charlie working over a minor key sonata they'd never heard him play before. When the music suddenly stopped, no one spoke. They stayed by the river until it got too dark too see and then drifted back to their houses beneath the silent sky. The next day they found Charlie floating in a red-water bathtub where his ebony fingers had played their final razor-blade symphony on the frail flesh of his wrists.

On another moonless night some good number of months later, the sharp-eyed reporter was taken down to look in the front window of the Dying House. What he saw was a man sitting at Charlie's old piano banging away on the keys. The man was named Graham Collins, and he didn't know a thing about how to play the piano or any other musical instrument. But that night it was his turn to continue the Dying House. So from midnight until dawn— the hours when the spirits find it easiest to return and roam their former realm—Mr. Collins sat and played the piano. It didn't matter what kind of tuneless noise it sounded like to earthly listeners; the music wasn't meant for them. It was meant for Charlie, who was hearing with a different set of ears.

Every night a different resident of River Town took his or her place at the piano and played from midnight until dawn. While they played, the continuers imagined Charlie not as he was, but as he could have been. They saw him beneath the spotlight at Carnegie Hall; they played the strains of that masterpiece sonata or jazz solo that sky-rocketed him to fame and fortune; they ran their fingers up and down the keys with the sweet certainty of success.

"What ... what's he doing in there?" the sharp-eyed reporter finally asked after watching Mr. Collins for the better part of an hour.

"He's continuing."

"What?"

"See, folks come to the Dying House for a reason. Maybe, like Charlie, they realize that dream is never gonna come true in the life they've been given, so they're ready to try out another one. Maybe some of them decide they want themselves and their loved ones going out of this world all together rather than waiting around to do it separately. Maybe some of them have looked in the mirror and seen something there too terrible to keep living with. Maybe some of them just got plain worn out with the business of waking up and facing down another day just like the one before it. No real way to know exactly why they come to the Dying House— just that they do."

"What does that have to do with—what did you say? The continuing?"

"That's right. The continuing. See, the folks that wind up here already gave up on something before they even set foot through the door—or something gave up on them, if you want to look at it another way. But the spirit is a tenacious thing, don't you ever think otherwise. Most folks don't know it, but it has the damnedest tendency to hang around looking for satisfaction even after the body has gone and given up. And the spirit gets especially determined when it's been forced out the door a little too early, you know what I mean?"

Inside the Dying House, Graham Collins banged away on the piano. Then all of sudden he dropped his hands from the keyboard and sat ramrod straight, his eyes far-away and dilated as if in a trance.

"What's happening?"

"Have to wait and see if Charlie's finally satisfied."

The reporter watched as the keys of the piano began to move up and down without Mr. Collins getting anywhere near them. Instead of the choppy, discordant noise of before, the night air now filled with a sweet-sad sonata in some strange and melancholy minor key. The reporter stood listening to that music until some of the sharpness went out of his eyes. Maybe he understood that he was the audience for Charlie's last, greatest performance ever; maybe he was just enjoying the song.

When the final note drifted out across the river and disappeared into the mist, Graham Collins stood up, walked out the door of the Dying House, and went back to his own house without saying a word. He sat on his porch and stayed there until the morning sun burned the mist off the river and his wife called him in for eggs and hash browns.

The reporter also left the Dying House and went and sat by himself down by the river. Everybody knew not to bother him, so nobody knew how long he stayed there at the water's edge, thinking things over. About a week later his name showed up on some big news story about pay-offs in the state capital. The story ran in all of the papers and eventually won the young fellow some kind of a prize; but he never did get around to writing that tell-all book or made-for-TV movie or whatever it was he'd been planning about the Dying House. Like sweet midnight sonatas in minor keys, there are things in this world that defy any words you try to put to them.

It's as quiet as ever in River Town these days. Once Charlie finished his masterpiece, Granny Blue's Swap and Pawn sent a van over to cart the piano away. Most times nobody comes to claim the things left behind at the Dying House, so the folks of River Town take care of it as long as it's still wanted.

The place has been empty for a good long stretch now. Somebody always makes sure to come by and mow the lawn and pull out the weeds and crabgrass. The inside of the house is kept just as clean and neat, with everything dusted and scrubbed and kept in order for the next residents. There's even been some talk about putting a team together to finally patch up that roof. After all, you never know when somebody might be in need of a quick move-in.

You can stop by and see the place anytime, if you're curious. Just cross the bridge and walk toward the east edge of town until you reach the overgrown railroad tracks, then take a sharp left at the end of the lane by the refrigerator graveyard and another sharp left at the first gravel driveway and you're there. If you're brave enough to come between the hours of midnight and dawn, when the spirits find it easiest to return and roam their former realm, you might peek through the windows of the Dying House and see an entire family together in the living room before a cheerful fire. Apple-cheeked children might be playing with their toys or dozing on a rug in front of the dancing flames. Sometimes a stray dog or prowling cat will even wander in and complete the scene. The man and woman might smile at each other, dreaming of a future that somehow or other slipped too far out of grasp for their original versions.

Maybe you'll see some dedicated soul hunched over a keyboard agonizing over those last perfect paragraphs of the greatest novel never quite written; or maybe he or she will be in the basement tinkering with that almost-finished invention that never quite changed the world. Maybe the folks inside will be continuing quieter lives—the taste of a good glass of whiskey and a home-cooked meal before the sickness stole all that away; the pages of a favorite book or a good conversation with a loved one before the brain cells checked out and never came back; the feel of cool night air on skin before the skin got too tired to feel anything anymore.

Or maybe you'll see two lovers curled up in each other's arms on a warm feather bed. They might not be married or even sweet on each other outside the walls of the Dying House. But when it's their turn to continue, they'll fill that bed with all of the love and promises and hope that got away from the young couple who curled up together on that same bed one last, final time. The next night, two more will take their place—young, old, those kinds of details don't matter. What does matter is that the lives that come to an end in the Dying House are continued until what could have been is imagined into being enough for the spirits to find some satisfaction and move on to some other home.

B. E. SCULLY is the author of the short story collection *The Knife and the Wound It Deals*, the acclaimed gothic thriller *Verland: the Transformation*, and numerous short stories and poems. Published work and other scribblings can be found at *bescully.com*.

ANDREW WOLTER

STAINING THE MEMORY

For Carlos

THESE FLOWERS WILL NEVER DIE. NEVER. NO.

Not like you in your tombless, backyard grave. You, in the hard desert earth—your only warmth, the springtime Arizona sun; your only comfort, the beady fire ants that swarm over you, stinging and nibbling on your decomposing flesh.

Perfect flesh! Always flawless skin, you. Androgyne with a square jaw and a richly dark goatee framing your lips. Lustrous black hair—short, soft, natural. Piercing emerald eyes; and I anxiously recall how they pierced me with love, wonder, and awful hatred. And in that rage, in those moments of complete monstrosity, you overpowered me; for your size was practically double that of mine. You, well-sculpted—robust chest, chiseled abs, and tight muscular calves. And don't forget about the tattoo; that was your insignia, yes! The tattoo conferred hope that you contained loving emotion somewhere within that hard-bodied shell. The irises on your left calf were purple, decaying from a love that once wronged you. Wrapping. Inky. Painful art designed from needle to flesh.

Then there was I, not comparable to you by far. Yet, my undying love for you was a quality all my own and it kept us alive. Almost.

It was I, 'Poor, lonely Patrick' or 'Patrick the Emotional,' as you'd said so many times with genuine disgust tainting your voice. It was as if you blamed your emotionless self on somebody who could care, somebody who could love the human body as well as the trees of which Mother Nature delivered from her earthen womb.

Patrick, that is I. Average in appearance, an artist of words—an aspiring poet. Scrawny, naturally defined body, and always having to work hard toward maintaining handsome looks. Marred face that seems to change on a daily basis; overly sensitive skin. Blond hair and blue eyes, an acolyte for Hitler had I been born many decades earlier.

Never good enough for you as you strove toward perfection. Too emotional was I and too blind to love were you. Always you, and you could've had the world if you asked.

Your pastime—reading your books of philosophy, of Jung and Nietzsche, and keying the chords of Beethoven and Bach on the baby grand.

No leisure for me. Interrupt. What would you have me do now that you have spent your time constructively? Oh no, no time for 'Poor Patrick.' Give me something; don't take all I have left. Hand me my books; let me browse through Dickens and Maupin and Rice. No, instead, let them lie on the carpet with their rich, hard covers. Let them remain half-read, those wondrous texts. May they keep me in frustrating mystery. Damn you!

Drip. Drip, drip.

Oh yes, the flowers. They drip to the floor as if weeping. The droplets are not clear, however. Rather, they are the deep, rich color of a fine Cabernet. The linoleum is red and sticky in places; the carpet is wet and cold. Who will clean up this mess? *Drip.* This mess, all because of you.

I call not your name. I will not speak it as I cling to your memory. All reference to you is made with a general pronoun, for I need not a name to remember your face. The memory is haunting enough; the bruises are yellow and almost faded. Then, of course, there are these flowers.

White roses are these flowers. They are not as sweet smelling as the Southern jasmine you once told me you desired. That was another time when you gave me more love than you did in the end. No, instead the flowers emit the subtlety of Wisdom, the scent of an old, wise woman. It is the scent of Lilith and all her power.

When I purchased the roses from Floral Direct, I was originally going to buy one. But one is lonely, solitary. I bought two, for two is a powerful number. Two is a number of balance, of positive and negative. It is representative of togetherness. It is the Tarot card numbered for the High Priestess. Two. One for me and one for you.

I preserved the flowers. However, water was not required. Nor did I need to arrange them in a glass vase, for I carry them with me as one carries a talisman. It wasn't the life of the flowers themselves I wished to sustain. Quite simply, it was the memory of you.

The one obsessed with love always longs for something to which he can cling, be it an article of clothing, a captivating photograph, or even a limb. I chose your blood.

Drip.

I recall when I approached your lifeless body with hesitation, before the digging, carrying a rose in each hand. Steady steps, slow pace like a bride who saunters to the altar on her wedding day. I knelt; the roses were still pure. I stuffed one of the blossoms in the gaping wound where the blood on either side of you ran in scarlet streams. Below your chest, above your stomach, a hole torn in your beautiful flesh.

I stained the roses with your memory. They were lacquered in red; silken petals heavy with sopping, wet weight. Their white purity took in the dark crimson and embraced the hue with no discrimination. Soaking. Your blood trickled from an overturned petal, traveled half the length of the thorny stem, and made contact with my forearm. Lick. That's right, taste the bitter sweetness that runs through all lives. Bitter.

No movement from you, no squeamish recoil. Open eyes that stared into some netherworld. How soon in death did your gaze extend beyond the spackled ceiling? Did your sight penetrate through the roof as if it a transparent model of the living world? Were you still here when I thieved your blood like a vampire in need of its nightly feeding? Or were you intimate with the stars and peering down at the geographical grid of Phoenix?

Yes, Central Avenue, Gay Central, always located in the center of this vastly growing city. On either side of Central, the Avenues and Streets shoot respectively to the West and East farther than the eye can measure. Central, the heart, and the adjacent Avenues and Streets are the veins. You, me, and the populous are the blood that travels through the large body of Phoenix. Love this city, yes.

Drip.

Only three days have passed and I can already sense your apparition. Were you that eager to avenge yourself? As if you have a right to. You do not scare me specter, you phantom horror.

I'll simply grip the flowers tighter, for they are the only memory I need of you; they project the good times only. The petals, only slightly moist now, still retain their bright hue. Heavy petals, sagging away from the center, like they are maturing and growing from the blood which has become their sustenance.

And what would you have me see? What would appease you so that you may pass on to the other side?

Your voice echoes an answer. It's different from the authoritative voice to which I'd grown accustom. Instead, it's a hoarse, bellowing cry into the night from a world beyond and it vibrates the atmosphere all around me. *Look what you've done to me! What have you done, Patrick? Remember?*

Of course I remember, but do *you* remember? Do you remember exactly? Oh yes, that is fine, take us both back to the night of your death. Propel us to a time three nights before, you haunt, so that you can observe how it happened for a final time. And, thus, shall you pass on to the afterlife that awaits you.

I remember the night you died.

As I walked in the front door, I paused and stood stock-still in the living room. I took in that haunting melody that you always played on the piano as I entered our home. It was as if you knew the musical piece made me tremble and you writhed in that.

I basted in the sounds of Beethoven's "Moonlight Sonata." You played the first movement so dexterously and in the key of C sharp minor. But as C sharp descended to B, the house became flooded in somber darksome. Chill me with your tempestuous chords, for this would be music of my funeral.

Taking a deep breath, I moved down the hall; the tones became louder, closer. Hand on the brass knob, I gently turned it to the right and pushed the door open.

You sat with straight posture and moved your hands up and down the keys. There was no recognition from you, no acknowledgment that I stood there observing as you played. Your almond face remained concentrated on the music, on each quarter note, on every measure. A smile fell upon my face. You, whom I loved, a passionate and studious artist as myself.

I was elated to see you as I had always been for the two years previous. Always a long day at work. Always, you, bringing the first smile of the day upon my face.

"I love you," I said.

You continued to play the classical piece and turned your head toward me. Squinted eyes and upturned lips. What had been wrong with you? Did you care no longer? Was our relationship tiring you? And that look on your face, each time, became more cruel.

You sourly stated not to interrupt you during your practice time. No 'I love you too, Patrick.' No, 'Please, I'm practicing.' Just your cold-hearted command. You directed your attention back to the sheet music. Although you were cruel, I had grown used to it. Yet, I was enraged and sick of the love I gave to you that was never returned.

I rushed out of the room and slammed the door shut.

Sometimes I wondered why I remained with you. Perhaps it was the good side you sometimes showed, for there were times we shared in which laughter and happiness coexisted. And although your dark side was monstrous, still, I stayed. My blood spilt over your sharp knuckles many times and I stayed. You knew how to keep me with your apologies and your attractive body and the great sex we shared. Lately, though, my body was becoming sick and my emotions tired of fluctuating with your mood.

So what would I do on that night, now that the mood was cold and the doors were slammed? That night, as many before it, already ruined before it could begin. And my heart murmured in dreaded hesitation as to what would occur when you emerged from your room. Soon would come the harsh exchange of words and then the horrific beating. Monster, ignore it all and let the night end.

No need for me to read that night or create poetry for another magazine to reject. Stress overcomes concentration; thoughts broken. And would it be that I opened one of the partially read books stacked next to the sofa, you would not have allowed me to continue. That's right, always you not wanting to see me flourish in the arts. Envy or jealousy, I knew not which it was that kept me from having leisure. Maybe it was control, for you prided yourself in having domineering power over me and, that, you always had.

So let me grab my goblet and drown my anxieties. Yes, the goblet, for it held more wine than the standard glass of rich etiquette. And grab the jug from the refrigerator, not from a cellar, not a thin bottle. No cork on the jug; no deep indent on the bottom. The vintage wines no longer matter. I drink, not to taste and savor, but to make my body numb. No breathing required, just twist the ticking cap and pour. Poison my viscera with your cheap vinegar taste. Soften the blows that are soon to come.

Scared me, you did, as your figure loomed over mine. Two more gulps, turn and, to my shock, you were standing there. I never heard the sonata come to a close. Tricky you.

"Drinking again?"

Yes, again. No more to do but drink and wait for your nice side to emerge. This, my thought as my voice remained silent.

Pulling back your hand, as if you would have slapped me, you catapulted it forward and knocked the goblet from my grip. I flinched as it collided with the wall and stained the area light purple. Not tonight. Not again. My body grew rigid, a lump swelled in my throat, and my forehead grew damp. My heart sped into a frenzy, for I knew the next blow would be to my own body.

I purposely kept quiet. No rebellious words from me and certainly no retort to your extreme action. No. I stood still, part of me consumed with fear and the other with the fleeting, heavy pounding in my chest. I prayed that only a few quiet moments would pass and then you would inevitably leave.

Your eyes probed me, intimidated me, and your face was blank of any recognizable emotion. Your monster was emerging. Your green eyes dulled, became dry; your gaze would not shift. Your eyelids would not flutter.

Cold sweat formed on my palms and I trembled as I endeavored to walk past you. A light graze of shoulders as I hurried around your towering figure.

Behind me, in the past, but you fiercely gripped my shoulder and forcefully turned me toward you. You yelled never to walk away from you and drew back your solidly clenched fist.

My world spun as the sharp contact of your knuckles met with my eye. I could feel my brow swell, the heat from blood rushing beneath and on the surface of my face. The vision in my right eye was blurred; a thin white haze lingered. My god, my eye! Why have you done this again? Once again, the victim of inferiority.

Dampness on my forehead and swollen high cheek—sweat, tears, and blood. Stinging sensation as the salty fluid singed my eyeball. *Make him leave. Bastard! Wish you were dead, yes.* But I loved you.

I bellowed choked cries. Surely my face was flushed with red. Red, a color of love and of pain. You left to another room and I collapsed to the linoleum floor, hesitantly deciding what I would do to make you the victim. To overpower you for once. Just to see you cry.

And those thoughts continued to play through my broken mind. You the victim, yes. Overpower you, yes. Cry, yes! Cry and let my vengeful thoughts compose a melody of dread. Let them haunt you in that same way as the playing of that particular sonata caused me to tremble.

Hitting me, always you. Hurting me. I, defenseless and with no recourse to take. Taking it in, always I, and morbidly using my pain as inspiration that was always brought on with closed fists and piercing words. Why didn't I see? I did not know if you had always been that way or if the change was gradual. I was so blinded by love! Had I known that it would have all turned out this way, the day you came into my life and came into my mouth, I would have treated you as nothing more than a one night stand.

Those rageful thoughts did it; they forced my mind to teeter on the edge of madness. I suddenly realized I had lost two years being a slave to your fury. No longer. No.

I had always felt that our love would've been magnificent if not for the abuse. Take away the physical and emotional pain, but leave the love. Preserve it.

It was then that I gathered my weak body from the blood-speckled floor. I rushed to the back door of the kitchen and quietly unlocked it. With the same tactfulness, I slid into the humid night, and pushed open the door to the storage shed. Reaching into the darkness, I grasped the long handle of the axe that leaned against the corner.

The axe had always been there. When we moved into the apartment, it was vacant and hollow. In the shed we discovered that axe, its sharp head in a corner and gleaming silver. It was as if it were part of another memory, it being the only item left behind by previous tenants. The weapon was meant for us, my hateful love.

My insides were fueled by the adrenaline of hatred, of rage, and of utter agony as I returned through the door leading into the kitchen. I saw you nowhere as my moist hands grasped the long, splintered handle of the fated weapon tighter.

Without warning, you barreled out of the hallway and around the corner. I recoiled from your strong, sudden entrance. Your face was hardened and enraged; your arms dangled on either side of you with tense fists. As you made your brisk approach toward me, I reacted by landing the flat blade of the axe against your forehead. It caught you off guard, for you fell to the welcoming floor.

You were quite possible in a daze, and you attempted to shake off the dizziness as your eyelids rapidly fluttered.

"What are you doing, Patrick," you pleaded. There was such a change in your voice. A soft whining tone. I felt triumphant as I had never experienced. You, the victim!

As I towered over you, I raised the axe high above my head, holding the very end of the handle with both gripping hands. Slight, uneasy shaking as I steadied the ten pound, silver head directly over you. Then I witnessed the terror in your glistening eyes and observed your upturned lips. Defeat, for once.

With all my might, I plummeted the axe downward as I gave off an exasperated howl of victory and thrust its shimmering head deep into the cavity of your chest. The blade separated your lungs and made a wet, hollow thud as a meat tenderizer does to raw beef. When the head penetrated you, your body reflexively gave off an instant jolt and then fell quickly still. You were defenseless and beaten, with a frozen expression of shock that sculpted your comely face.

Specks of blood from the initial blow formed a gory dot-to-dot around us. I gathered my strength and extracted the head of the axe. Visceral tissue seeped down and dangled from the blade. Blood founted and spat from the gaping black hole.

I cupped both hands over the fountain of gore that seemed to spurt endlessly from your chest. I became immersed in you, in your blood, as I steadily brought my hand to my face and smeared the rich redness over my lips, chin, and neck. Warm. Salty. Metallic. I ripped off my T-shirt and threw the stained, white cotton fabric aside. My hands returned for more of your blood and I brought it to my chest, close to my heart, then rubbed it over my hairless stomach.

My dick swelled and I eagerly stripped off my pants. I climbed on top of your lifeless body and moved up and down, pushing my stiff cock over the rough edges of your jeans as I bathed in the warmth of your blood. I felt my lips instantly curl, such was the instant excitement. In fact, I believe I was smiling more than I ever had in the time I'd know you. In was only a matter of minutes before I ejaculated. I stirred my semen and your blood together, mingling it with anxious hands and rubbing the slimy combination of fluids all over my stained body.

Lay still, I did, holding your corpse.

Scrub.

Get the flowers to preserve your love.

Drip. Drip. Drip.

Afterword, I used the head of the axe and tore open the earth in our backyard, where the dirt welcomed you. I returned you to Mother's womb.

Now was it enough to hear the story of your death from my point of view?

Your ghost no longer lingers. You must have certainly passed on to a place of ethereal setting and ectoplasmic kisses. I am left here with these flowers, these special flowers. These blood roses.

It is these flowery plants set with your life-blood that remain. And, no, I will not discard them when the blood crusts upon their petals and hardens them. They are the beautiful memory that I keep of you. In essence, they are a piece of you and they are all I can claim.

Although I will keep these flowers always, even in their most dried up and decrepit form, they will never have the ability to respond. When my hands grasp their limber stems and I cry myself to sleep in a lonely bed, they will not be able to hold me in loving return. When I throw them in a rage, they will not hit me back. And when I press my lips to their stained petals, they will never make love to me.

They are only a memory. They are not you. Not the real thing, no. Memorabilia.

And here it is, my own realizations after telling this story to your phantom. I've learned how intense love can turn into murder. I've learned how to preserve the memory of the one dearest to one's own heart. And, ultimately, I've learned how to miss the flesh.

ANDREW WOLTER is the award-winning author of *Haunt Me Again*, *Seasons in His Abyss*, and *Much of Madness, More of Sin*. In addition to his fiction writing, Andrew writes LGBT non-fiction under the pseudonym Tristan Wilde. An active member of the Horror Writers Association, Andrew currently resides in Seattle, Washington. Connect with Andrew at *www.AndrewWolter.com*.

MANDY DeGEIT

DESPERATION

HER HEART BEATS QUICKLY AS SHE GLANCES DOWN at the cell phone; the device is taunting her. She blinks her eyes and fights back the sting of tears. Her dripping hair sticks wetly to the sides of her face; the droplets accumulating in her lap go unnoticed as she toys with a box of matches. Her hands tremble, the tiny wood sticks clatter against one another inside their cardboard prison.

She was so close to seeing him again, her man in uniform, her white knight, her salvation.

She takes a red-tipped match from the box and strikes it against the rough side. The match sputters with life and she smiles as the tangy smell of sulphur permeates her nostrils. She places the box of matches carefully on the table and touches the flame to a gasoline-soaked tendril of hair hanging from her forehead. With a sizzle, the curl disappears upwards, in a stink of smoke and a pretty orange flame. She drops the burning match into her lap, watching soundlessly as her fuel-dampened jeans smoulder for a moment and start to burn. She looks at the phone on the table as the flames sear her tender skin.

If she calls him, he will come.

She dials 911, presses send and sets the phone beside the matches. Ignoring the searing pain, she sits back in the chair with a crooked smile on her blistering lips.

As the flames spread, she stifles a scream and silently waits for her firefighter.

MANDY DEGEIT, hailing from Ottawa, Ontario, Canada, is awesome, outspoken and spends most of her money on tattoos and traveling. When not writing, she's thinking about what to write next. You can find out what she's up to at *mandydegeit.com*.

K. ALLEN WOOD

THE AMAZING VINNIE STITCHER

1

CORBIN CARRIED THE ALLIGATOR-SKIN CASE down the center aisle toward the front of class. He would have smiled, but today wasn't a day for smiles.

Not yet, anyway.

His classmates whispered back and forth, wondering aloud what was inside the case. Some unconsciously held their breath and leaned away as he passed, as if what he carried was a living thing, able to clamp down and rend flesh from bone, bone from body.

The case was old and bore the heavy smell of damp, which weighed upon the classroom like stale attic air, an aroma that Corbin had grown fond of in recent weeks.

Two months ago, while searching for a hiding place for his adult magazines (because his bedroom held no secrets from his prying mother; everything he hid there, she inevitably found), Corbin had discovered the case tucked away in a small cubbyhole in the attic, blanketed in dust and spider webs and tantalizing mystery.

The attic ran the length of the house: a large open room with an angled ceiling, accessible to only the third-floor residents and spiders. The air was perpetually musty, dead. Corbin imagined it to be what the inside of a crypt might be like, if a bit more accommodating for the living. It was there, in the dank and dusty confines, that he found a sort of dark sanctuary, someplace he could dream in privacy.

And, to his surprise, make a friend.

He'd stared at the case that fateful day, after pulling it into the somber light bleeding through the attic's large dirt-stained window. In that moment, kneeling beside it, mesmerized—and just a bit apprehensive—it had been the most evil-looking thing he'd ever seen, as if it were made strictly to store darkness. But Corbin had found a twisted kind of curiosity swelling in him, rising to the surface of his consciousness, compelling him to peek inside. He knew, now, that something more powerful than mere curiosity had driven him to open the case and learn of its dark secrets.

Corbin gently placed the case on Mr. Feldman's desk, as if he were making an offering at the altar of some god. *As if.* Mr. Feldman was no god.

Mr. Feldman sat at the rear of class, tugging at one end of his wiry mustache, looking bored. He had squeezed himself into the chair of the small one-piece combo desk. The top half of his chest was near halfway across the desktop, which itself was pushing deep into his gut, turning it into a grotesque, toothless maw.

With his back to the classroom, Corbin ran his hands over the top of the case, his fingers tracing the intersecting ridges and grooves of its deep burgundy skin. The skin was tattered at the corners, revealing a yellow-brown wood that reminded him of the smoke-stained filters of his mother's discarded GPC Ultra Lights. A dark red flake of gator skin fell from a corner of the case, spiraling down like a drop of paper blood. He watched as it settled on the ground, thinking it was a good start.

He tucked his hair behind his ears, cracked his knuckles, flexed and stretched his fingers like a pianist preparing to play Mozart—or something much darker.

An almost palpable hush fell over the room. Corbin glanced over his shoulder to make sure the world hadn't disappeared. But his classmates were still there. His heart began to thrum within his chest; soft at first, then so strong he feared it would explode. Blood rushed to his head, down his arms and legs, tingling. A gentle warmth spread through his body as he looked from face to face, their eyes sparkling with eager delight. Most of them, anyway.

In recent weeks, since discovering the strange case in the attic, Corbin had told his classmates all about Vinnie, and retold the outrageous stories Vinnie had told him. Some had not believed—he'd seen it then as he saw it now—but they listened, and today they would have no choice but to believe.

"We haven't got all day, Corbin. This is Show and Tell, not Stall and Waste Time." Mr. Feldman rolled his hand—and his eyes—to emphasize the point. "Get on with it."

Corbin turned around. "Bastard," he mumbled.

Not only was the case housed in alligator skin, a small alligator skull—skin, teeth and all, save for the bottom jaw—covered the latch on the front. Its tongue (it was just a piece of leather, but a tongue sounded all the more wicked) was fashioned into a strap that connected to an old bronze clasp incrusted with green. Eerie, pale blue marble-eyes gleamed under the fluorescent lights, as if the case were eyeing its prey from beyond death.

Corbin turned the clasp, slipped off the tongue-strap, and opened the case. A rush of cold, stagnant air flowed past him. He had to grab the edges of the case to keep from shivering. He'd never get used to that. A shuffling from behind told him others felt it as well. Then they settled, *compliant*. All part of the show.

Inside the case, on a molded bed of smooth purple velvet, Vinnie lay still, eyes closed, but smiling. Always smiling.

Corbin closed his eyes, conjured an image in his head of an old man, overweight, waddling around this very classroom, his brow creased, disapproving, while he dished out vitriol in wheezy, stinky breaths; his foul, abusive mouth twisted into a perpetual scowl. Even in this quick, imaginary moment Mr. Feldman was shouting, the Y-shaped vein in his forehead bulging like an earthworm splitting in two beneath his pasty skin. Spit-bubbles collected at the edges of his bottom lip, and a moment later he was sucking it all in, like the last bit of drink being slurped up through a straw.

It was just a flash, a moment, but even in the personal hideaway of Corbin's own mind it was all too real.

Inlayed within the case, surrounded by soft velvet, was a small gold plate inscribed with six words. Running his finger over the inscription like a blind man reading Braille, Corbin whispered three times: "*Ano det liftu, ano sa tris.*"

The connection made, Vinnie opened his eyes.

2

According to Vinnie, he and Corbin's father, Charlie, had become friends in battle, long before Corbin was born.

"We fought the war for years," Vinnie had once said. "Countless battles, countless victories, glories worthy of kings, if you can dig on that."

He'd never mentioned any particular war because, to Vinnie, it was just the war. "The war is and always has been, always will be, you see. It is waged in the turbulent, spiraling wake of infinity." Whatever that meant. Corbin had learned that questioning too much seemed to only confuse and anger him, and though on the surface Vinnie looked plush and cuddly, he knew enough not to press the issue.

Corbin also knew his father had never been in the military, but during one of these conversations with Vinnie, he recalled something from a few years back: Most nights had seemed endless when his father was around—just a mirror of the night before and the night before that, all perfect reflections of each other—but one particular night had always stood out as a singular event, and much starker now. His father had been caught up in one of his drunken fits, but on this particular night he was spouting off nonsense about people dying for nothing, for the selfish whims of an evil man and a pointless war. It was new ground for Corbin's old man. For the first time in years, his father's anger and vicious words weren't focused on Corbin or his mother. For this one night, he was railing against an unseen demon.

The drink and drugs had taken his father's mind by then, and Corbin figured he was talking about politics or something. But now, looking back, he wasn't so sure. Corbin would have asked him about it, but his father had butted heads with the wrong slab of concrete not long after that night. His mother had told him it was a tragic accident, but Corbin knew falling from a third-story porch would kill a man just as good as a drug overdose—and his father had done both at the same time.

At the front of the classroom, Corbin lifted Vinnie from the case and set him on the floor before the desk. More whispers rippled through the classroom, and he heard a few derisive giggles and snorts. The non-believers. From another classroom, distant laughter could be heard. Corbin knew better, but he imagined that laughter was directed at him, and he used it as fuel.

Moving quickly, he removed a small pair of iron shackles from a compartment inside the case and placed them on the floor to his left and right. He kneeled down and looped the U-shaped pieces of metal around Vinnie's soft ankles, locking them in place with pins. He then wrapped the connecting chains around the thick legs of Mr. Feldman's desk. He secured it all with a heavy lock that used the biggest—and only—skeleton key Corbin had ever seen.

From behind him, Mr. Feldman grunted. Corbin turned and watched him stare at the desktop, peering into its glossy wooden surface as if it were a crystal ball. His legs strained, fat quivered, as he tried to piece things together in his mind, find a logical explanation for his inability to extract himself from his current position.

"It's no use, Mr. Feldman," Corbin said, and laughed. "Just sit back and enjoy the show."

Typically, Corbin feared this man. There was nothing rational behind it, as far as he could decipher, but it was there all the same. Maybe it was the shouting, the insults, the threats. Maybe it was the occasional tempered words, the rare off-balancing kindness that was quickly tainted by bitterness and contempt, like a diversion for some cheap, malicious parlor trick. Maybe he was simply a man to be feared and loathed.

Now, though, that fear belonged to the fat man wedged into a child's desk at the back of class.

Mr. Feldman looked up, and Corbin saw it in his eyes—panic, horror, fear. He smiled.

All at once he yanked and thrust his legs upward; the desk and chair jumped and bucked—a wood-and-metal bull trying to toss its rider.

"Jesus Christ!"

Corbin shook his head. "Language, Mr. Feldman. *Tsk-tsk.*"

Mr. Feldman tried to stand, but his bulk had swallowed most of the desk and it rose with him. He stumbled to his left, hunched over, the desk and chair clinging to his midsection as if he were some newfangled version of Igor. He slammed into a startled Gary Cook. "The *fuck* is going on?" Feldman demanded (as if Gary had a clue), confusion sizzling at the edges of his fiery words.

"I'm disappointed, Mr. Feldman." Corbin pointed to the sign on the wall that read BE POLITE. "You know the rules—*and* what happens when they're broken in *your* classroom." Corbin laughed again.

Gary—with some effort—pushed Mr. Feldman away, and both teacher and hunchback-desk crashed back to the ground. Mr. Feldman began clawing at his left ankle, but it remained firmly fixed to the desk's chrome frame. He tried to shout, but what came out was a bumbling, trilling sound that bordered on the hysterical.

Although Feldman's descent into madness was fun to watch, more important work needed to be done. From another compartment inside the case, Corbin pulled out a hammer. He set it on the edge of the case and watched another flake of skin drift to the floor. He kneeled down, and squeezed Vinnie's shoulder.

Vinnie's eyes were wide. Some would see that as an indication of fear, but his smile belied that notion.

"You ready, bud?"

"Let's go, daddy-o," Vinnie replied.

"Oh, my God!" a girl shouted.

Corbin turned around to see Katy Sue Boyle with her hands clamped over her nose and mouth, eyes as wide as Vinnie's. Beyond her, Mr. Feldman was huffing and puffing, ready to blow the house down. His face was bright red, lumpy jowls like mashed potatoes sliding off a spoon. The old bastard inhaled deeply, his nostrils flaring as if he were a dragon about to torch the countryside. Instead, he whimpered.

Mr. Feldman was beyond words.

He was terrified.

The other kids sat astonished. *Now they all believed*, Corbin thought. One by one they cheered him on, their eyes glassed over, dreamy. Under Vinnie's spell.

Corbin grabbed the hammer, recalling what Vinnie had told him, but still skeptical anything would happen.

He turned and paused before the class, raised an eyebrow and smirked. His classmates quieted as he hefted the hammer before them. Feldman's eyes stretched wide with horror; he knew what was about to happen to Vinnie.

"Gross! He peed himself!" Katy Sue said, pointing at Mr. Feldman's khaki pants and the dark stain spreading across the V of his inner thighs.

Everyone laughed.

Except Mr. Feldman. He sat frozen in the icy grip of shock and fear.

In one swift motion Corbin spun around and brought the hammer down on Vinnie's head—once, twice, three times. Mr. Feldman shouted as the first blow landed, but it came out muffled in the din of ecstatic laughter and applause—just another normal Friday before a holiday weekend to anyone within earshot. Feldman quieted after the second blow, and went still after the third.

Vinnie remained silent through it all, but continued to flash his plushy-whites.

Once done, Corbin surveyed the captivated audience, *his* captivated audience.

But the show had only just begun.

He stepped aside, bowed low, and said, "Ladies and Gentlemen, Boys and Girls, I present to you, the one, the only, the Amazing Vinnie Stitcher!"

Vinnie stood before the class, arms spread wide like a sideshow preacher. He basked in the ovation the kids were giving him. It was uplifting. He looked at Corbin, now seated, nodded, and winked an appreciative wink.

"Thank you, thank you. You're too kind. Please, please … right on, sweet thing, you're awesome, too!" Groovy. Vinnie felt like a member of the Beatles in their heyday. "Okay, let's get on with the show, shall we? We haven't got much time."

The kids jostled about, their enthusiasm rushing through their veins like speed. Some of the young fellows continued to gasp every time he spoke, their eager faces flushed pink, their eyes aglow, hungry.

"Now, which one of you cool cats wants to go first?"

No one moved or said a word. Total silence. Tranquility.

Corbin had turned around. Vinnie followed his gaze to Mr. Feldman. The teacher sat there, mouth agape with implied awe. His cheeks twitched and jiggled. He groaned softly. Drool hung from the side of his mouth and onto his lapel, shimmering like a fine piece of crystal.

Beyond the classroom windows, the blue skies had surrendered to gray and it had begun to rain. A light, midday spatter.

"Last one picked is a loser," Vinnie said in a mocking tone.

That did the trick. The tranquil silence shattered under a barrage of excited and pleading voices. Nearly every hand in the room shot toward the ceiling, arms thrashing back and forth like a field of wheat in a hurricane, thrust so high and hard that all the desks bounced and shimmied. It sounded like a stampede of grammar-thirsty fifth-graders.

But they didn't want education. Not today.

They wanted blood.

And Vinnie would give it to them.

He scanned their intense, hopeful faces, stoking their anticipatory fire. He stopped at a small redheaded girl. A ginger cutie, shy but intense. "What's your name, my dear?"

She caught his eyes for a split second, and then looked down at her hands folded in her lap. She plucked at the pretty, sparkly flowers on her shirt. "Susan Pilkins," she said, after a moment.

Too precious. "Well, Susan Pilkins," he said, gesturing with a puffy arm, "let's dance."

Susan clapped in excitement and jumped to her feet, her apparent shyness gone in an instant. The rest of her classmates groaned, the slap of disappointment sullying their just-happy faces.

"Settle down, settle down," Vinnie said. "You'll all get a turn."

Susan sauntered up to the front of class, her pigtails bouncing at the sides of her head like floppy dog-ears. She stopped in front of Vinnie and they both flashed devilish grins. She held a wooden ruler with a thin metal edge in her right hand. "Go on," he said. "Do your worst."

She cocked her arm back, ready to strike, and then seemed to think better of it. Tossing the ruler to the floor, she went to Mr. Feldman's desk, and from a cup full of pens, pencils and markers she removed an X-Acto knife. She held it up in front of her freckled face. Her eyes lit up as she turned the blade, the ceiling light glinting off its surface.

Her classmates collectively gasped.

Little Susan Pilkins waved her new weapon as if it were a wizard's wand.

"Oh, very good," said Vinnie. "Very good, indeed."

Susan stepped forward and leaned in. The dusting of freckles across her nose and cheeks seemed to grow as she drew closer to Vinnie's face. In a different setting, it might have seemed she was going to kiss him. Instead, she surprised him and grabbed a handful of his coarse brown hair, twisted his head down to her left, and stepped in even closer.

Oddly, Vinnie found himself a bit frightened as she glared down at him. Her lips contorted into a painful-looking grimace, teeth clenched tight.

She pressed the knife to Vinnie's right temple and slowly dragged it across his forehead, cutting deep. Vinnie—and surely everyone else in the class, given the way they winced, their bodies tightening and compacting with every measured, arching inch—could hear the rending of Mr. Feldman's skull as Susan split Vinnie's forehead into a gaping frown.

"Outstanding," Vinnie said when she finished. He blew up at a wisp of cotton that dangled across his eye. "Susan? Hi. Hello? You can let go now. Yoo-hoo! Susan?"

Bloodlust was a powerful drug, and little Susan had taken a big hit. After a few moments, she snapped out of it, and Vinnie's head did likewise out of her grasp.

Susan turned around and curtsied before the class, her fingers daintily holding up an imaginary dress. She walked back to her desk and sat down, folded her hands on the desktop as if nothing had happened.

It's been too long, Vinnie thought. This is what he had been made for; it was his calling, his purpose. This was war, the fight against the darker side of humanity. Oh, his methods were dark, indeed, but he was a tool for the good and the righteous.

Ano det liftu, ano sa tris. One will rise, one shall fall. Do unto others and all that sexy jazz.

A trickle of sadness slithered its way into his head. And anger. He was sad that Corbin's father, Charlie, was dead, and angry that he had abandoned Vinnie for so many years. After all they'd been through, Charlie had just shut him out, intending to shut him away forever. And to what end? His own. That cool-cool cat had turned into a mouse.

Vinnie pushed the feelings aside, tried to remain focused and just be grateful to be back, to feel alive again. Corbin was like a dapper dude from way back, and together they would continue to fight the good fight.

"Right on!" he said. "Who's up next?"

The class erupted into a cacophony of high-pitched shouts and laughter, arms again shooting toward the ceiling like rockets on tethers, everyone trying to stand out in hopes of going next.

And so it went …

James Wilton, a nasty little punk with bad breath and a left eye that twitched like a Magic 8-Ball refusing to give up its answer, stepped up and sheered off Vinnie's ears. Timmy "The Toad" Johnston (clearly nicknamed so for the crusty warts that peppered his knuckles and chin) sliced off Vinnie's lips and stapled them to his forehead, above and below Susan's lovely frown.

During it all, Vinnie watched Corbin, tried to gauge his reaction. The first battle was always a test: of will, determination, but mostly it was a test of heart, the strength to see things through. Once Vinnie was set in motion, victory was all but inevitable, but the scars of battle could reverse the progress of war in a blink. Charlie had never understood that.

Corbin was looking away, face unreadable, and Vinnie could only hope he was looking *at* Mr. Feldman, not through him.

Billy Greene severed Vinnie's left pinky with a pair of dull, squeaky scissors, and then super-glued it to his cottony crotch. Commendable, if a bit perverse for one so young. But the devious bastard couldn't let well enough alone. He tried to force Tara Summers—a dear, sweet thing—to kiss it. Vinnie tried to kick Billy in the nuts, but his legs were still restrained (and wouldn't have done much damage anyway). Instead, lipless Vinnie shouted something indecipherable, but the tone was enough. Billy stalked off, pouting, and Vinnie decided that probably it was best not to speak again.

A syrupy river of blood flowed slowly down the middle of the classroom, and a riotous frenzy ensued.

The number of Vinnie's injuries steadily rose to devastating heights. Four kids grabbed his arms and legs, one on each limb, and began to pull. Juicy, sucking-popping sounds echoed from the back of the room where Mr. Feldman was literally coming unhinged.

"Oh, yucky," Amanda Harrow said, burlesquing a shiver.

The kids giggled, then finished tearing Vinnie apart, ripping his legs right through the rings of the shackles. Drawn and quartered. Nice. That was a first.

His disembodied limbs strewed the floor of the classroom. Susan came back for more and split his torso right down the middle. His insides billowed out of his chest like an overflowing bubble bath. The maniacal look in her eyes still scared him. He worried she would turn the X-Acto knife—which she had yet to let go of—on her classmates.

Vinnie laughed. He had a soft spot for this twisted little minx.

His head went last, torn clean off by three ravenous girls—Katy Sue, Laverne, and Janet, Billy's cow of a twin sister. The class then played dodge-ball with it. Vinnie found it exhilarating as he zipped across the room; it was almost like flying.

And then it was over.

When the clock struck two, and the bell rang, signaling the end of class, the end of the day and the start of holiday break, Vinnie's body lay in ruins.

From the rear of the classroom, Mr. Feldman fared no better.

Everyone had been having a blast. Now the kids moped around in a stupefied trance, packing their belongings as if they were sleepwalking. A total downer. They looked dejected and sad. Vinnie understood their disappointment. He sympathized.

But class was over. The bell had rung. The hallway beyond the door filled with the excited chatter of children. Parents and buses waited outside.

"Come on, little guy," Corbin said, picking up Vinnie's parts and placing them in the case.

"Danks," Vinnie whispered from the corner of his mouth. He had no lips, his jaw was twisted, and the word came out in a drunken slur.

Corbin chuckled. "You bet."

Vinnie and Corbin were together, on the same page. It was real this time. Vinnie could see it in his eyes, and it made him feel good inside. He had accomplished something great today, greater than could have been expected. After so many years alone in his prison, locked away in that attic, he was proud of his—no, *their*—performance today. He was happy.

"Oo days, Corin," Vinnie blurted, a little nervous now. He needed to mend. Were he made from flesh and bone, there would be no coming back from his injuries. Such a fate was for the likes of Mr. Feldman, but still Vinnie needed time to heal. The kids today had been exceptionally vicious—he'd never had so many attack him at once before—and that meant his time sealed away in his case would be extended.

"Jush oo day inna cashe, desh all I need. Oo day. Good esh new."

Corbin nodded. "Two days in the case. I promise."

Vinnie would have smiled wide ... if his lower jaw hadn't been slit and stapled to his eyelids. But he believed Corbin. He would do the right thing, Vinnie knew.

Two days.

Then he'd be free again—*alive.*

Corbin closed the case and latched it. The gator-eyes flashed a bright blue, and then went dim. He stood up, hefted the case off the desk. He hoisted it a few times, chains dully rattling inside, until it felt comfortable in his arms.

He opened the door, and turned the locking mechanism on the inside knob. The room was already beginning to smell. It came in waves, a faint yet strong tang of blood and piss and shit. But there was something else, something stronger which only comes from a deeper, darker place. It was the stink of fear. Fear mixed with pleasure. It was the same smell that had filled the house when his father would force his mother into the bedroom during his drunken rampages.

The fear of the prey mixed with the pleasure of the predator.

Corbin shuddered. "See you on Monday, Mr. Feldman," he said without thinking. He stopped, still holding the door, and looked toward the back of class. Mr. Feldman—his ruined head on the desk, bulging eyes staring at the ceiling, his body slumped over in a glistening pool of blood and body parts—didn't respond.

"Or not."

Corbin laughed, flicked off the light, and stepped out into the empty hallway.

<hr />

3

Mr. Feldman's house was on Oak Street, two blocks from school. He often walked to work, and had done so on that fateful day. He lived alone. A janitor doing clean-up found his rotting corpse Sunday night. No one had reported him missing.

School was cancelled the following week, and in all likelihood Corbin wouldn't be returning.

The police had questioned him three times in the days following the discovery of Mr. Feldman's mutilated body. A few of his classmates had pointed a finger at him, but while their stories had similarities, they were all wildly different, confusing and unbelievable. "Sounds like twisted fairy tales concocted by friends and family of the real killer," Detective Bradbury had told Corbin's mother. The other detective—Olson, he called himself—put it in a more concrete term: "Lies."

Simple as that. Lies.

At Olson's request (he had to at least check, after all), Corbin showed him "the doll." He was kind enough to do this in Corbin's bedroom, while Detective Bradbury remained behind and spoke with his mother. By the way Olson acted, Corbin figured he thought he was probably dealing with some sort of doll-loving queer, still years from coming out of the closet and disappointing his sweet old mother. He almost laughed.

When Corbin pointed to Vinnie, inanimate on his dresser (the case was hidden under his bed, pushed back to the far corner, the shackles in the attic), the detective couldn't hide his immediate dislike. You could see it in the way he scrunched up his nose and his upper lip curled as he stepped closer. But Corbin could see it was obvious to Olson that, weirdness and ugliness aside, Vinnie was just a doll. And clearly he hadn't been torn to shreds, like his accusers claimed. The doll was in one solid piece, no new stitching or patchwork of fabric.

It was just a toy.

Olson nodded and returned to the living room without saying a word.

The main suspect in the murder was loved by all. The community was shocked and appalled.

"Small Town Rocked by Brutal End-of-Year Slaying" read the headline of Monday's Bridgetown Gazette.

The story had gone national, too, and probably global. "Pixie Killer Strikes Sleepy Massachusetts Town." "Killer Exhibits No Signs of Remorse." "Pixie Killer Accuses Murdered Teacher of Sexual Abuse."

The story was everywhere.

And the best part: Police were sure they had their killer.

For the first time in his life, Corbin enjoyed the "luxury" of having no real friends; he was a loner, the son of a dead drunk of a father and a pill-popping, jobless mother that probably loved him but surely didn't care about him, and in the eyes of Detectives Olson and Bradbury, a too-obvious scapegoat. It was clear to both his mother and the police that Corbin's accusers were trying to pin the blame on him and save their friend from her unfortunate fate.

Corbin was innocent.

"It's a terrible thing about little Susie," Vinnie lamented one Sunday afternoon in their attic sanctuary. "She was quite the firecracker."

He stood in the meager light coming in through the window. Dust motes swirled in the angled rays of sunlight trying to break through the grime. He turned and looked out the window. He chuckled. "The Pixie Killer. Ha! It fits, you know. I do say it has a nice ring to it, too, don't you think?"

"Yeah, I guess."

The week-long vacation—courtesy of the late Mr. Feldman— had passed and the following weekend was almost over, and Corbin was bored out of his mind. Vinnie was fun and all, but sitting in a musty attic got old, even if occasionally he did like the comforting solitude.

He couldn't go anywhere with Vinnie; not like a real friend, anyway. Vinnie was, after all, just a doll like the cops had said. Though Vinnie would argue that he was in fact a poppet, a living effigy, not a doll at all.

Corbin leaned back on a pillow, placed his hands behind his head, stretched his legs and crossed his feet. Cobwebs hung from rafter to rafter like ghoulish party streamers. He watched them sway lazily.

"Never even got rid of the X-Acto knife," Vinnie continued. "Ridiculous! And I imagine the bloody footprint didn't help her much, either." Vinnie shook his head. "Ah, maybe it's for the best. That little kitten had claws. Crazy written all over her."

Vinnie said nothing for a time, and Corbin found himself— as he often did this past week—replaying the events that led him to this point. He was surprised each time to find that he felt no remorse for what he'd done, what he'd caused. In fact, it gave him a strange sort of pleasure. Mr. Feldman had deserved it, he told himself.

It was only later, after embracing familiar emotions only a death could bring to the surface, that Corbin truly realized why he had feared Mr. Feldman so much: he had been his father in different skin, a nightmare come back from the dead.

Like his father, Mr. Feldman got what he deserved.

"So who's next?" Vinnie asked.

Corbin thought for a moment, mentally compiling a list. Then a name, a haggard face, jumped out at him.

Down in the kitchen, his mother walked the asshole from downstairs to the door. Corbin could hear them slobbering all over each other like animals. He paused, cocking an eyebrow.

Vinnie caught on. "Clean this time," he said. He looked around the attic, pausing here and there, and then locked his gaze on Corbin. "Hey now, daddy-o, that's a nice, thick pillow you have there."

Ano det liftu, ano sa tris.

Too easy.

Corbin smiled, and Vinnie smiled back.

He always did.

K. ALLEN WOOD's fiction has appeared in *The Zombie Feed, Vol. 1, Epitaphs: The Journal of New England Horror Writers, The Gate 2: 13 Tales of Isolation and Despair*, and is forthcoming in Apex Publication's *Mountain Dead*. He lives and plots in Massachusetts.

VICTORYA CHASE

SUKI

HER EYES DIDN'T JUST REFLECT THE MOON THEY HELD IT CAPTIVE, cloning the giant silver orb to cage in both of her eyes. She had no iris that Jude could see, just pure shining silver.

"Excuse me." Jude said, his voice breaking the moment's magic. The girl was in a tree, resting in the Y of the branches staring up at the night sky. Her long white hair hung down stringy in its dampness.

"Do you need help?" he asked.

The woman turned her face down to him, the two moons piercing through his thoughts. Her hands, so small, moved against the harsh bark to steady herself while she twisted her position. Then she jumped, landing before Jude without a sound.

"What did you ask?" she said, her voice a brook bubbling through a placid field, gliding over rocks slick with moss. A voice that seemed soft but held within it the strength to carve canyons out of stone if given the time or opportunity.

"Never mind," he said.

Her dress was thin and wet. He didn't want to stare but couldn't help seeing the curve of her breasts, her nipples hard in the cold air.

"Are you hungry?" the woman asked.

"I'm okay," he said, drawing out the 'O', wondering now if what at first seemed like a beautiful apparition was just a strung out junkie, a meth head oblivious to the cold that clung to them both.

"I'm hungry," she said, moving closer to him. He backed away.

"When was the last time you ate?" he asked. He wanted to keep her engaged so she wouldn't turn on him. He also wanted to play this adventure out. Something had brought him here; some willow-the-wisp had shone into his windshield driving him off the road and to the shoulder. He followed its blue bouncing light into the swamplands, past skunk cabbages and gnarled old trees and sinking earth, heart racing, and mind apparently not working. He was led by wild abandon and wasn't ready to discard it yet.

"Do you like the Metro Diner?" she asked.

Jude relaxed. Metro Diner was just a mile down the road. A greasy little place good for burgers that doubled as hockey pucks if you let them get cold. But when hot, they were the perfect mixture of grease and cheese and salt. Plus, it would give him a place to dump her, make her someone else's problem.

"I can drive," he replied. She smiled, hooked her arm around his and let him lead her out of the swamps.

There was a table at the Metro Diner reserved for the homeless. You didn't have to be homeless really, just in need of a meal. If you sat in that booth you didn't have to pay. When the lone waitress on duty saw the woman Jude was with, she immediately ushered them to that booth.

"I'm paying," Jude said. "For us both."

"No worries," the waitress said. "Suki here never has to pay." She winked and the woman blushed, her white skin almost glowing with the pink that came to her cheeks.

"I can't believe I didn't ask your name," Jude said when they sat down.

"Oh, Suki's more of a nickname," she said. "Feel free to call me that."

"I'm Jude," He said, extending his hand across the table. She took it and he was shocked at just how cold she was.

"So, you come here often?" he said, hating himself as soon as the cliché left his mouth.

"It's nice to get out sometimes," she said.

They hadn't ordered, but suddenly there were two cokes and cheeseburgers in front of them. Suki didn't talk while she ate, just looked around. Jude decided to see if her eyes still held the moon even inside the diner and saw that there were no pupils or iris, just white. There wasn't even a faint pink of veins. She put her sandwich down and looked up at him, head titled to the side, wet hair dripping down to the cracked red pleather booth.

"I can see just fine," she said, bringing a napkin to her lips. "It's just a, a condition."

Jude picked up his burger to try and look like he hadn't just been caught staring.

"You know, you can see the stars better from up in a tree," she said. "Do you like looking at the stars?"

"Sure," he replied, picking at his fries. "I mean, who doesn't? What, with them right up there, and us down here."

She ran her hand through her hair, dryer now in the air-conditioned diner.

"I have to go," she said after what was to Jude an unbearable amount of silence. She ran from the booth and out the door. He ran after her but all he saw was the silver of the moon as it reflected off her dress. Only then did he notice she was barefoot.

"Don't mind her," the waitress said, patting him on the shoulder where he stood, watching her disappear into the woods across the street. "She's a nice girl. Nicer than some of her sisters. Flighty, but nice. We think her old man is controlling. Never a bruise though."

Jude pulled a twenty out of his wallet and handed it to her.

"For a tip or the next person who needs the booth," he said.

It's hard to let go of a mystery no matter how bad it is for you. Jude knew this. While he sat at his desk crunching numbers he realized that he should let the experience with Suki go, but somehow her face and the need to reconcile her actions kept infiltrating his thoughts. He had a touch of the surreal and wanted more or to bring it back to the mundane of his life. Either way would lead to disappointment, but it's in the nature of humanity to tear down gods and build new ones, to declare saints and then drag them into scandal. We can't help but show that no one is above the baseness of ourselves no matter how fervently we pray for the opposite. So of course Jude went back to find Suki the next weekend. He was a slave to this lure for more in life.

The moon was just a sliver in the sky. He stopped his car and wandered through the marsh, cursing himself for not bringing a flashlight. Jude stumbled at the edge of a pond that was just a black shimmering pool when he heard singing. It wound its way through the trees and pulled him. It spiraled around his hand and he felt the grip leading him deeper into the woods, his feet sinking and tripping over brush. Then he saw her, eyes once more duplicating the moon, the fingernail shape making her seem even more ethereal, more feral, as it split the whites of her eyes in two. Her mouth, perfectly pale gray in the light, was slightly parted and he could see her song pouring forth in the cold.

"I was wondering if you would come back," she said.

"I wanted to make sure you were okay."

"Why don't you come up here, see the stars?" she asked, moving aside and gesturing to an open spot in the tree she was sitting in. His muscles struggled as they remembered how to pull him up the tree. It had been ages since he'd climbed anything, and he was always more into the cold steel of the jungle gym then the unpredictability of Nature's giants. Suki laughed and then reached out a hand to pull him up the rest of the way.

"What do you see?" she asked.

Jude looked around at the trees in the scant light, how the ground beneath him was pulsating with the heat of decomposition. A slight mist rose from the earth. Some bird swooped through the sky, screeching at the sight of its prey, invisible to Jude. The stars were like holes in a blanket, giving just enough light to see there was something beyond where he now sat.

"A marsh," he said. "I see the marsh and some trees. And stars. You do see more stars up here. But they're depressing. Dead. You know that, don't you? That the light takes so long to get here that the star that cast it is just a ghost."

"Yes," Suki replied. "But that's depressing, can we talk about something else?"

"Why are you out here all the time? Are you okay?"

"You keep asking me that," she said. "I wonder if you even know what 'okay' is."

"It can't be sitting all wet up in a tree homeless and shoeless," he said.

"Why not?"

"Because I'm an accountant and it's too damn cliché for me to fall for some free-spirited tree-hugging hippie in a wet white dress," he said.

Suki pushed him. He fell out of the tree, tumbling over and landing on his back. The fall wasn't far, and the ground soft, save for the gnarled root under his butt.

"If I ask if you're okay, is that cliché?" she asked.

"Yes," he said, dusting himself off. "Yes it is."

Jude wanted to resist Suki. She was probably a runaway or drug addict. Maybe she was some girl of the woods. He read about those abandoned and raised by wolves. Maybe she had escaped a cult or was still in one. Then there were those eyes. Those eyes brought to his mind dueling banjos. Some people still lived deep in the swamplands, just pure inbred scariness who eschewed modern life. Despite his reservations, the warnings gnawing at the reasonable part of his brain, he visited her weekly and then had the urge to go more often. Maybe she was the drug.

"My sisters don't like you," Suki said. They were in the diner, but not at the free booth. A young woman and her daughter sat there, the little girl digging into a sundae and the woman oozing tiredness but smiling. Happy that today her child could get a treat. Jude and Suki both had grilled cheese before them.

"Your sisters don't know me. And wait, you have sisters?" he said.

"A few," she said, picking up a fry and swiping it through the cheese melting out the side of her sandwich. "I lose track of how many sometimes. They come and go."

"What are their names?" he asked. "Of the ones you remember, that is."

"That doesn't matter," she said, waving him off with a fry.

"Okay. Why don't they like me?"

"Because you're not one of us," she said.

Jude felt vindicated. She was in some kind of cult or back woods family that kept women wet and in trees, apparently, since she was still leaving puddles every time they went to the diner. They probably didn't give them shoes so the women wouldn't run away. Jude kept slippers for her in the car, but she refused to wear them. She never toweled off either, leaving a damp spot on the passenger seat.

"What have you told them about me?" he asked.

Suki shrugged. "Just that we go to the diner. We talk. You're nice."

Jude bit into his sandwich to hide his smile.

"Do I need to worry that they don't like me?" he asked.

"Probably. Maybe. I've never liked a man before, not since we became sisters. We'll see."

Jude's smile faded. They finished their meal in silence and then he walked her back to his car.

"Would you like to go for a drive?" he asked.

Suki fingered her hair, always so damp. "Hold on," she said. She ran inside. When she came back her hair was dripping wet.

"Just for a little while," she said.

Jude's dreams began changing the first night he met Suki and were only intensifying as her mysteries deepened. He was falling for a woman in white who was always damp yet always clean and smelling of the musk of the wood, a smell that somehow engaged and attracted him. He had always hated the outdoors, the mosquitoes and flies and other things that were so unruly and didn't fit neatly into an Excel formula. Now here he was walking through the uncontrollable world with Suki.

Sometimes in his dreams Suki's mouth became that of a shark with rows upon rows of teeth. Sometimes she turned into a bear sitting in that tree, waiting for him. Sometimes all she did was cry in her dreams, big tears that caused more trees to grow, so many he couldn't squeeze through them to find her. And as the trees grew a lake formed beneath him, dragging him under.

"Are your sisters really your sisters?" he asked the next time they met.

"Or course," she said.

"Sisters how?"

"By fate," she said. 'They come to live with us and we're sisters. Some find another fate, some find peace. But while we're there, we're sisters."

"That's awfully cryptic,' he said.

"We're bound by blood," she said.

"Still cryptic," he responded.

"Do you love me?" she asked. This caught him off guard.

"I don't know you well enough," he said.

"Is love knowledge or emotion?"

"Both, or neither. It's repetition. Familiarity."

"I don't think I understand that," she said.

"Love isn't a flash but a slow burn. It creeps up on you until you realize this is the person, the thing, the whatever that has always been with you and you want to always be there."

"So you don't know what love is," she said.

"No one can, it's indefinable."

"I'd like to be loved," she sighed.

"By me?" he asked. She was silent.

"You're becoming familiar to me," he said.

"I think my sisters are jealous," she said. "I made them promise not to hurt you."

"And what would they do?" he asked.

"Bad things," she replied. "Very bad things."

The bad things started that night. Jude went home to find his house flooded. The sinks were all running, the toilet backed up and pouring out onto the tiles, and the basement filled. Not a single thing was dry in his house, even the clothes hanging in his closet were dripping wet. There were carp dying in his bed, beneath the covers, tucked into his sheets and pillowcase still struggling for breath, eyes staring up at him as they flopped about begging for air or the release of death. He picked up a particularly golden carp and brought it to the basement, it flapping him in the face the entire way down. He brought all the carp down, one by one, and watched them swim about in the murky water. Then he called a plumber.

"Those are nice fish," the plumber said, sitting on the top step and watching them swim about.

"You fix this, they're yours," Jude said.

"I'll still charge you."

"I figured."

"Maybe not as much though, if they're as tasty as they look," the plumber said.

"What did this?" Jude asked.

"Who did this is the real question. Place doesn't get this wet without help."

Jude nodded. He looked at the estimate the plumber handed him. It wasn't good.

"It was a warning," Suki said.

"I don't think I know enough about you to handle such warnings," he replied.

"What do you want to know?" she asked.

"Your name."

"It's Suki."

"You're real name," he said.

"Katie Meyers," she whispered, tears falling. Jude held her. She was shaking. Her hair was so soft down her back, and so very wet.

"I think they hate you," she said.

"Your sisters?"

"They're so angry. I try to not be filled with anger. There's only so many times you can hate someone before you forget who you are."

"I think I'm falling in love with you," he said.

"It's just that we talk a lot," she said. "Please, be careful."

Jude looked up Katie Meyers the minute he got home. It was a common name, and he found nothing about a girl with no pupils. There were no runaways with that name, no missing persons. But, on the tenth page of his Internet search, there was a death. A drowning. A late night party at a local college leading to students wandering to the pond not far from where he met Suki. The guy in the article with a familiar name, the story that he was drunk, it was a joke to hold her under. Then there was her picture, dead eyes staring up at the full moon. Her hair so long and limbs so slender even in the bloat of death. She did look an awfully lot like Suki. It figures he'd fall in love with a dead woman, not that it could be her. Katie might not be her real name; she probably just stole read the article and stole it. Plus, the boy who drowned her, Ryan Kerr, that was Jude's boss.

"What made you even look for this article?" Ryan asked. He had his feet propped up on his desk. He didn't look angry, but a furrow was deepening on his brow.

"I was looking for something else, and this popped up," Jude said.

"Listen Jude, we're friends, right?"

"Of course," Jude responded, lying. Ryan wasn't a mean boss, or an unfair one, but he made his feelings on professional distance known at all times, as well as his belief that staff were one type of people, management another.

"It was an accident. We were goofing around. I loved that girl. She was my sweetheart. And a good swimmer too. It took me a lot of therapy to get over this."

"I'm sorry I brought it up," Jude said. "It was just, well, I saw it and had to know."

"It's hard to keep curiosity to yourself," Ryan said, "no matter the pain it can bring others, right?"

Jude nodded and reached for the article, but Ryan was already feeding it to the shredder.

"Just try and keep it to yourself," Ryan said. "Moral is low enough as it is because of the economy. If people start talking about me being a killer, even thinking it, it won't do any of us any good."

"You talked to Ryan," Suki said that night. They were out walking through the woods he decided were somehow her home, or respite.

"How could you know that?" he asked.

"He still wears the same awful cologne. I smelled it on you that first night, but it's stronger now. Bastard, killing me like that and then just going on with his life."

"He says it was an accident."

Suki sighed. "Right. An accident that we were out and his car ran out of gas. That he threw me out of the car when I wouldn't have sex with him. An accident that he dragged me out into this horrid swamp and held me down in that pond while his friends, following their fearless leader in their cars, just laughed. They laughed, Jude. I could hear them through the water."

"You're delusional," he said. "You've lived out here for too long and developed this fantasy."

"I want to remember who I am but there is so much anger. Maybe that's why the others turn to hatred, it's their way of loving themselves."

"Then forgive him," Jude pleaded. "If you believe this story, that you're really Katie and were murdered, forgive Ryan."

"You wouldn't kill him for me, would you?" she asked. Jude shook his head.

"Yeah, you're a good guy. Pity," she said, resting her head against his chest.

"Do you seriously believe you're dead?" he asked.

"I thought I had accepted it. Death. Forever drowned. Just a light still somehow blinking in existence years later. But then I met you," she replied.

"Should I be afraid?" he asked.

"A little fear in any relationship is healthy."

"Is that fear of you or your sisters?"

"My sisters, they're always listening. You won't kill Ryan for me. You won't avenge my death."

"Would you love me if I killed him?" he asked.

"No," she said.

Jude was fired on Tuesday. Ryan cited a combination of budget cuts and higher productivity from other accountants. He apologized, and then had him escorted out of the premises. Jude then discovered his tires were slashed. When he got home there was a message saying the plumber was suing him; the carp made his whole family sick.

When Jude went to find Suki, biking the distance, he found two women who were not her sitting in the tree waiting for him.

"She told you her name," one said, sliding down from the branches. Her eyes were the same as Suki's, pure ivory orbs.

"You refused to help her," the other said. "She wants to be free and you deny her."

"What are you?" he asked, taking stock of their dripping hair, the same white dress Suki wore. They laughed, a deep damp laugh of the damned.

"We're the drowned. The unclean. The dead that are trapped in the kelp, in the undulating embrace of the water."

"The cryptic," he muttered. They laughed again.

"You can set her free," one of them said. She was taller than the other, who immediately began to talk, as if finishing the thought of the first.

"Either through your death or through his," she said.

"His. My boss. Ex. Boss," he said, correcting himself.

"Avenge her," the taller one said.

"I might love her, is that enough?"

They both laughed in unison. Suki came running over.

"Leave him alone!" she hissed.

"Learn who you are, girl," the shorter said, pulling Suki by the arm. The other lunged at Jude and cut his wrist with her fingernail.

"And you learn your place," she said to Jude.

Jude turned to Suki but she held up a hand, stopping him.

"I'm fine," she said, tears streaming down her face.

"You're not dead," he said, letting the dripping blood warm him as it fell to his fingers. "Can't you see that?"

"We all are," the taller one said. "Look around, what do you see?"

Jude turned and saw he was surrounded by ethereal woman, all so eerily similar to Suki, to Katie, in their wet nature. Their gowns. Their white eyes and naked feet. Children ran giggling. One pulled on Jude's shirt. Another caught a drip of his blood on its tongue and ran off.

"What in the hell?" Jude said.

"You have forty-eight hours to make your choice," the taller woman told Jude. He reached out for Suki but she was pulled back. She collapsed to the ground and a child ran up to hold her.

How do you kill your ex-boss? Jude had seen 9 to 5, snorted when the animation came up over the boss' poisoned coffee. He could buy a gun, become that fired co-worker who comes in to take everyone else out. Maybe cut the brakes. Jude dreamt of Ryan being pushed from a window, being squashed in a garbage truck. He imagined his intestines ripped out and then wrapping around his throat, choking him to death. He impressed himself with his ability to think of ways to kill his old boss, ways he could never follow through with. He wasn't a man capable of taking a life.

When his forty-eight hours were up, rather than run from fate, from the mystery, he went back to the swamp leaving his bike at the mile marker. Children were waiting for him. Damp naked children, running barefoot and somehow not sinking into the wet ground like Jude did with each step. They reached for his hand and he took one in each of his. When another reached up, a little girl with long hair that hung to her ankles and the moon in her eyes, he knelt down and picked her up, placed her on his shoulders. He had always wanted children. Mind you, not some apparently murdered ones. Another ran up to him. He saw the rope marks around her neck. The pudgy nature of children became less cute when it was due to post mortem bloat.

"You're all dead?" he said, reaching up to take down the child from his shoulders. She had slits up her arms, which swung unnaturally. Broken. A crowd had gathered around the lake where Suki, where Katie had been killed by Ryan.

"I knew you wouldn't kill him," she said, running to Jude, holding him.

"Is it enough that I love you?" he asked.

"In fairy tales it is," she said. "In fairy tales you could marry me, that would give me life again. The love of a man and betrothal before the God that abandoned us. A promise to keep me chained to you, to your life."

"Chauvinist wish fulfillment bullshit," one of the others said.

"So it's not enough," he said, taking Katie's hand in his.

"We're bound by blood," one of the ghosts said.

"If I kill you I can live," she said, pulling a knife out of her dress and holding it out to him. The blade was wavy and sharp. It could do damage.

"Love hurts," he said. She nodded.

"I'm glad I got the chance to fall for a good man," she said.

Children surrounded the two of them. They began pulling at Jude until he was kneeling in front of Katie. They held him there. She knelt down and kissed him, leaned in, and pushed the knife through her own chest. He screamed, fighting the children that were piling on him. They held on with an unholy grip, their faces changing from their previous frivolity to pain and anguish. Katie slumped forward onto his lap, water gushing from the wound.

"Poor decision on her part," one of the dead said, the tall one from before. She pulled Katie's body off of Jude.

"What will happen to her?" he asked.

"Nothing," a child said, pulling its fingers from its mouth. "She has become nothing. No body, no soul. She is only water."

"And now, for you," another said. A child was holding the knife, the girl with the rope burns around her neck. She was crying, her face contorted in emotion, her eyes squinted shut.

"Mister, did you really love her?" another child asked, his voice a gurgling toddler's.

"I think so," he said.

The crying toddler ran up to him in the unsure manner of young children and plunged the knife into Jude's throat, his blood a river frothing forth. Jude tried to speak, but had neither words nor breath. He felt the knife pulled out and then pushed through again. He could smell his iron mixing with the must of the swamplands. He realized that part of the rising mist was his own life reaching out to greet the cold.

"Say good night," a voice said, so soft even in its hatred. He realized that was how they loved, just as Katie said, through their hatred of the living, a feeling so familiar because it was all they had left. It was all they could look forward to each evening when they rose from the depths of death to see the world that had forsaken them. He took comfort that in his dying he was part of their love.

VICTORYA CHASE is a writer who lives and works in the mountains. Her work can be seen in *A Cappella Zoo*, *Lunch Ticket*, *Shroud Magazine*, and numerous other places.

MEGHAN ARCURI

MOMMY'S NOT PERFECT

HE'S HERE. I WAKE UP AND I KNOW IT. I can't see him. Or hear him. But he's in my room. The man from my dream. The drums pound in my chest. I'm shaking. I try to scream for Mommy but I can't. Why can't I scream? I look at the window. I see feet under the curtains. I close my eyes. Maybe the feet will disappear. I open my eyes again. The feet are still there. Should I move the curtain, just to see? I don't wanna look, but I get up anyway. My night light's on, but he doesn't care. He comes in the light or the dark. I move to the curtain. I don't wanna look. Is he gonna grab me? I don't want him to grab me. He'll take me away from Mommy and Daddy. I hear the drums in my ears. I feel them, too. Mommy says that's my heart beating. Maybe if I move the curtain real fast, he'll go away. I put my hand on the curtain. I don't want him to touch my hand. To touch me. As fast as I can, I move the curtain to the side. A face stares back at me. I scream.

"Mommymommymommy!"

The door opens fast. Someone turns on the light. It's Mommy. I jump into her arms.

"What's the matter?"

"I'm scared."

She hugs me. Puts my head on her chest. Wipes my tears from my cheeks.

"Why?"

I tell her about the man and how he tries to take me. I tell her that I saw his shoes under my curtains. That I saw him in my window.

She rocks me and tells me everything will be all right.

"But I saw the shoes, Mommy. I saw them."

"All right, sweetie. Show me."

I'm still afraid to turn back and look, but Mommy's here, so everything is okay. But I still don't look. I just point at the floor where the shoes were.

Mommy laughs. "Oh, sweetie. Those are your shoes. See?" She tries to take me out of her arms, but I am not letting go. She walks us over to the window and sits on the floor. She pulls my face toward the floor.

"See?" she says again, showing me my snow boots.

I giggle.

Then I remember the face.

"But he was behind the curtain, Mommy. I saw him."

She pulls back the curtain.

Two faces look back at me this time. I scream.

"Baby, baby. Shhhh," says Mommy. "Just look."

My cheeks are wet. I have boogies. But I turn my head to look. I see a little boy in his mommy's arms.

I smile.

"That's me and you, Mommy."

"That's right, sweetie. That's what happens when it's dark. When there's a light on, it's more like a mirror than a window."

She waves at us. I wave back.

She tucks me back into bed and pushes my hair off of my face. She kisses my forehead.

"Don't worry, sweetie. It was just a dream. It's just you and me."

"And Daddy and Katie?"

"And Daddy and Katie."

Katie is my little sister. She's two. She sleeps in a crib.

"Okay, Mommy."

"Good night, sweetie."

"Good night, Mommy."

––––––––––

The next night, I dream of him and I wake up. He's here again. He's back to take me. I know it. I pull the covers over my head. Maybe he won't see me. But now I can't see him. My hair is wet. I'm sweaty. I take off the covers. I pull my legs out from under them. My body is cooler. I flip my pillow over to the cool side. It feels good on my sweaty face. It helps me to relax. I get sleepy. My arm hangs off the side of the bed, almost touching the floor. Something fuzzy touches my hand. Is it my teddy bear? No, he's right next to my head. Maybe it's Katie's teddy. She's always leaving her things in my room. My body jerks. Like someone tried to pull me off the bed by my arm. I yank my arm up and pull the covers back on to me. I am wide awake. And I'm hot, but I don't care. The covers will protect me from him.

But he's under my bed. I know it. I can't get to Daddy. I can't get to Mommy. He'll grab my ankles and pull me under there with him. I can't get away from him. I don't know what to do. I scream.

"Mommymommymommy!"

The door opens fast. Someone turns on the light. It's Mommy. I don't jump to her this time. I'm not moving from the bed. I don't want him to grab me. What if he grabs Mommy?

"What's the matter, sweetie?"

"He's under the bed," I say through tears. "Be careful, Mommy."

"There's no one under the bed."

"But he touched me. He was fuzzy. And he tried to pull me off of the bed."

Mommy bends down to look under the bed.

"Baby," she says, smiling. "Come look."

"No," I say, pulling the sheets tighter around me.

"Come here," she says, picking me up and sitting me on the floor next to her.

"Look," she says, pointing under the bed.

I lean down to see what's there. I see some old Legos. And my Chewbacca doll. The one I couldn't find yesterday.

"Looks like Chewie was trying to tell you where he was," she says.

I laugh.

Then I remember the yanking.

"But why did my body jerk?"

"Sometimes, right before you fall asleep, your body is so relaxed that it forgets itself and twitches. And sometimes it can be a pretty hard twitch. It happens to me all the time."

"And Daddy?"

"And Daddy."

"And Katie?"

"Well," she says, laughing. "She's not old enough to tell me something like that, but I used to see it happen to her when she was a baby."

"Oh."

"Okay, sweetie. It was just a dream. Everything is all right. It's just you and me. And Daddy and Katie."

"Okay, Mommy. I love you."

"I love you, too."

I wake up during the next night. From my dream. He's here. Why is the closet door open? I know Mommy closed it before she left. Is a shadow moving inside the closet? I hear a stomach rumble. I ate all of my dinner. I am not hungry. It's not my tummy. I hear a sniff. I see an arm reach out of the closet. I see a hand. It has claws. I scream.

"Mommymommymommy!"

I close my eyes when I yell for Mommy. I don't hear her feet coming down the hallway. I don't hear my door. I don't hear her voice.

I scream again.

After the scream, I remember the flashlight Mommy put next to my pillow before tucking me into bed. I click it on and shine it in the closet.

No one is there. Just my suit for fancy stuff and a pile of blankets on the top shelf.

I still don't hear Mommy.

But I hear Katie. She is screaming. Maybe she is having a bad dream. Mommy must be asleep and can't hear. I am a big boy. Maybe I can help Katie.

I take my flashlight across the hall to Katie's room. When I get to the door, she stops crying.

I push open the door. When I peek in, I drop the flashlight. I am frozen. I am too afraid to move.

He is there. He wears snow boots. Like mine. But bigger. Much bigger. His hair is fuzzy. He wears a long, dark coat. He is standing over Katie's crib. Katie is not in it. Where is Katie?

He turns to look at me.

"Mom—Mommy said you were just a dream."

"Your mommy was wrong," he says. "I am not just a dream."

He steps closer to me.

"I was here last night."

Closer.

"I was here the night before."

Even closer.

"I have been here all week."

He stands right in front of me. He is tall. The tallest man I've ever seen. His breath is hot. And smelly. But I can't see his face. The room is too dark.

I can't move. I have an accident. My pants are all wet.

"I've already visited your parents' room."

"You took Mommy?"

"And Daddy."

"And Katie?"

He nods his head.

"Your sister was tasty," he says, leaning in to my face. I still can't see his.

"And now," he says, sniffing at me. "I am going to eat you."

"MOMM—"

MEGHAN ARCURI is new to writing fiction and poetry. Her first published story, "Inevitable," appears in *Chiral Mad*, an anthology of psychological horror. She also has a poem in *Angels Cried*, an anthology honoring victims of the Sandy Hook shootings.

ROBERT DAVIES

DEAD LETTER OFFICE

JOHN CHASE TUCKED HIS BRIEFCASE UNDER HIS ARM and reached down to pick up the package. Meticulously wrapped in thick brown paper, the small box waiting on the doorstep smelled odd. He peered at the address label, but did not recognize the handwriting. The postage was nineteen mismatched stamps. There was no return address.

Maybe Elise had been on eBay again, despite her promises.

Cradling the package under his arm, he let himself into the house, kicked the mail that had been shoved into the mail slot—mostly bills and baby catalogs, as always—aside, and threw his keys on the small end table. He held the box gingerly as he walked into the kitchen. A weight shifted inside, making the box wobble in his hand.

Chase tore at the paper and placed the revealed cardboard box on the counter. It struck him then that the box smelled like rotten meat. Annoyed, he reached for the paring knife. He carefully slit the several layers of cellophane tape along the top. He dropped the knife into the sink and flipped open the flaps. He stared for a long time. The tangible, sour smell of rot now poured from the box in waves, coating the back of his throat with bile.

The box contained the corpse of a gerbil. A fluorescent pink Post-it note was tacked into its skull with a blue push pin. The note read: "You slept with my wife."

The rough chatter of Elise's car struggling up the driveway startled him.

The kitchen seemed to shrink around him as his skin went cold. His heart pounded.

He could not explain this, not now. It was over. It had been over for months. Ever since Elise had learned she was pregnant, ever since he learned he was going to be a father for the first time. He had ended it with Michelle the very next day.

Michelle, a perennial mistress, had taken their breakup in stride.

Her husband, apparently, had not.

The trash bucket was overflowing. Coffee-stained business reports, week-old newspapers, and aluminum containers from last night's Thai food. Chase tried to pack the trash down, but there was no room. Not for a dead gerbil.

Elise's key rattled in the lock.

He turned to the sink. Panicked, he jammed the stiff rodent and the incriminating note into the garbage disposal and flipped the switch. The disposal kicked into gear with a loud cyclical roar. The taste of rotting muscle and congealed blood exploded in his mouth as gerbil innards splashed up in his face and splattered the inside of the sink. A gerbil paw gyrated wildly round and round before being pulled under. The disposal protested for a long moment, but the bones finally were splintered and went down. The sink resembled a perverse Spin-Art creation of sinew, fur, cold Pad Thai noodles, and blood. It smelled even worse. Gagging, he turned the faucet on full blast, splashing water on his face and neck.

"I'm home, Jon," Elise said, coming into the kitchen.

The rotten stench drilled into him. He threw up into the sink, his vomit and the water washing the last of the gerbil blood away.

"Are you alright?"

He stood shivering for a few seconds before he could make himself speak. "I had some bad sushi I think," he said, wiping his chin. He let the water run, using his hand to rinse off the stainless steel. "Went to lunch with Stevenson from accounting."

"Well, at least you don't have morning sickness," she said. She came up behind him and pressed against his back. "Jonathan, you're all clammy. Do you have a fever?"

"I just need a shower," he said. He tried to smile. "And a cold beer."

Chase stood under the hot water for a long time, letting it run over his shoulders and down his back. He would have to do something about Michelle's husband. It had been a quick fling. Nothing more. Mark would have to understand.

Running his soapy fingers through his hair, Chase felt a small lump. He plucked it out and peered at it. A small knob trailing stringy tissue.

The gerbil's eyeball.

Chase had tried calling Michelle all morning, but there was no answer. He had to set up a meeting with her husband Mark. Stop things before they spiraled out of control. Elise could never find out about the affair. She would be shattered. He hated himself more than he thought he ever could.

She couldn't be around when the next package came. And he was sure there would be another one.

Chase zoned out during a couple of client meetings, nearly getting busted a few times with annoying questions. Realizing there was no chance of getting anything done in the office, he skipped out at lunch and sped home to get the mail before Elise got home.

Another package waited on the stoop. This one was larger than the last, but the handwriting on the address label matched Mark's puerile scrawl. Chase hefted the cardboard box, wondering whether he should open it at all. It was quite heavy.

He took the box to his study.

He would just have to make Mark understand. Spouses cheat all the time. You get over it. A small bump in the road. Nothing to go overboard about. It all made so much sense when he put it that way. Surely, Mark would listen to reason. They would laugh it off even. Everything would be fine.

Chase tore at the tape and ripped through the cardboard, peeling a side of the box open. A red toolbox was inside, its lid held shut with two metal clasps. He slid the toolbox out and set it on his knees, snapped each clasp open, and lifted the lid.

A small white poodle with ruined paws lay inside, all its orifices sewn shut with fishing line, its wet claws splintered and torn. Its arms and legs were stained dark brown. The interior of the toolbox was covered with a crazy patchwork of deep scratches. The dog had been placed in the toolbox alive. Nestled beside it was a well-worn Magic 8-Ball, sticky with blood.

No matter how many times Chase shook the black orb, the prophetic white triangle always rose from the shadowy blue depths with the same message: "You Will Pay."

Chase buried the poodle behind the tool shed, finishing with only a few minutes to spare.

Elise pulled in the driveway as he was washing the dirt and blood from his fingernails.

———

Chase called in sick to work the next day. He had to convince Elise to go down to the boutique, told her he just needed to catch up on his sleep. He had that nasty head cold that was going around. Maybe it was his allergies. Maybe, he thought, there is some fucking madman with too much time on his hands, and a fucking hard-on for scaring the living shit out of me.

Maybe he should just go over and see Mark in person, talk things over.

That thought quickly left his mind. The idea of facing Mark Edgars, a man who was not all there, a man who clearly was insane, did not sit well with Chase. At least the things Edgars sent through the mail couldn't hurt him. Scare the hell out of him, sure. But here in his own house, Chase was not in danger of bodily harm.

It would be better to call.

He made a few phone calls and was able to get Mark's cell phone number from an old high school friend.

He sat around in his silk pajamas until he worked up the nerve to call. A few times he started to dial the number, but got cold feet before the seventh digit. Once or twice he let it ring once before slamming down the receiver. Finally, he put the phone on speaker, dialed, and stood up, pacing the room. One ring. Two rings. Each ring seemed to grow louder and longer. Seven rings. Eight. No answer. He waited for the machine to pick up, but it just kept ringing.

He knocked the phone off the table.

He decided to write a letter.

———

Chase met the mailman at the door and exchanged the letter for a small brown package.

"My wife ordered like crazy from the baby catalogs for our first kid, too," the mailman said, grinning. "You better hide the credit cards."

Chase just nodded, taking the package. "Yeah, thanks."

He closed the door. Sweat was already on his forehead; his ears were ringing.

He almost threw the package in the trash unopened. He would show Edgars who was in charge. He wasn't playing the game anymore.

He then saw the postmark. It was dated 1981. Terra Haute, Indiana, his hometown. How the hell had this gotten through the Post Office?

He sat at the kitchen table, waiting, waiting. Finally, he opened the box.

Chase had never really believed his mother when she had said his pet turtle had run away. He had assumed that his pet had died of old age or because he had forgotten to feed it, and his parents had been forced to throw it out with the trash. Even at that young age he knew how things worked. But he had been so very wrong.

It wasn't age or hunger that killed Mr. Tippy. It was Mark Edgars.

The turtle's shell had been cracked open along carapace, and the pale yellow, striated plastron on its underside had been splayed open. The strangely man-shaped gelatinous body of his beloved pet turtle was pierced with ten hypodermic syringes filled with gasoline. A matchbook hung in its beak.

There was a single match remaining. On the inside cover, the word "cheater" was written in dark red lipstick.

He drove over to Michelle's house, the house where they had met in secret all those many afternoons. Maybe he could catch her at home. At worst, Mark would be home and they could settle things man to man.

He saw the For Sale sign on the manicured lawn first. He parked at the curb and jogged up to the front door.

Through the front windows he could see that the house was empty.

The mailbox was empty, too.

"Yes, I want all my mail held," Chase said, his voice echoing with the bad connection. "Letters, boxes, whatever. I do not want them going to my house. Do you understand? I want everything held."

"Yes, sir," said the postal worker, annoyed. "I can understand you. I'll put the change in."

"Please do," Chase said. He slammed the phone down.

Something moved by the front door, throwing a length of shadow across the floor for a brief moment. Chase ran to the door and threw it open. The yard was empty. The walkway, too.

There was another package on the doorstep. No address, no postage, only "Jonathan Chase" written in black marker on the side.

Suppressing tears, Chase sat on the doorstep and slit the box open with his key.

Crumpled up newspaper soaked in blood filled the box. The cloying sweetness of it filled his nose. Several pages were wrapped around a fist-sized something. As Chase peeled the sodden layers away, he saw the masthead of the newspaper and nearly jumped.

New Boston Times, June 26, 2059. The fragment of headline not obscured by blood read: "Third Mars Colony Needs..."

Chase didn't even take a moment to let the fact sink in. He tore at the pages with pent up anger, the blood tacky on his fingers. Buried at the heart of the paper was a dead Martian rat. It was clearly identified "*Rattus Arianus*" by the label dangling from its right hind foot.

A typed note from Edgars lay at the bottom, protected in cellophane wrap. "You have taken something precious from me."

Chase sat on the stoop and cried.

After a time, he again made the walk to the tool shed and took out the shovel.

"Elise, I think we should take a vacation."

She nodded, chewing her pizza.

"I mean now. We can leave tomorrow."

She smiled. "Can't. We are swamped down at the boutique. Lisa would kill me."

"She can handle it," he said. "We need some time away. We won't get many more chances."

"That's another thing," she said. "I have an appointment with Dr. Brown on Monday. I've already rescheduled once. Maybe in a few weeks we can go down to the Cape. OK?"

He wasn't sure if it really mattered. People got packages all over the country. Global Priority. Overnight Express. Edgars could reach him anywhere on the globe. At any time. It was no use running.

"Sure, honey. Sounds great."

His heart hurt with the pounding. His throat was always dry now.

Chase called in sick for the rest of the week.

A UPS driver with bad acne arrived early with a large wooden crate teetering on a metal dolly. The crate was covered with a rainbow of customs stickers and stamps from different ports. He glared at Chase as he waited for the required signature.

The driver nodded and mumbled thanks as he took the electronic pad from Chase's hands and wheeled the dolly down the walkway. Chase pushed the massive crate into the house, barely making it through the doorway. He managed to shimmy the crate onto an old red blanket and slid it into the living room.

As Chase stared at the crate, looming like some strange monolith, it struck him that it was the ideal size for a body. He remembered the last note and froze.

He couldn't bring himself to open the crate.

He got himself a shot of Bushmills, sat in his leather chair, and stared at the crate for several minutes.

An hour later, Chase was drinking the whiskey straight from the bottle. It emptied far too quickly and with too little effect, but he somehow found enough liquid courage to get up and make his way to the tool shed. It smelled like freshly turned earth. Brushing away cobwebs, he rummaged through the dark, damp shed until he found the crowbar. He hefted it as he made his way back to the house.

He marvelled at the size of the wooden box in the living room. It was a gravestone for a giant.

No, he couldn't think of graves. Not now.

Gritting his teeth, Chase worried the large black nails off of one side. He pried at the wooden panel, cracking it in a few places before it finally came loose. He let it crash to the floor.

Inside was a large blue barrel with the words "Sorrow!" spray-painted in black on the side. Dark dried rivulets ran down from the "S" and the exclamation point. He rolled the barrel out onto the hardwood floor. He was sweating now, his palms soaked. He knew what he would find.

He popped the top open with the crowbar. A violent smell like spoiled fruit and sweat rose off the corpse of the 20-foot anaconda.

123

It lay in the barrel like the senescent lime green phallus of some ancient, unwashed titan, its lifeless eyes black marbles. Chase tipped the barrel over and spilled the snake onto the floor. To his increasing dismay, a great bulge swelled about halfway down the snake's body. Had it been pregnant? His mind filled with the image of hundreds of tiny black snakes coiling in the dark, cold amniotic slime.

At once he was filled with relief that it wasn't Elise and wild rage that it easily could have been.

"You bastard!"

He slammed the crowbar into the tough flesh of the snake without pausing to think. He had whiskey reasons now. He just hacked away with malicious glee, opening the snake like some macabre piñata. Finally, the snake's gullet split open. A day-old goat, its fur slick with digestive juices, sloshed out onto the hardwood floor. Cold gore splashed onto Chase's shoes and soaked the cuffs of his chinos. He slumped down in the leather chair and threw up on his shoes.

That was it.

He called Elise at the boutique and told her to come home.

Even though he had no intention of ever returning to the house once they left, he spent the time waiting for Elise by spraying an entire can of Lysol onto the sordid mess already staining the pinewood floor. He covered it with a few towels and the red blanket. Satisfied, he went upstairs and calmly began packing.

He met Elise at the door. The suitcases were already in the car.

He told her he didn't have time to explain, told her not to touch anything. They were going to stay at a hotel until they could find a new place. The movers would handle everything else.

Let them deal with the mess.

"What's going on?" she said. He blocked her from entering the house.

The phone rang. It sounded like a scream.

Chase grabbed her by the arm. "Don't answer that. Please! Come on, let's go."

A brown UPS truck was pulling up behind her car. The same driver hopped out, his acne-ridden face red. "Sorry. This was behind my seat. Almost missed it."

He shoved a medium-sized cardboard box into Chase's hands. "No need to sign."

The box felt slightly damp and warm, hot even, the cardboard mealy in his hands. It weighed about eight pounds. The postmark was dated three months from today. His ears began to ring, his mouth went dry.

"Honey?"

He turned to his wife, tried to stop her from speaking. Tried to stop time.

She smiled, beatific, confused. "Honey, I just felt a kick."

ROB DAVIES writes weird fiction. His stories have appeared in *The Year's Best Dark Fantasy & Horror, Weird Tales, Interzone, Black Static, Shroud Magazine, Murky Depths*, and *Pseudopod*. He is the author of *Hiram Grange and the Digital Eucharist*.

Scott Christian Carr

M.A.D.D.

THAT FIRST DAY, NO ONE HAD ANY IDEA WHERE ALL THE BODIES *could possibly have floated in from.*

Men and women. Mothers and children. Brothers, sisters, husbands, wives. Old, young. Babies, grandmas. Every one of them, mangled and half-eaten. Bloated and waterlogged and pale.

Hundreds of corpses, at first, washing up on Staten Island. Then thousands clogging the East and Hudson Rivers. Millions up and down the Eastern seaboard—bobbing about the Florida Keys, flooding the Jersey shore and lying frost-covered along the white beaches of Maine.

Human flotsam and jetsam.

That first day, no one knew who any of them were, it all happened so fast—as the impossible body count drifted to shore, no one could guess how many more might still be out there. All those sea-soaked, tidal bodies washing in from the horizon.

The West Coast, more of the same. The Gulf of Mexico, clogged with bobbing, broken flesh and limbs and unrecognizable people-parts from every continent.

Not drowned, but mauled. Closer forensic inspection would reveal puckered, venomous injection sites. Reptilian scales wedged under the bloody fingernails of the victims' death-gropes. Bite marks and claw rakes. Skin burned by stomach acids. Severed limbs, partially digested heads, intestine-trailing half-torsos.

Asia had gone offline just sixteen hours before the first body hit Staten Island. In a flash, the world's most-populated continent was severed from the rest of the planet—no phones, no Internet. No radio or television waves. Satellite imagery revealed no light or power of any kind. The Ukraine had followed minutes after.

It had happened so fast—the only clue, a five second clip from the cargo freighter Tusko off the coast of Dakar.

Appearing on YouTube in the same instant that the Orient went silent, the grainy iPhone footage depicts a tremendous swell of waves rising against the starboard side of the rusty ship's deck. The wave continues to rise, never crashing—a shimmering mountain looming over the Tusko. Deep in its shimmering tides—shadows and silhouettes. Reflections of the terrified crew rippling on it surface.

Frantic Chinese, rushing water and gale fill the background. The five-second clip ends in crackling static. The only intelligible bit, roughly translated as,

"The jelly! The jelly! My God! The jelly is filled with people!"

"Have you been ... Are you drinking?"

"I'm driving."

"That's not what I asked."

"Mom ..."

"You have been, haven't you? Don't lie to me. A mother can tell ..."

"Mom! I'm not—"

"You can't be drunk when you're supposed to be saving the world, Gordon!"

"Jesus."

"Do you know even where you're going? Do you?" Gears and Mother's voice screech and grind as Gordon wrestles the clutch into second, cradling the iPhone between shoulder and ear. The M.A.D.D. lurches and pivots—swings an oversized mechanical foot wide to avoid a burning dumpster. "Do you even know what you're looking for?"

"Of course I do. I—"

"How much have you had to drink?"

"Giant monster, Mom. I'm looking for a giant monster. See?" Gordon turns the iPod away from the *glug, glug* as he tips the bottle to his mouth. "Stone cold sober." He hopes Mom can't hear the empties rolling around the cab of the mech. The beer had since run out, but there was plenty of vodka on hand. 'The first rule of successful alcoholism,' Gordon believed, 'is always to be well-stocked and prepared.'

"Of COURSE you're looking for a giant monster, Gord," Mom spits exasperated impatience. "But do you know what level? What genus? Do you know where, or are you just in S&D?" she hmphed. "Or is all that still too classified to share with your mother?"

"It's not search & destroy, mom. I know where I'm going."

"Do you?"

"Yeah, I do ..." Gordon was careful to articulate and not slur his words. "611 Riverside Drive."

"That's not even remotely funny, Gordon. You're drunk." As if to drive her point home, she continued. "Daphne called. Your wife, she doesn't think you should be driving, either."

"Ex-wife, Mom. She's with Hammerhead now."

"Don't call him that."

"FUCK THEM!" Gordon winced. Shouldn't have said that. Now there was no doubt Mom knew he was drunk, and not just because of the angry, indignant slur in his tone.

Even inside the M.A.D.D. he could smell the stench of Bayonne and Staten Island, see the fires lighting both the eastern and western skylines. They had been (mostly) evacuated when the monstrous jellies that had followed in the wake of the bodies crawled out of the ocean, but there were still stragglers. Survivors. And more bodies than you could count—piled at intersections, burning in dumpsters, splayed on sidewalks. Rotten and rat-bit in the shadows of alleys. Suicides hung from lampposts and tenement windows. Blood soaked the streets in a metaphor of biblical magnitude made literal.

The Mechanical Assault Destruction Device—the M.A.D.D., the mech—could easily push and plough through the piled bodies with hamfisted steel reinforced tractor hands. Could easily climb over the corpse-heaps with magnetic-corrugated spiked all-terrain stomping feet. But Gordon preferred, whenever possible, to swerve around them. Even from the insulated cockpit, the squishing give of the dead flesh was unnerving.

Even the rubble and crumbling architecture was no obstacle for the mech. Piston-powered jackhammer fists, hip-rockets, groin grenades and artillery would cut through concrete as easily as the jelly-flesh of the monster invaders.

And he was almost through the thick of it. Uptown, near the Safety Zones, the roads would be clearer. In the protected and cordoned blocks between the devastation of lower Manhattan and the Tree Faces and Perle Oysters of Central Park, there would be precious few bodies. And even fewer monsters ... Save for one. No, make that two.

Named for Dr. Ungar Perle—the scientist who was first to identify and classify them, and who famously lost an arm to one—the oysters were actually bisected, self-feeding eggs. Appearing in freshwater everywhere, lakes and streams, sewers, reservoirs, swimming pools and bathtubs and toilets, they had all but infested the parks and rivers in and around Manhattan. Filled the sewers and aqua-ducts, clogging the city's water supply. Flooding was imminent, but as of now the uptown Green Zone remained miraculously untouched. Even the grope-tendrils that reached up from curbside grates and out of faucets had been kept at bay. The forty-foot tall jelly behemoths had been fought back to the water by the Zone's missiles and M.A.D.D. Defense squadrons.

Only two monsters had infiltrated uptown. And they weren't on any scientific or military classification system.

"Yeah, Mom ... It's classified." Gordon took another long pull from the vodka bottle. It was nearly drained, but there was plenty more."

Uptown, Mom," Gordon knew he was saying to much, but sometimes it was just better to let the alcohol talk. "I'm goin' uptown ..."

The Blockade was in sight. An over-powered Master-Mech with painted red shoulders and twice the size of his own spotted him from a block away and gave a mechanical salute. Two sentry M.A.D.D.s turned and gripped the Gate in hydraulic claws, pulling the razor wire and iron from the road and waving for him to pass.

"Gordon ..." unbelievably, his mother was at a loss for words.

Gordon furrowed his brow, squinting and plumbing his booze-addled brain for just the right clever insight, admission of wrongs done to him, betrayals suffered, indignities endured, to put words and poetic righteousness to what he was about to do. To make Mom understand. Prove that romance wasn't dead, revenge was best served cold, breaking up was a bitch, and that no one cheated on Gordon Boswell—screwed his wife—and lived to tell about it.

"Fuck 'em," he said."

Gordon ... I'll call Daphne."

"So call her," Gordon shouted. 611 Riverside Drive hove into view. Apartment 43B. Twelfth Floor.

Gordon opened another bottle and armed the anti-tank shoulder scrappers. The high-gauge ballistic bunker busters.

The self-imploding mini-nukes. The sticky-napalm hydrant hoses. The nerve-piercing gas canisters. The high-rise demolition zonkers. The anti-ex-wife and cheating bullshit boyfriend fuck-me-all go-for-broke barnyard blasters.

He took a long, burning pull from the bottle and armed all offensive systems. Grinned as the other M.A.D.D.s and mechs swiveled to see what the hell he was up to—Gordon could almost imagine the shock and awe and admiration—the respect of, 'a job well done, Good Show, Sir. Bravo!'—on the metal and glass cockpit faces.

Gordon placed a trembling finger on the Big Red Button.

"Tell 'er to give Hammerhead a kiss for me ...!"

Scott Christian Carr lives on a secluded mountaintop deep in New York's Hudson Valley, where he spends his time writing novels and stories, producing for film and television, and enjoying the country life with his kids. He is the cocreator of The Learning Channel TV series *Dead Tenants*. His fiction & nonfiction have appeared in *Shroud Magazine*, *Withersin*, *GUD*, *Horror Quarterly*, *Pulp Eternity*, *Weird N.J.*, and assorted anthologies. His novels *Champion Mountain* and *Hiram Grange & the Twelve Little Hitlers* are currently garnering favorable reviews.

T. G. ARSENAULT

MY ACHING BLACK HEART

As I spend another day waist deep in the Missouri River, questions plague my mind, tease the folds of memories buried within, and penetrate the deepest senses of my being. Fly fishing relaxes me, allows my mind the freedom to venture beyond flesh and bone, purges the pressure that nearly drives me insane. It also numbs the pain. It's all I can do to avoid clenching my teeth around six inches of blued steel.

The sun has barely risen above the horizon, its shape oblong, its rays struggling to push through the low-lying haze of distant Montana wildfires. Even in the foothills, the smoky taste sits heavily on the back of my tongue, something I've long since gotten used to. A lime green floating line whispers to me as I judge the current, stripping its length through the eyes of a nine-foot rod with a pause every few seconds. Bugs dance around my face beneath the brim of a stained and tired New England Patriots cap that also protects the whitish glow at the top of my thinning dome of hair. Gnats and mosquitoes test the wrinkled creases of my flesh, repelling as the smoke of a Swisher Sweet forces second thoughts among the small army of flying projectiles. I don't inhale, never have. A habit taught by my father, the white tip of the cigar is there only to bite upon and survive the hatch; the only way to spend the day on the river this time of year and still go home with eyes not swollen shut.

As a father to an only son myself, I had only one chance to do it right and failed miserably. It hurts to think about, causes me to squint against something more than the rising sun as I attempt to quell a sudden wetness from brewing for fear that another thought would allow the weight of retrospect to fall in the form of stinging tears.

Memories.

Some witnessed in person, most imagined from distant cities that had no plans of entering my future when I first plunged into the perplexities of pharmaceutical sales. I only wanted to put a roof over my family's head, ensure food always lined the shelves of the refrigerator, and never have to worry about the thermostat setting. I accomplished all of these things—and more—for most of my life, lived in a home well beyond anything I would ever need. I was good at what I did, usually to a fault. As fate would have it, I needed to be.

Five years ago, as autumn quickly turned to fall, my wife became a victim of an invisible sheet of black ice on her way home from getting a gallon of milk. A goddamned gallon of milk changed our lives in the mere seconds it took to complete a three-hundred-sixty degree turn smack in the middle of 10th Avenue South and slam our Impala head-on into a semi full of cattle. She survived, but paralysis spread its wrath from her waist down to her toenails that she sometimes let me paint on cold winter nights.

Hospital bills led to required, expensive home improvements and more adjustments for the family as a whole. Quite simply, I needed to make more money, which required me to step up my game among obsessively driven pharmaceutical reps in order to ensure that our family survived. To guarantee my family got the best of what a radically changed life now had to offer, I had to *be* the best.

With a drive for success came enjoyment, then fulfillment, then a craving that spawned a hunger for more. And with success came sacrifice.

When a new client needed schmoozing, the company called. When another deal needed closing, the company called again, sure of my success as evidenced by my very profitable and growing track record. No longer did I have the time to spend on the river with my son, teaching him the art of fly fishing and how to appreciate the simple things life had to offer, or discuss those sacred questions a growing boy asked a father.

One day on the river once puffed my chest out and squared my shoulders with pride, but now only leaves me feeling deflated with skin hanging loosely from shattered bones.

I watched as my son Anthony contemplated how to get to an exposed rock, too far out into the river, without getting wet.

Too short for any waders I could find, he wore just a tee shirt, jeans, and a beat up pair of hiking boots. Still learning, he always convinced himself that the perfect fishing spot was just a bit further. Sometimes, he was right.

I could almost see the cogs turning in his brain and smoke starting to drift out of his ears as he faced his dilemma. I let my fly drift to the side of the banking behind me and watched, anxiously awaiting his solution. Chewed on the end of my cigar and silently encouraged him.

In a sudden moment of revelation, Anthony dropped his rod and searched the ground nearby, then a little further, certainly searching for the best tool to accomplish his small mission. He was right again as he bent to pick up a rock of perfect size and dimensions—flat on the bottom and large enough to give him plenty of stepping room. He sauntered to the river, hunched over and grimacing, but never asked for help. Then dropped the rock dead-center between the riverbank and his target location with a splash that certainly startled any fish away.

So enthralled with his problem, he never realized I was watching the entire episode unspool before me. I could see the biggest smile stretch to each side of his face as he topped the elusive rock that was now within easy reach. A short time and a five-pound brownie later, he was right ... again.

Those days ... those days are long ...

Gone.

My steadfast work ethic prevented me from refusing the work when I knew I instead should be showing my son how to tie a new fly to match the hatch, tucking presents under the tree before dawn, or showering the bed with rose petals, though our lovemaking days were long gone. Thoughts of commissions and advancement continuously cluttered my mind, always wanting more, and, to be honest, a much needed escape from a lifestyle change that I couldn't handle. Every successful business venture only lent itself to a driving need to prove myself again, like an addict in need of a fix. Right before a deal closed, my limbs got to tingling and my heart picked up a steady hammer within my chest as the need for even more reared its ugly head.

During a rare meal at home, on the eve of another promising

business trip, I noticed my son's changed complexion. Teenaged years were proving unkind as acne started to dot his face and neck, enough to produce small sores and scabs where he had scratched. His water glass clattered against his teeth before he managed a sip, the tips of his fingers quivering ever so slightly, almost tipping the glass as he tried to set it down and quickly place his hand under the table. Matted, sweat-stringy hair hanging in front of his face, he picked up his fork, only to fiddle with his mashed potatoes and gravy, seemingly fascinated at the food pushing through silver tines.

I don't think I ever saw him take a bite. Or swallow. Or notice the way his shirt appeared a little baggier on his frame. Nor was I aware of the increasing use of methamphetamines among teenagers, even away from the big cities. Montana, of all places. Meth labs were now as prevalent as the oriental massage parlors.

A quick glance from my wife over a wine glass told me there was more to discuss. I let it go unsaid beneath a few gulps from my own glass, certain all would be well upon my next return.

In the middle of dinner with a potential client, my cell phone vibrated in the pocket of my suit coat. I could feel it rattling against my reading glasses in my breast pocket. I kept on talking, ignoring the gentle buzz, talking a little louder about a new psoriasis medication so the person in front of me couldn't hear the sudden interruption, sure whoever was calling would leave a message. I relaxed when the buzzing stopped, felt my blood pressure dip to a comfortable level, then spike with a vengeance when the phone buzzed again.

Beads of sweat gathered at my temples as the buzzing continued. And continued, dripping into my ears, down the back of my neck, and along the sides of my chest. I talked louder, faster, in a rush to close this lucrative deal, my limbs tingling with excitement. Loosened my suffocating tie. Out of sight, my hand squeezed the dinner napkin into a sweaty ball as the incessant buzzing toyed with my temper. My tongue disobeyed the messages my brain attempted to send to the man across from me—so close to finally shaking hands on our agreement—but my words only tripped over each other, stringing into nothing more than a nonsensical babbling of syllables. Three times I tried to begin my speech anew, a rote script easily tapped into—usually—but it only exacerbated my frustration. With a dramatic roll of his eyes, my client left the table, tossing his napkin in disgust.

I choked the cell phone out of my suit coat, tempted to throw it at the back of my client's head as he exited the restaurant and raised an arm to hail a cab.

"WHAT?" I screamed into the phone, ignoring the sudden silence produced among the other dining customers, still feeling the cold November breeze from my client's sudden exit ripple along my flesh. I glared back at them—each and every one of them— telepathically forcing them all to start chewing again and mind their own fucking business. Slowly, they did, but failing to resist a few smirks around mouthfuls of food. My jaw clenched; teeth produced tiny squeaks.

"It's Tony," she said in barely a whisper, but exuding a tangible panic within three short syllables.

My stomach lurched; faced flush with a heat that knew what would follow would not be good. The smell of my untouched salmon made me nauseous. I took a deep, needed breath; let it out with a fluttering hiss.

"What happened *now*?" I asked, unable to keep the accusatory tone out of my voice. His behavior had been on the verge of ridiculous recently, not belonging to the same little boy that once loved little league baseball, fishing, and boiled peanuts at the circus. Now his interests involved ... absolutely nothing. Behind his bedroom door, he spent most hours of the day locked away from humanity, from us. Steady pounding on the poster-plastered door only produced muffled grunts beneath the raucous of maniacal music. He would disappear at night, sometimes for hours.

"He didn't come home last night," she said, choking back a sob.

As expected.

"THAT's why you called?" I said, and seethed, pinching the inside of my thigh to keep from bursting. "Why the hell—"

"He left a note," she butted in, ignoring me, surely knowing not to let me keep going. It's what she did. "It's the only way he knew how to talk to you."

I chewed on this and felt shame burn my cheeks.

"Well, what did it *say*?" My jaw was starting to ache, pulse pounding at my temples.

"I think you need to come home," she said with an irritating nasal slurp, then delivered a constant tone with a single click of a button on her end.

I slammed my fist upon the table, water seeming to boil out the top my glass, silverware making a sudden bounce to the left. Those around me jumped in unison. Fuckers.

A master of living out of a battle-scarred suitcase, I quickly found myself on the next flight back to Montana, still livid about my first utter failure of a business trip. Tie loosened around a wrinkled collar, whiskey in hand, every bump of turbulence ignited my fury. Every screaming baby and food cart bumping into my foot poured more fuel onto the inferno that already blazed inside.

Three teeth-grinding hours later, I reached my destination.

With a jarring dip of the hood of my car as I stood on the brake pedal, I had barely removed the key from the ignition before I had one foot on the driveway. The garage door made a sickening grinding noise, taunting me with its geriatric rising. I always used the door through the garage to avoid walking up the wheel-chair ramp in the front of my home, think I was actually embarrassed to use such a thing. So I waited, hands opening and closing at my sides, the scent of clean mountain air trying to dissuade me from my current mood—impossible.

I spotted a shoelace first, untied and dangling, as the garage opened its gaping maw with more than its customary creaks and groans. Then the wheels of a chair.

And the body of my son, hanging from one of the tracks of the garage door opener, his weight bending the metal in its place, where a leather belt was fastened and stretched to wrap around his neck. The door met the kink and started coming back down. I slapped an automatic hand to the inside wall of the garage to stop its descent, only to wish the groaning motor still infused my ears with its discord.

The squeaks of twisting leather seemed so much louder, magnified within the small enclosure, pausing for too short of a moment as my son's body changed direction. His tongue, impossibly swollen and flaccid, drooped from one side of his mouth. Worst of all, his eyes seemed to pop with accusations that had built exponentially, ultimately erupting on this fateful day. I turned away, not from disgust, but guilt. And shame.

Then fell to my knees.

My wife sat in her wheelchair, slumped over and crying, one hand caressing the leg of my son, shoulders rising in twitching hitches as she appeared to strangle on her sadness. An envelope weaved through the fingers of her other hand as her fist pounded against her chest. Hair disheveled, nightgown haphazardly draped around her body, she raised a tear-streaked face.

"He's home," she said, and handed me the envelope. In bold letters, DAD appeared in shaky script.

I couldn't open it.

My aching heart dropped to my feet, where I wanted to stomp on it for all the blackness it contained in my desire for career versus family, knowing no amount of dedication or drive or will to succeed at mending our lives back together would ever work.

Unable to accept our loss, share a consoling embrace, or speak a single word to each other, my wife left soon after, using my time away to have someone move her things.

I sold the house, quit working, bought an Airstream and a plot of land where the Missouri River provided a wishing well of requests that would only wash downriver.

Like the river itself, my grief ebbs and flows. Certain times of the year—like today, the anniversary of my son's death—it swells enough to overflow and give birth to a desire to end it all. Instead, I continue my penance, letting myself burn with insurmountable guilt, searching for answers, for reasons why.

Sometimes I see him before I go to sleep at night, hanging from my short ceiling with those hauntingly accusing eyes, a blackened tongue hanging to one side, his body swinging in a gentle circle, sometimes touching my toes with a cold, mottled hand.

The note still rests inside its unsealed envelope, unread, kept as a constant reminder on the refrigerator like a self-inflicted lashing with razor wire.

So many painful questions, some of which I'd rather not know the answers to.

As the sun touches the horizon with an ethereal glow I used to enjoy, I climb into my Airstream and gaze upon the river before closing the door with a congested sigh, wondering if the river will provide the answers tomorrow.

Or if one answer will eliminate the need to ever ask another.

Author of *Forgotten Souls* and most recently, *Bleeding the Vein*, T. G. ARSENAULT resides in upstate New York with his wife and son. His short fiction has also appeared in multiple online venues and anthologies. Visit T.G. Arsenault at *www.tg-arsenault.com.*

KEVIN LUCIA

DOWN IN THE DARK

Hell's Half Acre
Fort Sumner, New Mexico
March, 1887

"TORN DOWN THREE YEARS AGO," SAYS THE FARMER NAMED FIGGY, standing in a square depression filled with knee-deep grass, surrounded by crumbling foundation walls. "The Maxwells wanted it gone. Don' blame em. Bad mem'ries, here."

He stares at the ruined foundation. "It happened here?"

"Yessir. There inna corner. They was waitin for him. Out onna porch." Figgy steps forward. "An this. This right here."

Though he knows Figgy's playing the showman, he looks to the ground where Figgy points. "Right where that sacatone's growin? That's where he came through the door. Right here where I'm standin? That's where he died. Shot inna heart."

He looks around. There's lots of grass and scrub. Not far away, cows graze. Beyond that, the river rolls along.

Nothing much remains but a bare stage. All props gone, all actors retired to their dressing rooms, moved on to other dramas far away yet somehow, the spot pulls at him. Bright sunlight shines into all the shadowed places. Walls long gone spring up. Night falls.

And *he* is here.

The Kid.

Moving silently across the yard in the moonlight, his step ghostly. *El Chivato*, they called him. "The artful sneak."

But there's a rustle, and a youthful rasp: *Quien es?*"

Who is it?

A pistol roars.

And in the sudden muzzle flare he *sees* the Kid, already moving, Colt up.

But too late.

And then it all goes away.

Present day and noon again, too hot and bright and humid.

"Right here," Figgy says, holding his hand level with his breast, "was where the bullet tore into the west wall, after blowin out the Kid's heart. Not long after, I wallpapered right over that bullet hole myself."

He nods.

Raises his head, glances at the modest herd of grazing cattle. "His grave. Take me to his grave."

Quarter a mile away lies what must be the loneliest cemetery ever. A half-acre enclosed by rusted barbed wire, it looks more like grazing for chickens than burial ground.

Flat, sparsely covered by grass, sagebrush and Spanish gourd. Here and there graves are marked by weather-beaten and tilting crosses. Even in the high noon sunshine, the plot looks damned.

Figgy sidles up alongside, hands jammed into his pockets, shoulders hunched, as if against something cold ... despite the day's heat. Jaw tense, body rigid, Figgy's nonchalance has vanished into a wary unease.

Or maybe he's just that good.

"This cemetery usta have an adobe wall 'round it with an arched gateway an a cross on top." Figgy glances at him, offering something between a grimace and a smile. "Know it don look much now, but looked right nice for a spell. Had graveled paths. Them wooden crosses usta have names an dates on em. Looked right purty. But not no more. Goes by 'Hell's Half Acre', now."

He licks wind-dry lips, swallows and manages a skeptical frown. "Folks don't believe it's ..."

"Cursed?" Figgy shrugs, glancing back at the cemetery. "Who knows, mister? Place looks sick, right? All that weak lookin grass. Things usta grow here well nuff. Folks usta come an leave flowers. Not no more. Folks say it's haunted. Some'll ride miles outta their way at night to keep 'way from it."

He snorts. "Haunted. You believe that?"

Figgy grunts, turns and fixes him with his pale blue, watery eyes. "Don rightly know what I b'lieve. But in one year, some violent men died violent deaths an was buried here an sure 'nuff, place went to hell. No one took care of it no more. An look at it."

Figgy waves a leathery hand, staring at the graves, as if expecting something to claw its way from the earth any minute. "Jus look at it. That groun look healthy to you?"

He looks at the small cemetery.

At its cracked ground and the brittle grass and stunted brush. Looks at the much greener, healthier looking growth outside it and sees, running along the cemetery's back edge, mounds of earth boasting no crosses.

"The back of the cemetery," he murmurs.

Figgy nods uneasily, as if he's been dreading this question all along. "Tha's where he is. Buried with somma his pals. Woulda liked that right fine, I think."

"Yes. He would've." He stares at that barren row. "None of the graves are marked."

Figgy shrugs. "Most of em was buried by their killers. Wasn much cause for markin their graves. Well, suppose you wanna see his plot. C'mon, then."

They enter, walk clear to the cemetery's back, cut right to the far corner.

And stop.

Figgy turns, points down to a strip of yellow, sun-cracked earth that looks strangely bare.

"Here. Un'er here is the Kid."

The bare space runs the length of a short man's body. Unhealthy, straggling grass and burnt shrubs grow around it, but stop short at the naked rectangle's edges. Not a blade sprouts within it.

"S'always looked like this, since 'bout a week after they buried him," says Figgy. "Don know why. Nothin grows onnit. Like the groun's poisoned or somethin."

He stares at the naked strip of earth, entranced. Narrow cracks made by the blistering sun have outlined what looks like the crude suggestion of a human figure.

When Figgy speaks again, his voice has regained a confident thrum, again the tour guide. "If'n you stan' at a certain angle, them cracks over there look like a skeleton hand. Over here a bit."

Though loath to humor the farmer he finds himself entranced by the cracked portrait carved into the dead earth. He steps aside, following the farmer's finger.

"See? Them four lines there look like a dead man's crooked fingers reachin for somethin. That short line there looks like a thumb. Spooky, ain't it?"

Against his will, he peers at the sun-etched portrait, shuddering as he sees the uncanny resemblance to bony fingers reaching ...

He closes his eyes.

Breathes deep.

And feels angry.

At himself for allowing this two-bit vaudevillian to spook him, and at Figgy for stooping so low for quick coin. The idea that he's let himself be taken in leaves him feeling cheap and ashamed.

And if he were a different man?

More like the Kid?

Maybe he'd have the strength to put this grubbing little farmer out of his misery.

But as quickly as it comes this rush of anger fades, leaving him weary and defeated. Of the many things he is, he's not the Kid. Never was.

And that was always the problem.

Still sickened by the farmer's shameless performance, he wants to be done. Without looking at Figgy, never taking his gaze from the cracks in the ground, he sticks his hands into his pockets. "Like to be alone."

He doesn't see Figgy's expectant stare but says, "I'll pay you. Swear. Jus' leave me be. Please."

Figgy grunts and without another word brushes past him, towards the cemetery's entrance in quick, nervous strides.

As if relieved to be leaving.

———

As he stares at this this blighted grave, emotions surge within. Grief. Regret. Guilt.

And sadness.

He sighs. Reaches up and rubs the back of his neck, working a sore muscle. Time to leave the past to rest, finally.

But before he turns, he hears it.

A rustling scrape.

And his heart flutters when he hears that smooth, clear voice over his shoulder, along with an icy cold muzzle pressing into the back of his neck.

"Long time, *pal.*"

He winces as a hammer clicks and reaches for the sky, arms and legs trembling. "Wassa matter," that voice purrs, "aintcha happy to see me?"

He closes his eyes.

Somehow manages to rasp, "You're dead."

A dry-leaf chuckle. "Sure bout that?"

He swallows but his throat feels raw, cut by jagged glass. "That's what they've all been saying. The papers and books and all."

The muzzle presses harder. The smooth voice slides in his ears, this time a little steel vibrating in it. "An why, pray tell, are YOU here?"

"I ... I ..."

The muzzle jabs harder. "C'mon. Don' waste my time. Why you here?"

He sags, hanging his head. "I ... don't know. Somethin just made me come, that's all. Guess ... guess I wasn' sure it was true. Guess I didn't believe."

And suddenly the muzzle's pressure vanishes, along with another dry chuckle. "All right then. Tha's all I wanted."

He spins and backs away, hands immediately dropping to his holsters. He doesn't draw them, however, because there he is, silhouetted by the blazing sun, features cast in shadow ... and his guns drawn, dead bang.

Him.

The Kid.

"Now, now," the Kid drawls, shaking his head, looking as disappointed as a grade-school teacher might with a pupil, "let's not get hasty. Ya ain't never out-drawn me, an ya ain't bout to start now."

He knows this. But he leaves his trembling fingers on his revolvers' butts, because no matter what, he'll go down shooting, even if he isn't the Kid.

"How?" he rasps. "How are you ... I mean, you died. They say you died."

The Kid nods, smirking beneath the shadows crawling over his face. "Came to a few days later. Dug myself out, filled the grave back in."

He shakes his head, trembling and shaking all over. Even if the Kid did draw and he was able to get his guns out, wouldn't matter. His arms feel so heavy and limp. "But ... how?"

The Kid shifts, manner softening. "Well," he said, voice more somber, "it's right hard to 'xplain."

He flashes a smile. "But hell, Ah'm right glad you come. Been waitin on ya. Figured you'd show, eventually."

Something icy ripples down his back and he shivers. "What ... what do you mean? You've been waiting here ... for me?"

"Yeah. Off an on ... but yeah."

He swallowed a hard lump. "Wh-Why?"

The Kid steps closer., his eyes shining. "Because," he rasps. "This strange thing? Happened causa *you*. Happened that day out inna Capitan Mountains. When the sun was blastin everythin hot an white ..."

Capitan Mountains
Arizona Desert
1879

The sun blasted everything hot and white.

Rifles cracked.

Lead zipped by and blew out chips of rock in small geysers.

The Kid dove, mind wheeling and confused. He hit the hard-packed ground with his shoulder and rolled clumsily behind a rock outcropping. Scrambled to his knees. Crawled behind the rock, far as he could go, squeezing himself into its corner, wrapping his arms around his knees and hugging them to his chest, heart hammering, breath thundering, ragged and harsh in his ears.

More rifle cracks.

Lead sang and slapped the top of the rocks he cowered behind, spraying him with dust and gravel.

"Didja see im?!? Where'd that little pissant go?"

"Think he's behin them rocks! Prob'ly scared shitless, goddamn thievin little bastard!"

Loud, braying laughter.

Another rifle shot.

Blasting dust and chipped rock into his face, eyes and nose. He pressed his face into his arms, trying to breathe.

"Hey! You see that other'n anywhere's near?"

He shuddered.

John.

Him and John hit Fort Grant last night. Rustled some horses. Turned out they'd rustled *rustlers*. Mean, rattlesnake-nasty fellas that caught up with them at dawn, out here in the Capitan Mountains, where they started blasting away at them, cutting down his mount right off, leaving him sliding and rolling down a hill until he'd found this little hidey-hole.

And John?

Why, he'd done the only thing he could, what the Kid woulda done himself, other way around.

He'd run, cut his rustled horse loose for the hills, straight off leaving him here alone, with no guns. He'd lost them when he'd fell off his horse.

Another shot.

Rock exploded.

One of the rustlers, creeping closer.

"Mackie? Rode up in them hills. Prob'ly long gone b'now. But we'll take good care of this'n! String im up at Fort Grant, so everyone can see what a thievin little bastard he is!"

Another blast.

Rocks shattering and dust flying.

Making him choke and gag.

"You hear me, Kid? Picked the wrong hombres to rustle from, that's for goddamn sure!"

Another blast. Rock fragments sprayed him. Cut into his cheeks and forehead.

"Cover me, Bob! He puts his head up, you blast it the hell off. I'ma gonna end this. Teach 'im the last lesson he'll ever learn!"

And now footsteps.

Jogging across hard-packed dirt towards him. In a few minutes, either they'd drag him outta here by the ankle, hitch him to their horses and drag his ass all the way back to Fort Grant, or they'd just blast away at him here in this little crook where he had nowhere to go, end it right quick, just like that.

Cold desperation filled his guts.

Made him right sick to puke.

He'd almost died plenty times before this. Now, looked like it'd really happen, unless …

He scanned his surroundings.

Nothing but high smooth rock wall to his back. Nothing he could grab hold of and anyway, even if there were, would just leave him hanging out in plain sight. So he had to go forward, risk running in the open and dodging clean shots, before that rustler rounded the corner and cut him off … .

And then he saw it.

Maybe a hundred feet away, downslope from him. Nestled at the base of another steep rock wall reaching up to the Capitan Mountains. A little black mouth.

A hole.

A cave?

Mabye only a shallow one. Hell, maybe only eight or ten feet deep leading to a dead end with nowhere else to go, and then it'd be like shooting fish in a barrel. Or he'd get stuck, leaving them rustlers his ass a target to shoot up as they pleased.

But it was his only chance.

He closed his eyes.

Breathed deep.

Pushed off the ground. Dashed headlong for that jagged black circle that might mean freedom … or the final nail in his coffin.

Bright, furious cursing. Jagged yelps.

"There he goes!"

Rifles cracking. Revolvers snapping.

How many rustlers had chased him down?

Didn't matter. Rock and dust plumed up in geysers all around his feet. Lead sang by. Slammed into rock. But a few more steps … .

He launched himself forward, hands outstretched, plunging headfirst into the hole. And panic squeezed his heart, his shoulders catching on its jagged sides. He wriggled and pushed, lurched and finally scrambled all the way through.

Only to hit the ground a mere six feet deep.

He cursed.

Rolled onto his back. Looked up at the bright, ragged circle of light above. Footsteps and rustlers yipping and yelling outside. Getting closer. Any minute they'd be here, and his fate wouldn't be no different. Either they'd blast him where he lay, or drag him up and out to work him over.

He rolled onto his hands and knees.

Desperately scoured the small little alcove.

He'd fallen on broken pottery, old bones, tattered cloth and chipped flint instruments—maybe even an old tomahawk and a few chipped spearheads.

An Indian burial mound.

He'd fallen into an old Indian burial mound, just deep enough to get trapped in.

No escape.

Footsteps pounding closer.

"Prob'ly an old Injin mound! Bet it ain't more'n man-high! Ain't nowhere for the bastard to go, neither!"

The hungry glee in the rustler's voice spurred him on. He scrambled away from the jagged, irregular opening above, diving for the mound's farthest corner. Rock and dirt looked different on that end, more crumbled and cracked, as an opening had collapsed long ago. Damned thin odds, but his only chance in hell, so ...

Feet skidded on the gravel outside.

Spurs and gunbelts jangling.

"There! See im! Shoot his thievin ass..!"

Billy dove forward.

Leading with his left shoulder.

Eyes squeezed shut.

"DAMN! Blast 'im!"

Rifles and revolvers thundering. Sounding like cannons in that small space.

He slammed into the crumbling dirt wall shoulder-first. And all his wild, desperate speculations came true as the wall disintegrated and fell away.

As he pitched forward into a deep black nothing.

Falling.

Down in the dark.

Sudden pain.

Bright and stabbing. Behind his eyes. Throbbing in his head. He coughed, licked his lips. Swallowed, jaws aching, and he gagged on the metallic taste of his own blood.

He breathed. Ribs hurt, but seemed fine. Nothing broken. Didn't feel shot anywhere, neither. Just banged and bruised some, after falling ...

Falling.

Falling *down*.

He coughed again.

Turned his head and rested his cheek on cold, smooth stone.

And opened his eyes.

To the dark. Not complete dark, though. Thin, pale and ghostly slivers of light cut a path through the darkness to pool on the ground near him. From the hole he'd broken through above.

Joints groaning and creaking, he crawled to his knees. Kept his head down, brow resting on that smooth, cool floor ... which felt wrong, somehow. If he'd broken through to some sorta cavern or burial ground, floor should be rocky, bumpy. This felt smooth and flat against his skin. Almost slippery. Like it'd been buffed or polished or some damn thing ...

And then he heard it.

Whispers.

From somewhere above. Men whispering or cursing from far away ...

He froze.

Guts churning.

Heart pounding.

The burial mound. The men outside it. RUSTLERS. And they were coming in after him.

Frantic, head pounding with fear and adrenaline along with pain, he staggered to his feet. Swayed just a bit. Everything spinning and tilting, like someone was shaking the whole goddamn world.

His stomach lurched.

He gulped. Closed his eyes and squeezed his head between his hands, trying to push everything back together. *C'mon. Pull it together ... or you're a fuckin corpse.*

"Hey! Dammit to hell'n shitfire ... there's a goddamn hole inna backa this thing ..."

The rustler's angry voice echoed and bounced around the great expanse. Escalating fear drove the pain and dizziness away. His hands slapped his empty holsters without thinking.

Feet, knees scrambled in dirt and gravel above him. "Well I'll be fucked! There's goddamn steps goin down there, somewhere!"

He spun, searching as best he could in the dimly lit space. Couldn't tell for sure, but looked like he'd fallen into an underground grotto about the width of a hunting cabin, twice its height. And there, behind him, what looked like a flight of steep, rough-cut stone steps leading up to the hole he'd fallen through. Past that, through that gray, hazy hole ...

He squinted. Couldn't see much, just shadows and shapes moving, but he heard more scuffing of dirt and gravel, along with the jingle of spurs and gun-belts. That, and the rustlers arguing over who was going down first.

"Like hell, McCready," a deeper, gravelly voice rumbled. "Ain't goin down there. That there's an Injin cave or somethin. Prob'ly cursed. You kin kiss my ass, go an git yer little horse thief yerself, all I care."

Another voice, high and thin and reedy. "Dundon's right, McCready. No way in hell I'm goin down there inna dark. Sides, dumbfuck only stole a horse an saddle. Waren't even worth shaggin em this far, sure ain't worth goin down in *that* damn thing."

He thought fast. Trying to figure some angle, anything ... make himself do something ...

Away from the light, fool.

Move away from the light, out of sight into the corner. Behind one of my totems, if you want to survive this ... boy.

He glanced around.

Sure enough, in the corners loomed tall, shadowy forms that had to be totem poles or something. Sure. That's what they were, specially if this thing *was* some sorta strange Indian burial place. Maybe if he could wedge himself between one of them and the wall ...

"Erb! Goddammit, man. Seen me some deadwood out there. Go snag a branch, get it lit so I can get some light. Fuck y'all. I'mma gonna finish this bastard. *Nobody* steals from me."

Fast and quiet as possible, he scuttled away from the pale streams of light towards one of the closest totem poles. He sank against it, and as his desperate hands reached around the back, he almost yelped in relief when he found space between it and the wall. Not much, to be sure, but enough for him to squeeze into, out of sight.

As he jammed his back into the small space, he didn't look too hard at the totem looming high above him. Hard to tell in this hazy dark, but he didn't like the looks or even *feel* of this damn thing. He'd seen his share of totems, real ones in villages and on reservations and ones made in the city for selling to dumbass city folk, but for some reason, *these* here totems didn't seem like them others at all. They just didn't *look* right.

He shivered.

Felt kinda sick and even dizzier. Thinking about them other totem poles and this one he was hiding behind. He tried to forget them, though. Thinking instead on how the hell he was getting out of here.

Odd. He waren't so scared of McCready and his boys. But this damned place, these totem poles ...

He squirmed. Skin itching and crawling when he pressed against the totem pole. Had to get outta here. Maybe he'd die down here, maybe not. But some icy sensation crawling along his spine told him bein down here was worse than anything McCready's boys could conjure.

Way worse.

Fact, he thought he'd rather face McCready and his boys dead bang with nothing but a soup spoon and a dull eating knife than stay in this damned hole one minute longer.

And a rustling at the top of the steps said he was about to get a chance to do that very thing ... except without the spoon and dull knife, of course.

Bright orange-red flickered down the steps. Playing and flowing over the floor where he'd landed. He peeked around the totem best he could, as the light thrown by McCready's torch illuminated the room.

Under the flicker of the descending torchlight, he saw the room was about the size of a hunting cabin. And, as impossible as it seemed, almost perfectly square. Walls as flat and smooth as the floor had felt.

And that waren't right.

Not at all.

No way someone dug this thing out by hand, cause the walls and floors all looked rock. No way anyone blasted this thing out, then chipped and filed it down so smooth and flat. Waren't possible.

Waren't it?

"Go on, McCready. We'll cover ya up here," that rough, gravelly voice said from above, "but we ain't goin down there. He stole *your* horse. Y'all go get 'im."

"Buncha fuckin women." This from McCready, descending slowly, complaining loudly. "I swear. Y'all ain't nothin buta buncha fuckin women, for sure."

Boots scraped down the steps.

Spurs jingling and jangling.

Gravel and rock whispering down. Red-orange torchlight flickering as McCready descended slowly.

Biting his lip, squeezing his hands into tight balls so hard his fingernails bit into his skin, he peered around the totem pole, mind working feverishly. Needed some guns above everything else, so maybe if he rushed McCready, knocked him off balance and grabbed one of his guns, maybe throw that torch in his face ...

No way. Would never work.

His breath hissed between his teeth. Skin crawling and shivering. He wanted outta this hellhole. Right. NOW.

McCready neared the floor. Holding his torch high. Made in a hurry of some old cloth wrapped around a deadwood branch then lit with a match, it was already fading, but even so, as McCready stood where he'd fallen, he got the best look of the place yet.

Like he'd thought.

Almost perfectly square.

Smooth, flat rock walls and floors. And where he'd fallen, an almost perfect circle of gleaming black stone the likes of which he'd never seen before, polished to a shine.

And he couldn't rightly tell from his hiding spot ... but it looked like something had been carved into that black circle. Lines. Shapes or designs, etched there or something.

"What ... what the goddamn *hell's* all this?"

At McCready's rasp, he peeked further around the totem. There stood McCready. Dimming torch held high, facing a totem pole. As the red-orange flickers of McCready's torch played over curved and weirdly angled lines and shapes, something *greasy* turned in his guts. A sick kinda fear or dread. The kind that wakes children from sleeping to screaming, makes grown men piss their britches.

But sick as he felt, much as he wanted to look away from that totem, he couldn't. Couldn't stop staring at the looming monstrosity.

McCready stared, too. With slack jaws, eyes big and round, face pale in the torch's dying flickers.

He shivered. Hating the looks of that totem pole. Them waren't the usual animals carved into most totems. These was ... different, somehow. Wolves that looked more like men. Hawks that looked more like deer. Blobby things—didn't know how else to describe them—with gaping holes where mouths and eyes should be.

Some of the totems had arms. Kinda. Reaching and grasping and flailing, though he got the idea them arms were more like tentacles. Thick, coiling, snake-like things, frozen in rock as they whipped and lashed the air.

Impossible.

How the hell could *anyone* carve something all curvy and twisty like that, even from the softest wood or lodestone? Just waren't right.

The worse part of the totem, though, was the wings.

Goddamn wings.

One or two of them heads didn't have arms or tentacles at all. Just gigantic, spreading wings. Not like birds or hawks or nothing else he'd ever seen. And even crazier, in McCready's dim light them wings didn't look rock. More like leather or dried rawhide or ...

He swallowed.

Guts churning and swirling.

Like skin.

Those wings looked like dry, pebbly-lizard skin, even from here. They looked *alive*.

And McCready was reaching for the closest pair. Slowly, as if drunk, hand outstretched, fingers spread ... to touch it.

Rub it.

And then, something crept over *him*. A strange, weird, cold sensation that filled his belly and burned in his blood, freezing away his fear and leaving nothing behind but a deep, emotionless, fearless cold heart.

No fear.

Just cold.

Ice cold.

He liked that. Very, very much.

His hands hung loose. Flexing. Every part of him relaxed, feeling nothing but cold inside.

McCready stiffened with a cry.

Went rigid. Muscles stiffening in his arm and neck, as if something powerful coursed through him, holding him there while he fought with every muscle he had. Jerking, twitching, holding that wing, mouth open wide but quiet. Not screaming or whimpering.

Nothing.

With a rush, that cold, unfeeling ice pulsed through his veins. Pushed ALL his fear and unease away. He leapt away from the wall and flung himself across the small room. Silent. Cold and deadly.

And slammed his shoulder into McCready's chest. Wrapped his arms around McCready's waist. Whatever had frozen McCready there disappeared. His hand jerked away from that godawful wing as he twisted and tried to swing at his head.

But they was already crashing to the floor.

McCready's boys shouted from outside, their voices far away.

Him and McCready hit that hard rock floor, knocking the wind out of McCready. His hand banged against the rock, forcing it open. The torch rolled away, guttering, fading.

A hazy darkness fell over them as they kicked and fought and rolled. McCready grunted. Flailed and punched at his head. Billy kept swinging, trying to keep McCready's hands busy, away from his shooters.

Shouts drifted from outside. Rock and dirt rustled. And they fought. Struggling and kicking on the smooth, cold rock floor.

And something else.

Just below all that.

Whispering. Soft and far away. Like someone whispering through gauze. And humming. Buzzing. Drums, dammit ... drums beating in the distance.

McCready rolled on top of him, but he thrust his knee into McCready's groin, pulling another long gasp from the big rustler. McCready sagged limp for just a minute. He flipped him onto his back. Scrambled on top. Swung a wild right that connected square with McCready's jaw, drawing a cry and grunt of pain, cracking the back of McCready's head against the rock floor.

"McCready! What the hell's goin on down here?"

He planted his knees on the rustler's chest. Grabbed his neck with both hands.

And *squeezed*.

McCready's eyes bugged. Mouth gaping as he gasped and fought for air. He squeezed harder. What little torchlight remained cast McCready's face in dull red. Like blood flooded his skin as he held on and choked the life outta him ...

But McCready was bigger.

Way bigger.

The rustler bucked. His grip loosened. He fought to re-establish his hold but before he could, McCready bucked again.

Wedged his knee up between them.

Jammed it into his gut.

And kicked him away.

He flew back, arms flailing. Landing on his ass. Rolling to his back. The impact knocked wind from him, but that cold and fearless thing inside still pulled the strings. Pushed him off the floor. Flung him at McCready even as the rustler rushed forward, one of his Colts free from its holster.

And rising.

He slammed into him.

Right hand locked around McCready's left wrist. Holding that Colt down. Left hand clamped on McCready's right wrist, pushing it away from the other Colt strapped to McCready's hip.

They struggled and fought and pushed against each other across the room's middle.

"Hey! McCready! What the hell!"

McCready grunted but oddly remained silent. Just pushed and pulled, shoved against his own slight frame. Trying to break free.

McCready kicked at his knees. He danced away, still clamped onto McCready's wrists.

McCready heaved with his left shoulder. Creating space space between them. And slowly, McCready's greater size and strength won out as he edged his Colt's muzzle up.

He wrenched. Trying to force the muzzle back toward McCready. Push. Shove. Pull.

Lean and turn. Lean and turn.

McCready kicked at him again. Pushed, shoved, and pulled. He leaned and turned, hard as he could.

While those soft gauzy voices whispered and something hummed and those drums banged, far away.

Another push and shove and pull and twist and turn ...

And McCready's Colt banged.

It's echo slamming off the tight, stone walls.

Booming, back and forth.

Filling the world.

McCready grunted once and sagged against him.

Eyes wide and disbelieving. Scared shitless.

Like he'd seen something, just as he'd passed on.

Something he hadn't expected. Something that had scared the ever-living piss out of him.

He staggered under McCready's dead weight. Released McCready's wrist. Stepped back. And let the rustler's body slide down with a *thud* to the floor.

He stepped back, farther.

Almost slipped on something slick and wet. Looked down and saw that he and McCready had wrestled their way across the room onto that black stone circle set into the floor.

And the blood.

From McCready.

Pooling around his feet. Spilling into the lines carved into the floor, but not just spilling. Pouring. *Flowing.* Neatly, all McCready's blood filled them carvings and crevices like they was being poured there by some unseen hand, even worse: no way that much blood could gush from McCready's gut *that fast.* Or neat. Not from one shot. Not like this.

Something pulled the blood from McCready.

Pulling it through cracks and lines that formed weird shapes and designs. Triangles and circles crossing over each other and such, designs carved in the black stone circle, right under his feet and McCready's crazy bleeding body. And something else.

He could *see.*

Somehow he could *see* everything, clearly: The black stone circle and them weird etchings, McCready lying at his feet, blood pooling and flowing so neatly into them etchings and tracing them designs in all different directions, like them streams of blood was alive and racing towards each other.

He stared down for another second or two. Crazy as it seemed, light came from that black stone circle. A cold, greenish light. Glowing. Throbbing. Brighter and brighter. Making everything look green and cold and strange. The cold light pulsed like his own damn heartbeat. And as it pulsed and grew brighter, that cold thing inside him pulsed and spread and filled him.

All the way up.

Till there wasn't much of him left, inside.

And that felt very good.

As he stared at the streams of blood racing along those etchings towards one another. Somehow, the etchings were connected, with no breaks, and the closer them flowing beads of blood got to each other, faster the light throbbed. Wasn't gonna be long before they met, and when they did ...

Something cold pulsed inside him.

And he felt very fine, indeed.

Staring at them blood beads racing towards each other as the black stone circle glowed brighter and brighter and dimly, in the background, he thought he head screaming somewhere above, maybe in the burial mound where McCready's boys had been ...

All the blood beads met and pooled together at once.

All the etchings filled with neat, shivering little rivers of blood.

And everything got very quiet and still. The black circle dimmed.

At last.

Thank you.

Green light the likes of which he'd never seen before *blazed* up from the black stone. Burned the etchings into his brain. He threw up his arms, closed and covered his eyes but it didn't matter. Even in the dark behind his eyelids he saw those designs, glowing and pulsing and he wondered if he'd always see them now, glowing and pulsing in his brain whenever he closed his eyes.

Something howled all about him.

A great rushing of wind.

A great *opening* filled him. Slammed his heart against his ribcage. Something *roared* and a great coldness passed through him, surged upwards and away.

And then he heard them.

Screams.

Shrieks.

Voices gurgling from mouths filled with blood. Wet, sloppy sounds of something being torn apart ...

And then nothing.

The light faded.

Didn't die out right away. Slowly dimmed down. Gave him time to collect himself off his knees where he'd fallen. He sat back on his haunches. Blinked and listened. As the light from the black stone circle slowly died out.

The small room was still empty, except him and McCready's body. Even more, it *felt* empty. Emptier than before. As if that *wrongness* had left with the rushing cold he'd felt pulsing through him.

He nudged McCready's body.

Felt light as dried firewood, now.

Like it'd been drained of half its weight. It rustled and crackled, too ... like McCready's whole body had been dried out, somehow.

When he stooped to pluck McCready's Colt from his hand, his finger's brushed the rustler's skin ... and felt something dry like old parchment paper flake away.

He felt very glad he couldn't see the rest of McCready.

He straightened and hefted McCready's Colt. Felt solid. Grip felt cool and smooth. Ivory, most likely. On a whim he turned, searched as best he could in the rapidly dwindling green light, and just before it winked out, found the Colt McCready had dropped. He scooped it up, twirled it once, then stuck both into his empty holsters.

And they fit just fine.

Like they'd been made specially for him.

Whistling some jaunty tune he couldn't name, he stepped over McCready's body—now only a shadowed form on the floor—and headed for them steps. Carefully, he made his way up, out of the dark, into the light. Whistling the whole time, feeling free and easy and relaxed.

And ice cold inside.

When he scrambled into the burial mound and saw the other dead rustlers—their flayed, stripped and gleaming skeletons still wearing rustler clothes, all piled on top of each other, like they'd been fighting each other to flee—he didn't miss a note.

And after he climbed out of that mound, using several hand-holds he found in the wall, and found the rustlers' dead horses—stripped down bare to their skeletons, gleaming in the sun as if they'd been there for years—he kept right on whistling.

Feeling cold and empty and just fine, indeed.

He pointed himself south.

Ambled off in that direction, walking free and easy, loping along. Whistling and thinking he'd been damned lucky to escape them rustlers, though he waren't quite sure how he'd done it this time. Head felt all muddled and hazy on that point.

Course, he was the Kid, right? Escaping tight spots came natural to him. What he did best, actually.

One thing for sure. He was gonna have a talk with John when he caught up with him, who probably felt plumb sorry for leaving him high and dry like that. Probably bent all out of shape over it.

And if John waren't?

He smiled at the weight of them new Colts hanging heavy on his hips.

If'n John waren't sorry, right and proper …

Well.

He walked on, started back into whistling.

As the coldness inside him spread and hummed.

He opens his mouth to speak, but there's nothing to say, because the Kid's right. Whatever happened to him, down in that cave ...

Was his fault.

Cause he'd left him behind. Abandoned him. Rode off, without ever looking back. "Kid. Ah'm sorry. Really. Always felt horrible bout leavin you like that, always meant to find ya afterward, see if ... "

The Kid shrugs. "As it turns out, I got kinda busy later. An then, after I came back from bein dead ... well, figured I'd just wait. See if you'd come."

"But ... what happened? Down there inna cave? What ... what *was* all that?"

The Kid stands still for a moment, staring with dead-light eyes. Then he twirls his Colts showman-like, slips them into his holsters, smooth as butter, and hooks his thumbs under his gun belt, a picture of ease and confidence. "Don' rightly know. Been doin some reading since then. From old books I've dredged up. Lookin up all them symbols an other things I found down there."

He shakes his head.

Looks off to the horizon. "Real confusin. Lotsa talk bout Old Ones reclaimin the earth an all. Best I can tell, I accidentally let one a these old things out. An when it passed through me, it left somethin behind in me."

The Kid fixes him with that dead-eye stare. "An now, for some reason, I can't never die. An I tried, since diggin my way outta that groun. Trust me. I tried."

He frowns. Stands a little straighter, folds his arms across his chest. "So ... you can't never die? Never?"

"Nope."

"Well ... hell, Kid," he stammered, desperate and anxious to turn this around, somehow. "That ain't so bad. I mean ... you can do whatever the hell you want now. Right? Ain't no one's gonna stop ya if'n ya can't die."

The Kid nods, slowly.

Sizing him up like a buzzard does fresh kill. His stomach sours at the thought. "Yeah. Reckon that's true. Cept ... for all the livin I'm gonna be doin forever ... somethin's missin inside. An where it's missin ... ain't nothin but cold, John. I ain't nothin but dreadful cold an empty.

158

"An I figured, seein as how it'us *you* brought me to this, John Mackie, for leavin me on my own like that … if'n you ever came lookin to see if'n I was really dead, I'd bring it to *you*."

The Kid flickers.

Twitches.

And in a heartbeat is on him. Clutching him close, bending his neck back, exposing his throat jamming that Colt's cold muzzle into his guts. He thrashes and squirms, but the Kid's grip holds like iron. Unrelenting, merciless …

And cold as hell.

"Billy," he whimpers, hating the sound of his high, shrill voice, "pu-please. Don' kill me."

A hammer clicks back.

As The Kid's icy cold breath brushes his throat. "Oh, don' worry about that," the Kid whispers. "Killin ya's that last thing on my mind."

The Kid's Colt roars.

And all is black.

He wakes up much later, lying on his back on the cold, hard ground. It's night. The window is blowing. Stars shining.

He sits up. Pulls his knees to his chest and feels cold inside, a cold that has nothing to do with the breeze that washes over him. This cold runs deeper.

Down to where something is now missing.

And he pulls his knees to his chest and weeps. Because he knows, somehow. That the Kid has gone out. And has left him here, all alone, down in the dark.

Just like he deserves.

KEVIN LUCIA is the author of *Hiram Grange & The Chosen One*, Book Four of The Hiram Grange Chronicles. His first short story collection, *Things Slip Through* is forthcoming in November. He's currently working on his first novel.

Tracy L. Carbone

The Freeze

Paige awoke in a panic filled with dread, the kind that comes from forgetting to turn the stove off, or picking up your child from daycare. Only it was stronger, incapacitating. She lie in bed, covers pulled up to her chin, her black Lab, Tanner, asleep at her feet.

It was too quiet. Snowstorms brought this level of silence. When the snow insulated the world from sound, the birds hid themselves away, and people remained in their houses, it would be eerily still like this.

But Paige looked out the window, and the ground was clear. She stood there a couple of minutes checking for signs of doom: an orange or green sky, trees knocked down from wind, airplanes colliding. But there was nothing. Only a strange stillness, and bitter cold.

It was early morning. The dim light from outside partially lit the room. *God it's cold in here.* She flicked the light switch but it didn't take. Power was out. She used the light from her cell phone to check the thermostat, fifty-three degrees. She set it at sixty-nine last night.

She peeked outside again. No one else's lights were on but that didn't mean anything. It was early for people to be up and about. Her phone vibrated and shut off. *Damn it, out of battery.*

"Ivy!" she called down the hall as she ran to her daughter's room. Danger. That word was forefront in her mind. *Danger.* As plain as the skull and crossbones on a rat poison package. There as something deeper than the power outage, something she couldn't put her finger—

Ivy was gone. Paige's knees buckled and she fell onto the bed. *What the*—? Her bed had been made. Tight hospital corners. In all her seventeen years the child had made her bed only a handful of times. Ivy's clothes were generally strewn on the floor, and her bed a tangle of sheets. She hated her top sheet and it was usually on the floor with her clothes, a pink polka dot protest to cleanliness and order.

The room was spotless. Sterile. Each surface scrubbed clean, all the items in the room fronted, faced and perfectly aligned. *Danger.*

Paige checked her bathroom. "Ivy?" No answer.

She's run away.

No. Not Ivy. They were too close; she would never—

A rustling noise came from Ivy's closet. Paige dashed from the bathroom, opened the closet door, and found Ivy huddled in the corner, wrapped in a down comforter. Her knees were pulled to her chest, so she resembled a big white ball with a head. Her eyes relayed terror when she said, "I had the dream about the bears again. They're coming for us."

Paige knelt down next to her daughter. Until a week ago, Ivy loved bears. Had stuffed Poohs and pandas and black bears on her shelves and bed. But then the nightmares began. Always the same, a large bear growling and thrashing at her with giant claws, trying to kill her.

"Something's wrong," she said. "I woke up ... it's the bears."

Paige shook her head. "The power's just out, that's all. Come downstairs and we'll sit in front of the fireplace. We'll warm up and figure this out."

"Nothing to figure out," Ivy said as she walked down to the living room. "It's the bears."

Thankfully the gas fireplace kicked on. Paige lit the gas stove and made them tea. Ivy huddled in front of the fireplace on the floor. The breath puffed in front of them. The thermostat on that floor didn't register a temperature. Battery must be dead. Couldn't be a coincidence, Paige thought.

"I'm taking Tanner out."

Paige walked to the back door, donned her parka, hat and boots. Tanner, an old black Lab with white whiskers, shivered, maybe from cold, maybe from the same unidentifiable fear they felt. He backed away from the door. "What is it? Come on, time to go pee pee." The dog dug his feet into the floor when Paige pulled at his collar.

She tried to turn the knob but it was ice cold, penetrated straight through the gloves. "What the hell?" She looked back at the dog. "Tanner, let's go pee pee outside. Now!" She held the door handle again and the dog stared at her glassy eyed, then urinated on the floor. "Great."

Paige cleaned up then walked back to Ivy, who leaned against the glass front of the fireplace. Tanner ran over and lay down next to the girl.

"I'm going to check outside again," Paige said. She opened the blinds. No one on the roads. By now it must have been about 6:30. The high school kids should have been walking by towards the bus that picked them up outside their house. The neighbor's car should be running, warming up for his ride to work. *But no. Nothing.*

She stood watching for signs of life, the sound of a car rushing by, or the cracking sounds of leafless tree branches blowing in the wind. *No movement. None.*

"Ivy, come here. Look outside. Tell me I'm not crazy."

The girl rose, still wrapped in the comforter, and now wearing gloves and a ski hat with a sock monkey face.

They both peeked out the window. "Don't you think it's weird there's no one out there?" Paige asked.

"The bears are coming so the people are hiding." The words were nonsensical but Ivy uttered them with such conviction that Paige's fear spiked. She felt her daughter's forehead. Ice cold.

Maybe this was the danger, that Ivy was losing her mind. But that didn't explain the scene outside. "Look," Paige said. "The trees. Nothing's moving at all."

They waited, studying the street, the blades of grass, the curled and dried dead leaves. Not a whisper of movement. "It's like a nightmare photograph," Ivy said.

"Look at that cloud. It hasn't moved. I've been lining it up with that fence post."

"I'm afraid," Ivy said. She was and always had been a stoic child, but she sensed the enormity of the mysterious stillness. The feeling Paige had when she'd awakened grew stronger as they witnessed ... nothing.

They were stuck in this period of time, just after nightfall, just before dawn, with only enough light to cast the world in gray.

Paige placed all the couch cushions on the floor in front of the mantle and wrapped herself in a matching version of Ivy's.

"It's just a power outage," she said. A lie but who knew the truth?

"No. I woke up scared. Like something was going to happen, like a bomb or something," Ivy said. "And my room—did you clean it while I was sleeping?"

Paige shook her head. She couldn't have gotten it that clean without a crew. The night before it had been a cluttered mess.

"Who did?" Ivy asked. Paige shrugged. A clean room should not be a thing of fear, but it was hospital-clean. Unnatural. Just like the scene outside.

"Is that why you were in your closet?"

"Yes. No. I woke up and my room wasn't, wasn't my room. It was so cold. And then I—" She flinched. "I felt the bear; it touched me. So I hid in my closet until you came to get me."

A loud humming sound echoed around them, like an elevator or the hydraulics of a dumpster truck.

"What was that?" Ivy asked, cuddling close to her mother, something she hadn't done in a couple of years since she'd started asserting teen independence. Paige opened her blanket and wrapped it around the two of them.

The fireplace went out. *Shit.*

Paige got up, checked the stove. No gas at all. She looked out the window again, hoping to see a sign of life, maybe a utility truck or a police car. Instead, the desolate road iced over while she watched, barren winter trees freezing and splitting apart. She closed the shades before Ivy could see.

"Let's go back into your bedroom closet," Paige said, attempting and failing to sound calm. "Heat rises and there are no windows there. Bring the blankets. I'll grab candles and flashlights."

Ivy pointed to the windows.

"Nothing to see out there. Please go upstairs. It's getting too cold down here."

The shadow of a giant claw shone behind the shades. "Bear," she whispered. Tears flooded her eyes and ran down her cheeks. Ivy stopped trying to be brave. "Mom?"

"Go upstairs now!"

Ivy ran up, Tanner followed, and Paige filled a bag with supplies. She found a stash of hand and foot warmer packs she'd bought last year when Ivy was a football cheerleader. Like striking oil.

In under two minutes, they huddled inside the closet, which was indeed warmer than downstairs. She stuffed every blanket and pillow they owned in that closet, and sealed the edges. They made a circle in the middle and lit a candle.

"Here's put these in your shirt," Paige said as she squeezed the heat packs to activate them. She did the same and put one under Tanner, who stayed under the blanket with only his head peering out. They agreed not to leave their annex until … until they knew it was safe.

"What's the last thing you remember?" Ivy asked.

"What do you mean?"

"Before we woke up. Do you remember yesterday?"

"Of course. Don't you?"

She shook her head. "Tell me what you did yesterday," Ivy pushed.

"I went to work and came home."

"How did you get there? What do you do for a job?" She raised her voice and Paige began to argue back but caught herself.

"I—I went—" *I have no freaking idea.*

Something scraped the outside wall of their house. A series of scratches against the siding.

"It's the bears," Ivy whispered.

"You've been having nightmares for a week. I can remember that."

"Are you sure it's been that long, and not just last night?" Ivy asked. Paige couldn't reply. Time blurred.

The claw dug deeper into the exterior wall and board games fell from the top shelf. Tanner pulled out from the blanket, sat, and looked up at the ceiling. He didn't bark, never had, and Paige was grateful for his silence.

She drew Ivy closer. If they were going to die, at least they'd be together.

Paige didn't believe there were giant bears outside trying to kill them. The bears were merely Ivy's phobia. They didn't explain the power loss, the temperature drop, or the fact there were no signs of life or movement outside the home. Well, except for the claw. She shivered.

Paige struggled to recall last week, last month, where she went to school, who her husband had been. Did she have one? Ivy was her daughter, no doubt. But the past was fuzzy.

As she held her daughter, she couldn't help but wonder if any of this was real.

"You don't remember either do you?" Ivy asked.

""No I don't. But maybe—maybe it's the carbon monoxide. Maybe we breathed it in and we're dead." For some reason that seemed a happier option than the unknown.

"All of us? Even the dog? All of us ghosts together? Mom this is real! What are we going to do?"

"I don't know, okay? I don't know. All we can do is hide and stay warm."

"I don't want to die," Ivy said.

"Me either."

"How come we can't remember anything? And where are all the people?" Her voice grew hysterical. Paige had no words to offer that would ease her fear, but actions were necessary.

"I'm going to take a look out there. You stay here. We can't just hide forever. Maybe everything is okay now." Paige smiled but doubted Ivy believed the happy façade.

Paige wrestled out of the blanket and opened and shut the closet door quickly. The trees, houses, and cars had frozen and shattered, as if they'd been dipped in liquid nitrogen. A pile of red broken glass was all that remained of the neighbor's Jeep. Impossibly though, the temperature inside the house seemed to rise ever so slightly.

Without buildings or trees, Paige could see for miles. In the distance, warm yellow light rose from the horizon. The sun was finally rising.

She wondered if whatever cataclysm had occurred was all over the town, the world, or just what she saw from this vantage point. She ran down the hall and looked out her bedroom windows. Clear as far as she could see. Dots of shattered homes, cars, trees, and maybe people.

This can't be real. Can't be. It's in my head. A tear in my imagination caused a spiral into madness.

Suddenly there was music, faint but clear, coming from outside the window. Soft soothing piano. But like everything else today, the presence of music booming around her couldn't be real.

Paige went back to the relative safety of the closet.

"What did you see out there?" the girl asked.

"We're still okay. That's all we can worry about." She looked down at her daughter's sad face and realized Ivy had barely changed since her toddler days. Sure, she was tall but she was the same.

The music grew louder and thankfully Ivy heard it too. *It's not in my head.*

"What's that music? Is someone out there? Someone to save us?" Ivy asked hopefully.

They both heard a quiet beep. Steady, like a life support machine. Then Paige heard it and felt a loud buzz on her wrist. She looked and saw a thick black bracelet strapped on. "What is this? Has it been here the whole time?" It lit up and vibrated, the way restaurant pagers do when a table is ready.

Ivy pulled her hand out from under the comforter. "I've got one too. Mom, what are these things? What's going on?"

Paige sat next to her. "Did we have these this morning?" Paige asked again. She tugged at it, tried to unhook it, but it wouldn't release.

"I can't remember," Ivy said, crying. "But it's there now. Mom, what are we gonna do?"

Tanner nuzzled Paige's other hand. "Good dog." She patted his head and then spoke to Ivy. "It'll be okay. Whatever is going to happen, we're going to be all right."

The scraping outside became louder, rattled the house.

Paige hugged Ivy. The dog had crawled under the blanket with them and stayed close.

The bears were on the roof. Scraping. Gouging. Plaster fell from the ceiling so Paige covered their heads with the comforter. They burrowed under the pillows. But still the bracelets buzzed and lit up, revealing their location.

A bright light shone from the edges of the blankets. "Keep your eyes closed, Ivy."

The music blared. Beautiful but deafening.

"Time to wake up Numbers One Forty," a woman's voice said above the sound of the music, which faded as if someone lowered the volume.

A force pulled the blanket off. Paige tried to fight but her arms had been pinned down. She and Ivy screamed; their only defense. Tanner remained quiet.

Paige opened her eyes.

She found herself lying on a cold metal table. A woman in an elastic white suit watched her. "Number One Forty, welcome to the future," she said. She had a hard to place accent. English but a monotone. A robot? "Don't be afraid. You will remember soon. Don't move too quickly. Just relax. I'm going to unfasten your wrist alarm and your belts but please do not try to move." She released

Paige's limbs and she gently moved her hand and foot restraints. "Are you warm enough? We've been gradually returning your body temperature to normal. You're almost there."

Paige was warm but didn't reply, and instead rolled her head to the side and was relieved to see Ivy. She was asleep but moaning. *Still in our dream state. In our other life?* Ivy's wristband buzzed, and another worker approached and woke her up. Paige's fear lessened considerably. She wondered if they had given her a sedative.

"Welcome to the future Number One Forty-one," the man said to Ivy.

"Mom?" Ivy's eyes met Paige's.

"I'm here," she said. "It's all right. We're all right." Somehow she knew it was true. No lies this time.

"Where is here?" the girl asked.

"I don't know," Paige replied.

"Where are we?" Ivy cried. "We want to go home! Please don't hurt us!"

The male worker removed Ivy's bonds as he spoke. "You won't understand when I tell you where you are, just know that you are in a better place and safe." He and the woman slid the beds together. Paige took Ivy's hand.

"You and your daughter, and a thousand others, won a lottery back on your planet. You were chosen to come here, to be frozen until you could be transported to a safe haven."

The male pressed a button on a large panel and very slowly, the tables raised upright and then folded to become reclining chairs. Paige felt light-headed but soon her head cleared.

"You will need to move very gradually," he explained. "You have been in deep freeze for two hundred and fifty years and we only started to thaw you this morning. You will need to acclimate to our gravity, and to walking again. Please stay seated."

Grrrrr. Grrrr. An animal growl reverberated from a large brown cat on the floor. It was almost feline, but had a large shiny black snout. And the sound was all wrong. More guttural than a purr, closer to a roar. It jumped onto Ivy's lap and rubbed against her. It must have weighed thirty or forty pounds. Ivy was clearly still groggy and confused but calm. They must have dosed her with something too, thought Paige.

"Bear is one of our therapy pets." *Bear.* "He calms the Transports as they thaw. He's spent most of today assisting your process."

Ivy smiled and petted the cat.

"We entered a lottery?" Paige asked.

"The government recommended residents who met certain criteria. You were not made aware of the plan. With the others, you were *taken*, by surprise, on the last possible day," he said. "The situation was not ideal, but beyond our control."

"Last day for what?" Ivy asked before Paige got the chance.

"The last viable day on your planet," the woman in white said. She handed them sunglasses and pressed another button on the vast panel. "Your eyes will need to adapt. Please put these on." Electric blinds opened onto a vista of flowing fields dotted with colored flowers. The colors were unfamiliar and indescribable, but soothing. Their rhythmic movement denoted harmony. Paige considered that perhaps her serenity was inherent in the environment and not a drug.

The male walked to the window, which was also a computer monitor. He used his fingers to enlarge the view until he zoned in on a small house surrounded by others. It was round like a scoop of ice cream or an igloo, but open on top.

"Number One Forty and One Forty-One, that is your new home. When you have built your strength, you will be released into the outside with the other Transports."

An animal that resembled a dog, sort of, walked to Paige and rested his head on her lap. "That is Tanner. He will be your guide." *Tanner. Of course. He wasn't part of our past after all. He was part of our present.*

Oddly, Paige did not feel sadness or pain that her planet was gone, with most of the people. Who was there left from her past she would miss? She couldn't recall anyone now, except Ivy. She looked back out the window. A clean slate. A new chance. She looked to her daughter who smiled at Bear. They would be all right here.

"Will our memories come back?" Paige asked.

The male shook his head. "No. It was decided that mankind would fare better, and last longer this time, without a past. You have important memories of development of your daughter and yourself, maybe some disjointed flashes of your last day on Earth, but no world or personal history. You know the names of things that you will need. The rest, you will learn." He smiled then and Paige wondered if he was a living being and not an android. She supposed it didn't matter away, so long as he showed kindness.

For a second, there was a pang of sadness and longing for a life and past she could not recall, but it was gone just as quickly. Part of the procedure no doubt, the inability to remember or feel upset. She smiled as hope filled her. Already the fear she felt in her dream, or her memory of her last day there, was fading, giving way to the life before her.

"Your future starts today," the female said. "Come, I will take you to meet the others."

A powerful hydraulic sound and vibration led to a platform opening in front of them. Their recliners became wheelchairs. The male and female pushed Ivy and Paige down a ramp and into the sunlight and swaying grasses of their brand-new land.

TRACY L. CARBONE is a Massachusetts native whose has published dozens of short stories. Her novels to date include *The Soul Collector, Restitution* and *The Collection and Other Dark Tales*. She is a member of the NEHW and HWA.

TIMOTHY P. FLYNN

DARK SONG FOR ICARUS

so easy to create you: a rib
not broken; the manufacture
of design. false pride,
taken for granted—
selfish desires, demonize
the ideal of creation.

how do you get rid of memories?
stillborn offspring of a conscious
mind; forever eternal—
fused and binding.
supplied with the means to soar
you chose to ignore the lectures
wisdom derived through painful
salvation, scars of the past
passed down—ignorance
was your death ...

broken, shattered pieces of me
inherited into you, viral blood
pulsing in veins—mind too naïve
to realize this path of
isolation

gouge out these eyes, tear out
this seared heart to not
see or feel, the pain: overpowering
burden of righteous guilt
cursed for eternity; the vivid
images {eyes, face, your smile}
steal me awake ...
from every restless nightmare.

TIMOTHY P. FLYNN resides in Haverhill, MA. His previous poetry has been in *Space and Time* Issue # 115, and the first annual *Anthology: Year One* edition. Tim is a husband and father of three, member of the NEHW, and an online student at SNHU.

ERRICK A. NUNNALLY

HAROLD AT THE HALFCOURT

TO ANSWER THE QUESTION: our lives—human lives—are nothin' but choices. You think the law is what keeps you safe? Nope. It's other people choosing not to ruin your day. Push comes to shove, though, other people wouldn't give you the time of day if it meant the difference between keepin' an appointment to save your life or lettin' you die. Folks tend to suck and they suck harder the poorer they get. Suck the life out of everything around them. Entire neighborhoods full of colored folk, robbed of color. When the life laid out for you is nothing but a maze of profit-driven dreams— what was it that cat in that movie said? "You think that's air you're breathing now?"

Yeah, that flick was Harold's favorite movie and I do mean favorite. The counsel of a movie character meant more to him than anyone else's words—even his coach's, even his mother's. The man Fishburne portrayed in that movie delivered straight knowledge to Harold's cortex. He knew, deep down—the way a truth can warp reality around a person—he knew that he was a better baller than anyone else, knew that this particular reality was his to mold if he were disciplined enough, if he were true enough. Wait up.

You knew Big-Time NBA Star Harold Thompson, right? That's what they used to call him 'round here anyway. He learned true truth the hard way: he met the biggest lie you could ever meet. Right over there. On Halfcourt.

Everyone calls it 'Halfcourt' because it's the only thing you can call it. Part of a city park rebuild, it was the best The Man could do with half-assed planning and a cup of guilt that'd been used up over twenty years ago. See, they fucked up. After cleaning out the field for soccer ('football' those crazy-ass new-to-the-ghetto islanders called it) and putting in a tennis court (tennis ball, I guess), they didn't leave enough room for basketball. 'Ball' the original ghetto-ites called it. A sport so near and dear you don't even have to call it by its full given name. Just say: 'ball' and everyone knows you're talking two holes and a rock. Don't even need nets, little ninjas will play on cut out milk crates nailed to leftover sheets of particle board. The compromise for the park, as you can see, was to put in half a court. Don't think too wrong on this: even though it was born of error and a deep-rooted, misunderstood malice, the court was good for some things. Practice, for one, small games, for two. One-on-one, two-on-two, and a crowded three-on-three if the natives were feeling charitable.

The nearest full court, for Harold, was at his high school. Being a senior, and living where he did, classes didn't start until later in the morning, leaving him time to bounce a few in the early morning, maybe catch a pickup game with another early-to-rise aficionado. Y'see, Harold had game to spare, enough game to ignite The Dream the geniuses in NBA marketing feed to the hungriest of masses. Harold had his sights set on pro. Not before college though—nope! He was smart enough to want the college experience for 'maturity' as his coach put it, 'a real ticket out' as his mother referred to it. 'Whatever' is what he muttered under his breath when he didn't think anyone was listening. The boy wasn't sure if he was going to be able to finish four college years knowing that he would be recruited—his poor reading and comprehension skills notwithstanding. To start, he planned on going to Indiana or Louisville—they had top-rated programs. He'd already been working with his coach to catch recruiting eyes. (Maybe Kentucky, if he felt like slumming a bit.) From there, he planned on the East Coast remaining his home. Historically thinking, it was the Celtics, the Bulls, or the Nicks. He did one season with the Bulls, by the way, but you knew that already. Right?

Harold didn't smoke or do drugs, didn't drink, got plenty of sleep, ate all his vegetables, and supplemented his endless ball playing with regular exercise. In short, Harold was driven with a capital

'D' and he loved the game. Loved. It. He did have one weakness, though, but we'll get around to that.

This particular morning, Harold found the court empty. Nothing but a weak mist blowing across the slightly moist court. He arrived at a light jog to warm up and planted his feet on the foul line to practice foul shots. The first two thumped off the hoop, sending a low hum through the park. The third was a brick off the backboard. But let me tell you: Harold took a moment to remind himself that he was the best there was at basketball and sank the next five. All net. That sound so very satisfying every time. The sixth shot swished through and that's when he saw the tall, dark dude standing at the corner of the court.

This brother—get this—wore his skin like classic Dr. J: the afro, thigh-high shorts and—no shit—knee-high socks with red and white stripes. He was givin' Harold the 'slow clap,' grinning through thick lips under a wide nose; dark glasses hid his eyes.

"Nice shootin', little brother." That clean baritone made Harold's guts vibrate, a smooth delivery, verbal butter, The Force was strong with this one. "Got time for a game?"

Now, Harold nodded acknowledgment for the compliment, but he looked this old-school cat up and down on his game request. The neighborhood was full of O.G.s and leftover wannabes that never made nothin' out of themselves on the streets. Most of them were out of shape, out of time, and stayed out of sight, normally. Here comes this dude: slim, way behind the times, and thinking he was going to put Harold to The Test. Some older guys liked to do that; see what Harold was made of.

The younger man checked his watch, he had time, so he waved the 'fro over.

Before trotting on to the court, Mr. Time-Traveling Pimp Ball Player, popped his glasses off and slipped matching sweatbands on to head and wrist. Then he clapped once, causing a sharp retort that surprised Harold and made him flinch. "Let's do this, little bro'. Play to twelve, no threes, ball-check on points, you dig?"

"Uh, yeah." Harold nodded.

Cool, grey eyes in a smooth, dark face fixed Harold at Halfcourt. "Cool, m'man. Think you can be a gentleman on fouls? No time for hack-a-hatchet brother on the court, sly."

Harold smiled. He didn't typically foul, but he was respectful enough to make the call or allow the call when it came.

"A'ight, slick, let's do this."

Harold never expected to be stripped and out dribbled like he had been. This old dude moved like an oiled snake. A street-livin' octopus, he had long arms and legs, big hands—he was built for ballin', and he knew how to, in Larry Bird parlance, 'Make the ball go in the hole.' This crazy rapid dribbler was a fan of wraparounds and crossovers, nearly threatening to lay the Gilmore on Harold more than once.

No inflatable, ass-donuts for our boy, though, Harold stepped up his game; 'cause before he knew it, he was down by two. Then four. What to do? Double the usual effort, squeaking rubber on asphalt, strip, post, check, rebound. Rinse and repeat. Win.

When it was over, Harold took the game by two and was shocked to find that it was twenty minutes of the hardest ball he'd ever played!

They'd also picked up a small, but shapely audience.

Three girls he'd never seen around before. One, the color of coffee with too much cream and a shape like a bottle of Co-Co-Coca-Cola. Number two—Harold didn't recognize her either—stood by the fence with them, talking and looking in their direction. The second was an impossibly curvy, caramel-colored, smooth-skinned cutout of heaven. Harold wanted her in ways that should've been illegal. He wouldn't mind a bite of all of them. The third girl appeared to be molded from milk chocolate, with a small waist, perfectly curved hips and just the biggest, roundest pair of—you get the idea: she was stacked, built for booty-duty.

"You got my brains blown; you're good, my man."

This tall dude, makin' time on the asphalt like he'd been born there, had been watching Harold watch the ladies and now drew his breathless gaze.

"Thanks. So are you," was all the boy could manage, addled as he was by the fine young flesh that had just burned the back of his dome through his eyes.

"Ah, the young prod finds his voice and the ladies do come to the mountain! Call me Dee." Dee's smile dazzled. Impossibly straight, impossibly white teeth, glowed at Harold. The man offered his knuckles. They bumped.

Harold breathed his name out there, distracted as he was, in a kind of little-kid puff of air. "Harold."

"See you 'round, Harold, m'man." Dee carried an old-school, canvas, gym bag. He stuffed his sweatbands into it, slipped on the sunglasses, and pulled out a washcloth to mop up a bit before zipping a bright green, skintight Adidas jacket over his torso.

Harold saw an opportunity for improvement. "Uh, wait. Tomorrow? Same time? Wanna go again?"

"My brother, I thought you'd never ask." Dee blessed Harold with another dazzling smile and took his leave, promising they'd meet again tomorrow, same time.

They did. And the day after that and the day after that and the day after that. Harold's game improved, much to his delight and the anger of his opponents. Dee was relentless, the cat pulled moves out of nowhere, taught Harold a few things, but never dunked. He finger-rolled like he was laying the finest slice of cake in front of the Queen Mother, but never dunked. For his part, Harold took the cue and kept his mitts off the rim too. Classic play, the real deal, nothing but skill, no trash talk. Respect.

Harold soon made serious skin time with Valerie (Ms. Too-Much-Cream in Coffee). And eventually Solina (the caramel one). Those girls both did things with their bodies and mouths that—ohmygod this one time—barely a day apart! Harold. Playah-playah, right? Thank Dee. Harold knew it—knew that his one-on-ones with Dee were puttin' extra weight in his jock that these vid-e-hoes was bound to recognize. Except number three. Lucy. She who was cast from milk chocolate. Harold never found his rhythm with her, couldn't lay game on that one. That's what he thought, anyway.

So. The rest of the last semester of Harold's home life wound its way to an end. No one was aware of Harold's early morning "training" sessions with Dee. No one but those girls.

A few months before graduation, Harold got some serious proposals from college recruiters. He found he had his pick and he picked Louisville. Despite having "made it," he trained harder. The day before graduation, Harold met Dee at Halfcourt, never expecting that it'd be the last time.

The court was hot that morning, no breeze, and only one spectator: Lucy. Dee was different then, more intense. It was as if the light bent around him, taken in by his gravity. He was heavy, to say it simple.

"Heard you got recruited by Louisville."

"Uh-huh."

"Lucy girl up there is goin' to Louisville too."

"Yeah?"

Harold didn't think to ask how Dee knew what he did. Just like he didn't question what came next.

"Yeah, you gon' get yo' chance wit' dat. Now, how 'bout we make our last game interesting, bro,' a little wager?"

"Dee, you crazy, man, I ain't got no money."

That dazzling smile cracked Dee's face. It always surprised Harold how Dee could switch from the Wisdom of Solomon to Caligula in no time flat. The younger man was like a mouse in the beam of that smile, well-timed as it always was. Harold wondered if this was what a movie hero felt like the first time a punk got up in his face. If so, he knew he was going to shut the whole thing down, bend the outcome more to his liking. Harold knew in his heart of hearts that he was in control.

"Don't want yo' money, young blood, don't want that at all. I got a mind on somethin' more interestin', if you willin'.'"

The smile again. Harold didn't know what to think, but he wasn't taking Dee's offer seriously.

"Okay, whatever, it's my last day 'round here, things 'bout to change f'real."

Dee nodded, he knew. "Just to make it interesting, put it all on the table for me. Everything you have up to now, all this, whatever heart and soul you put into things up to now, lay it on the table."

Harold just grinned, bouncing the ball lazily, physically confident. "And what's in it for me?"

"Your future, blood, everything that's to come. I give you my blessing. And I know some folks in Louisville that might could help you out, they got connections to the NBA too."

Harold suspected as much, he knew Dee had too much game to not know some folks somewhere. Not that Harold could suss the whole thing out, but he trusted Dee at this point and that meant more to him than facts.

"You wanna play ball or what, Dee?"

"We got a deal?"

Harold went with his trusting gut. "Yeah, man, we got a deal. Check!"

They played. A fierce game, a leave-it-all-on-the-court game, an asphalt-melting, dehydration nation bomb out! More hoops than the WNBA, more moves than a game o' checkers with multiple jumps and unlimited kings, and someone's heart sure got burnt into the paint.

With eighteen points on both sides—game to twenty, win by two—Dee had a few words for Harold. The first time ever that he'd spoken during a game.

"Don't forget what you playin' for, young blood, make it count."

Harold just grinned, he had a lock on how things turned out when he was feelin' it. Time meant nothing, the size and speed of his opponent meant nothing, skill meant nothing. His head was so far into the game, he already knew he'd won it. The physical part was a technicality for Harold. He faked right, rapid dribbled between both legs, made like a wraparound, but instead elbow passed to himself in a spinning move that nearly broke Dee's neck trying to keep up. The ball slid through the hoop in a backboard slapping finger roll that had Harold hopping on his toes grinning and Dee slow-clapping the end of an era.

The tall, older man pointed at Harold, nodded, scooped up his canvas bag and, slipping on sunglasses across a sweaty brow said, "You earned it all, baller, I'm a make some calls for you soon." With a head nod, Dee was gone, leaving Harold breathless on the court with Lucy.

Harold and Lucy were married in a simple ceremony, one year after Harold skipped out on a stunning winning streak in college for a fat NBA contract. Six months after that was when he got the first summons from his pregnant mistress. This incident didn't end his marriage, but the child that turned up from a one night stand in Washington did. This caused no end of evil in his home life, especially since his first child with Lucy was on the way.

You think Hell hath no fury like a woman scorned? You ain't never met an angry black woman. There's nothing meaner in the world 'cause they start out mean comin' from neighborhoods like the one that molded Harold and Lucy. Now he had three at his throat. (Yes, the chick in Washington was white, but she come up black, so there you go.) Playing ball became his only escape. On the court, he was a god, twisting outcomes in his favor.

Another year passed. He was still at the top of his game when summonses from Valerie and Solina made their way to his doorstep. The legal paper informed him that he had five-year-old sons back in the neighborhood and that he'd neglected them. It broke his heart, his bank, and what little resolve Harold had left. Getting on the court was starting to feel like being moved from gen pop to solitary. Each day he dragged feet onto the wood, moved a little slower, lost the shine that made him one of the brighter stars in the sky. His game suffered. There was a lack of support coming from the head office. The owners had put a fat contract on Harold, to the detriment of the rest of the team. He had been that good, but now his game withered like day old collards in the fridge while a less-than-stellar team struggled to pick up the slack. They hated him before, but now they really hated him.

Still, he found solace in the arms of a woman. Between a vasectomy, a condom, her use of the pill, and the amazing fact that their relations were nothing but oral—according to Harold— he never expected the pregnancy. She chose to keep the baby. He denied being the father. DNA proved otherwise. Around that time, Harold frequently thought back to the morning before graduation when he'd last played Dee. Everything had felt right that day, he'd played his heart out and won that game. He beat Dee, won their little bet. Not that he believed the older man was responsible for his poor fortune nowadays, but he'd won that last game. Right?

Last time I saw Harold, he was right over there with a ball. It was his old morning routine time, smack between when the young kids go to school and the older ones are still munching on their pillows. Slunk his expensive ass right up to the foul line, planted his feet and took the shot. Brick. Banged right off the back board, rattling the pole. Come right to his feet off the fence. He didn't scoop it up, just stood there lookin' around. Seemed to be waiting for something to happen. He stood there a long time.

A native of Boston, Massachusetts, ERRICK A. NUNNALLY served in the Marines before attending art school. Having some talent in design and illustration, he chooses instead to write stories and study Krav Maga with kickboxing. Visit *erricknunnally.squarespace.com* to learn more.

DAVID BERNSTEIN

IT'S NICE NOT
TO HAVE TO SHARE

I STUCK THE NAIL FILE INTO MY SISTER'S TEMPLE, poked her a few times to make sure she was dead. I knew she was gone, her lifeless eyes staring at nothing as they bulged from their sockets, but it's always a good idea to be thorough.

The prosecution, my neighbors, newspaper reporters (via the articles), even my Dad, believe I'm evil, but I can assure you that I'm not. My mother's too medicated to have a true opinion so I'll leave her out of this. The only other person to substantiate my claim that I am not evil is my psychologist. As a Harvard educated man—the degrees hanging from the walls of his office telling me so—he doesn't believe in evil.

I have supporters, people that truly understand my plight and know how hard it was for me and my sister, Sally. None of them, of course, had the courage to do what I did. Don't get me wrong, I loved her with all my heart and with every breath I inhaled. We had a bond unlike normal sisters, but it was that bond that inevitably broke us.

Everywhere I went, she was there like a freckle on my nose. I, we, never had time apart. We always watched the same television programs, each having to endure the other's bad taste as we took turns with the remote. Showers were terrible, intrusive, to say the least—most people using that time to unwind, wake-up, refresh or pleasure themselves. Not me. Not with her always there.

Going to sleep wasn't much better. Countless times I lay exhausted, wanting to drift off into a soundless slumber, but she wasn't tired and kept me up, always talking or needing the light on. I punched her in the face once to show her I wasn't playing around, but it was like hitting myself—her pain was mine. I learned to live with her, but the final straw was pulled when Gerri, my true love, came into our lives.

Gerri and I had an immediate connection. I had never believed in love at first sight, but the clichéd saying proved to be true. We fell deeply in love.

Gerri was beautiful, full-figured, and curvy like a back mountain road, but with the muscle-tone of a professional dancer. She had luscious full lips, perfectly shaped as if sculpted from Cupid himself. Her skin was smooth, like the finest Mulberry silk, and had the hue of fine Italian porcelain.

Gerri was a genuine soul, looking at what a person was on the inside. She was kind-hearted and selfless, spending a good portion of every week with the elderly at St. Peter's Memorial hospital, making sure they weren't alone on birthdays and holidays.

My jokes were corny, or just not very amusing, but she always laughed at them, making me feel special.

My sister and Gerri got along well, and that was important because Sally and I were always together. With my being a lesbian, and Sally liking men, we had to come up with a deal.

Whenever Gerri came over I would wait until Sally fell asleep before we made love. The same went for my sister when she had a man over—they would wait until I was asleep. She was my sister and as much as a man's penis made my skin crawl, I accepted her heterosexual desires and needs. And as strange as the situation might've seemed, we managed well enough and had a nice routine going—until the night I caught my sister with Gerri.

I had my suspicions, wondering if Sally had been awake while Gerri and I made love. I could have sworn she moaned a few times and that it wasn't Gerri, but Gerri assured me that my sister was sleeping.

One morning, early in the a.m., I awoke to find Gerri and Sally going at it. They had tried to be quiet, speaking in hushed whispers. Their breathing was heavy and rapid at times, with the occasional moan sneaking from one of their mouths. Gerri was too good in the sack for whomever she was with not to make any noise. I wanted to scream out, to rake my fingernails down my sister's face, but I was frozen, numbed with shock.

My heart sank and I felt like crying out, but I remained still, and allowed them to finish. *My* Gerri was a two-timing whore. I should have known, with her acceptance of my situation and all ... She was, obviously, turned on by the two of us, had a fetish for our kind, and bid her time well until she could have us both. I trusted her; loved her with every ounce of my soul. My heart ached like a rotting tooth—the pain unbearable. I chose to say nothing, waiting to see if Sally's or Gerri's guilt would cause one of them, or both, to reveal what they had done. Neither said a thing, and my sister went about her business as usual, seeming more joyous than was customary.

I let it go, chalking it up to a first time offense. I loved my sister and I was in love with Gerri. No one was perfect, myself included. But a week later, to my dismay, I caught them going at it again. Once more I said nothing, letting them finish as I felt myself dying inside.

I waited until morning, after Gerri left, before confronting my sister.

"I know what's been going on with you and Gerri," I said, lying in bed.

"Oh?" she responded.

"I caught the two of you twice now."

"So. What's yours is mine and what's mine is yours," she said, not even turning to look at me.

"We had a deal," I reminded her, as I climbed out of bed. "An understanding." I wanted to kick her, but I played it cool.

"Well, Georgia," she began, "since we're always together, I figured we should share; like we do everything else."

"Absolutely not," I shouted. "And since when do you like women?"

"Since Gerri's tongue whisked me away to a place no man ever has."

I had to sit, the room was going out of focus and my legs felt like jelly. "How can you be so cold?" I asked. "She was my love, the other half of my heart, and you ripped her away from me, the only thing that I could call my own." Tears began to well, blurring my sister's face, melting it. I didn't want to cry; didn't want her to see me hurting, but the pressure was building within and needed to be released.

"It was impossible for me to sleep while you were having sex," Sally told me. "The sensations drove me wild, your lover's touch making me want moan, to cry out. I could only go with it."

"No," I yelled. "You have to stop." I pounded my fist against the dresser. "I'll drug you if I have to."

Sally stood up, taking me with her, dragging me to the bathroom. In front of the mirror, she said, "Look at us."

There we were, conjoined from the waist down with two upper bodies. It was the moment I realized I'd never have anything to myself, except for my thoughts. The deep, dark, ominous feelings, torturing my every breath, making me hate my sister—*myself.*

I stared into her spiteful eyes, seeing nothing. She was a completely different person than me, a different soul. We had become two people who spoke languages the other could not understand. She no longer knew me, nor I her.

Later that night, after she fell asleep, I tied my scarf around her delicate neck and strangled her. She awoke during the deed, fighting futilely against me, but to no avail. I still have a few scars on my wrists and face from where she clawed me—reminders of the night I killed her.

I was arrested and nearly prosecuted, but having been declared legally insane by a multitude of quacks, I was sentenced indefinitely to a psychiatric hospital where I would remain until deemed fit to re-enter society. I considered my sentence lucky, because I'm not crazy. For is it crazy to want independence?

I've had five surgeries so far, each a progression towards my normality. Sally's dead weight had been lopped off within hours of her death. The surgeons cut bone, reconstructed parts of my body, re-routed blood flow, and sealed off the pathways that had led to my sister. They told me that I had been close to death more than a couple of times, and that I was strong, a fighter.

I tried contacting Gerri, for I still loved her, but she never answered my letters. With time, I hope she can see past what I had to do. I did, after all, forgive her for her indiscretions and hope she can do the same for me one day.

I'll never be completely normal. No one is. But I'm emotionally free now, soon to be physically free once the doctors believe me to be well-enough for society. Then, I'll be able to help others like me.

DAVID BERNSTEIN is the author of *Damaged Souls*, *Machines of the Dead*, *Tears of No Return*, and *Amongst the Dead*. You can visit him at *davidbernsteinauthor. blogspot.com* and email him at *dbern77@hotmail.com.*

DAVID NORTH-MARTINO

THE INTERLOPER

"WHY ARE YOU BACK SO SOON?" Jared asked me as he fidgeted with his experiment. He played with dials and pressed at flashing lights. I stood in the messy laboratory with my hands crossed and my eyes downcast. I still felt so numb.

"Why aren't I home mourning, is that what you're asking me?"

"It's a natural process," Jared said. He stopped what he was doing and looked at me. I couldn't meet his gaze. "You mustn't blame yourself."

"I was driving the car, Doc," I said feeling the anger welling up. I didn't want to talk about this. Jared Brandon held multiple Ph.D.s to my one, but a psychologist he wasn't. "Anyway, I don't want to sit at home. I need to keep busy. And I think I have a lot to do."

"Then can I ask why you're in my laboratory instead of your own?"

"Because I have something I need to do, but I don't know how to do it. You're the one with the expertise." I was having a hard time containing myself. I wanted to get straight to the point, but didn't want to scare him too quickly. He wasn't going to like what I had to ask of him.

"What are you thinking of doing, Carl," he asked. "Rumor has it that the government commissioned you to conduct some time travel experiments."

"It's impossible, Carl," he said gently. "We were never able to go backward in time. Even if we could I wouldn't advise it. Some things are better left the way they are."

"I don't want to go back. I want to go forward."

"Forward? That doesn't make any sense. And even if it did, you can't stay on the same timeline. You'll end up in a parallel dimension."

"That's exactly where I want to go: a parallel dimension—in the future."

"Why?"

"In this world Cheryl died, but in another dimension I made a different decision. I came out of that skid and she survived."

I watched him as his mind took it in. His face slackened. He knew I was right.

"Yes, dimensional theory states that every time a decision is made alternate realities are created and the other possible decisions are played out in these other dimensions. But it's just a theory."

I could tell by his expression that he knew more than he was letting on. I finally found the courage to meet his eyes and then stared at him until he averted my gaze.

"Okay," he said stammering. "I'll tell you the truth, but this is highly confidential. We sent two military men into another dimension, but we were unable to recover them. One moment they were here, the next they had vanished. If they survived they're living life in some other dimension.

"That's only if they survived. The military finally couldn't see an application for sending people into a different timeline, especially when we couldn't get them back. They didn't feel it had any real world uses for war, so they took the funding from their $500 screws and $900 hammers and ended the project."

"But you could do it. You could send me to that other timeline?" I felt hope as I said it, and I had thought all hope was lost.

"It is doubtful that you'll survive the journey, and even if you did you'd have to stay there with her. She's dead in this world, Carl. And you haven't thought of the most important obstacle."

"What's that, Doc?"

"There's another you out there and he's in love with your wife, too

———————————

I wouldn't let anything Jared said deter me. And in the end he gave in. I had been contemplating suicide anyway, although I didn't tell him that. So he wouldn't lose his job at the university, I made sure to make my disappearance look natural. I contacted friends and relatives and told them I was going on a trip. My will was in order so everything would be taken care of when I was finally declared dead.

"When you get to the other side let the me there know. He'll be able to help you," Jared said as I reclined in a cushy chair that reminded me of the one my dentist used.

"Will do, Doc." He placed electrodes on my temples; the glue used to apply them felt warm and sticky.

"And give him this," Jared said handing me an envelope.

"What's in it?"

"The information on that paper will make him believe you—especially when he sees it was written in his own handwriting."

"Thanks for everything, Doc."

"I'm going to miss you old friend. I hope you find what you're looking for." If I didn't know him better I would have thought his eyes went misty, but then he turned around and rotated a few dials on the machine. A feeling of vertigo overcame me; the world doubled and then righted itself.

I found myself in the same room, sitting in the same chair, and holding the same envelope, but I was alone. The electrodes and the glue were gone as well.

The walk down the hall to Jared's lab seemed to take forever. My heart thumped and my mouth went dry. I could only hope that I didn't run into myself out for a bathroom break, or worse—in Jared's lab.

Too impatient to knock I barged through the door. Jared looked up at me in surprise from his lab bench.

"Carl, you look grim. What's the matter?"

"You're not going to believe it, Doc."

I told him everything and he laughed, but after he read through the contents of the envelope he stopped.

"How did you get me to consent?"

"You know how stubborn I am—or maybe you don't. But in my time and my dimension you had done this before so I figured you couldn't see the harm."

"I doubt that very much. The harm to this time stream could be irreparable. If you touch your other self you might both blink out of existence or create the equivalent of a nuclear explosion. What do you expect to gain by doing this?"

"I've come back for my wife, Doc."

"Don't you realize you were never without her. It only feels that way. When the Carl from this time stream goes home, he goes home to his wife. Will you make your other self suffer so you can be with your wife? You both can't be with her at the same time."

"How do I know my other self didn't blink out of existence as soon as I passed into this time stream?"

"That's a very good point. There is one way to find out."

Jared pick up the receiver from the phone on the bench and dialed my extension.

"Sorry Carl," Jared said. "I must have dialed your extension by accident." He put down the phone, his face now pale.

"Are you okay, Doc?"

"I'll be fine. Talking to your other self with you in the room shook me up a bit more than I expected."

But I was shaken, as well. I had hoped that I would just replace my doppelganger when I entered the time stream. Now I had to figure out what to do next.

"You know, the Carl from this time stream is you, feels the same happiness and sadness as you do. You made your choice, don't ask him to suffer the consequences."

"I have to see my wife, Doc," I said. I couldn't listen to this any longer. I turned away from him and strode out the door.

"She's not yours anymore, Carl." His voice followed me out into the hall, but I immediately broke free of it, leaving him and his objections behind.

The neighborhood lay quiet in the early afternoon. My street ended in a cul-de-sac and was lined with newly built million dollar homes. The economy had kept some of the houses unoccupied, others temporarily stood empty while the residents were dutifully out to work paying off the mortgage.

Little sun found its way into the interior of my home, but I resisted the urge to turn on the lights.

Upstairs I grabbed my .38 snub-nosed revolver out of the gun safe and loaded it. Bringing it downstairs, I fixed myself a scotch on the rocks and sat on the couch. The crackle of ice in the glass the only thing breaking the silence. My hands shook but the alcohol eased my anxiety.

I didn't have to wait long. I heard them at the door. My wife and my double. I put my drink on the end table. They entered the foyer and then stepped in the living room. I stood up. My wife gasped and stumble back into the arms of the interloper.

"Get away from him, Cheryl," I said.

"What's going on, Carl? She said, looking back at him then at me. "Carl?"

The other Carl pushed her away from him. It's exactly what I would do. And that made sense since he was me. I hesitated but only for a second. I pulled the trigger. The gun went off, the blast making my ears ring. The interloper slumped to the ground. My wife screamed. I had put him out of his misery. Cheryl ran out of the house still screaming.

I fell to my knees as a wave of information and emotion rippled through my mind and body. And I absorbed the other Carl's life, the car crash. His pain and longing became my own. Tears turned to sobs as the other me faded and then completely disappeared from this time stream.

Jared had warned me that the other Carl, the interloper, had gone to find Cheryl. I didn't believe him at first, but then he took me down to the security office and we reviewed the tapes from the surveillance cameras. When I saw the other me, a traveller from a different time, a different dimension, I knew what I had to do.

My wife called the police, but her story sounded crazy. The police couldn't even find a bullet, but they still charged me with discharging a firearm within the city limits. I had gunpowder residue on my hands, an empty shell casing still in the wheel of the revolver, and they could tell the gun had been fired. I paid a fine and was released. Then I was truly on my own.

My wife never returned. Two weeks later she filed for divorce. I heard she had moved back in with her mother for a while. I've lost track of her in this time stream.

Jared's stubborn, but he's not that stubborn. I've convinced him to let me travel into another time stream. I lost my wife in another world and she lost me in this one. Next time things will be different

DAVID NORTH-MARTINO's fiction has appeared in *Epitaphs: The Journal of the New England Horror Writers, Daughters of Icarus, From Beyond the Grave*, and *Dark Recesses Press*, among others. He lives with his very supportive wife in a small Massachusetts town.

T. T. ZUMA

THE SOLDIER'S WIFE

A PAINED SMILE ETCHED CLAUDINE'S FACE as her fingers lingered on the small box in her pocket.

She supposed that if her father-in-law had been gazing her way he surly would have mistaken her facial expression for a frown. With the corners of her mouth pulled back and the worry lines on her cheeks so prominent, only a close look into her eyes would have given him any clue to the contrary.

"I'm sorry, Claudine, you deserved better," he murmured through barely parted lips as he stood before his son's grave. His stiff posture and his droopy head made him appear as if he was staring at his shoes.

"Frank—" began Claudine, but she had barely gotten his name out before he interrupted.

"He was a shit to you!" His voice tinged with restrained anger. "He couldn't provide a decent home or even hold a job long enough to feed the both of you, but he had no problem finding the cash to buy booze or drugs, though, did he? How many times did he come home late stinking of cheap whiskey or so high he couldn't even make it to his bed, Claudine? How many times did he even bother to come home at all? And when he did come stumbling in late at night, what about the arguments, the fights?"

He made a point of looking disgustedly at the bruises around her neck.

She shrugged him off. "He had his problems Frank, I know that, but he loved me and he was faithful."

Frank's face turned a deep shade of red and his voice rose. "The only thing he was faithful to was a bottle or those drugs he took! He didn't give a crap about you, me, or anyone else. When did he ever go out of his way and put that damned bottle down or say no to a drug dealer? When did he do a single good deed for another human being? Look around you, Claudine! We're the only two people who bothered to come to your husband's funeral."

She sighed as Frank turned from her and looked back toward the grave. He focused on the small flat stone that simply bore her husband's rank, name, and two dates. Again, he hung his head, burying himself in thought.

Claudine continued to run her fingers over the small box in her pocket. The exterior of the box was covered with deep purple velvet and was stamped with a U.S. Marines' insigne. Inside was a medal, a Silver Star for bravery. Her husband had been awarded the medal for having saved eight men with disregard for his own life who had been ambushed on a routine patrol mission in Afghanistan. On the very day of his return home from duty, her husband had casually tossed the medal on top of a bureau and remarked that he had refused to attend the award ceremony. They had sent the medal to him anyway. He had also told her that he would have gladly given it back in exchange for the ten lives he hadn't saved in that ambush. He hadn't touched the medal since then, nor had he ever spoken of it.

Their relationship had been strained since his return from the war; her husband having suffered terribly for his heroics. The emotional abuse toward her had started early, and occasionally, it had become physical. She'd borne the insults and the drunken violence, understanding their source. She knew he still loved her; their crying jags left no doubt in her mind. So she had willingly shared his burden, knowing the day would come when he sought help, and things would be as they were before he had enlisted. He was a hero, and she loved him all the more for it.

After a few minutes, Frank walked limply away from his son's gravesite. With his shoulders sagged in defeat, Claudine thought he looked much older than a man in his early fifties should. He stopped several yards away and leaned heavily on a headstone. Claudine barely heard him as he spoke, "Only two of us to send that poor excuse for a son away."

She was ready to go home, content to leave the old man ignorant about his son, and to let him wallow in his misery.

When she turned from Frank to begin the trip back to the car, she stopped short. There was a haze of some sort, a fog-like substance swirling in the air a short distance before her. As she stared, the haze grew denser, and she thought she could make out shapes within it. Her eyes must have been playing tricks, she reasoned, so she rubbed them with both hands and then looked back. In the few seconds it took to rub the disbelief from her eyes, the shapes had taken ghostly but distinct forms. Claudine gasped.

Before her stood the shades of ten men in service uniforms, their visage like waves of heat rising from a sun burnt blacktop. They were smiling, wholly formed, and walking toward her husband's gravesite in formation. When they arrived, they broke rank and formed a broad circle around the grave. They stood there, rigid and unmoving, all of them gazing at the flat stone. As if a silent signal had been transmitted, they all went to their knees, and in unison, ten hands reached down and disappeared into the dirt. When their hands withdrew moments later, an eleventh hand could be seen floating up through the ground, clinging tightly to the others. They pulled Claudine's husband up, and he now stood with the ten, grinning and looking as handsome as he ever had. The ten welcomed him as only brothers could.

Claudine smiled. A warm feeling, centered in her chest, began to spread throughout her body. However, as she continued to view the scene playing out before her, something made her pause. Something didn't feel right. Her smile began to falter when she discovered what it was; there was a subtle change occurring on the men's faces. She noticed their smiles turning harder, their eyes narrowing. She blinked rapidly in confusion, unsure of what she was seeing. She focused, squinting at their hazy forms, and she noticed that their spectral hands, so welcoming only seconds earlier, were now curled into closed fists.

The ten servicemen began to move closer to each other, tightening the circle around her husband. She watched as his grin faded, confusion clouding his features. Soon, a look of panic overtook him. A chill worked its way up her spine when she saw his fear.

In a fury, they descended on him.

With unrelenting precision, the dead servicemen savagely raked and pummeled her husband's ghostly form. They tore the limbs from his body. From the empty sockets, wispy streams of pearl-colored fluid spurt through the air. Claudine thought her husband's pain couldn't have been any worse, but when his arms and legs drifted back toward his body and then reattached themselves,

191

she knew she was wrong. The scene repeated itself as the men inflicted the same damage on him.

Claudine continued to gape at the carnage silently. When some of the men plunged their hands into her husband's stomach, forcibly ripping it open, she stopped breathing. When his vapory intestines tumbled freely to the ground, her head began to swim. Bile rose into her throat when his entrails floated back up into the cavity and the wound resealed itself. Even in a daze she couldn't help but notice that the soldiers seemed to delight in their ability to disembowel her husband, over and over again.

Claudine began to sway in place. She took deep breaths. Her face felt tight from a mixture of surprise and shock. She had never thought to wonder if the dead could feel pain, but if she had, the answer was plainly spelled out before her. Her husband's agony was obvious and intense. Teetering, she watched as the men continued to torture him. And when a hand rested on her shoulder, Claudine jumped and screamed in terror.

Turning in a panic, she saw Frank standing behind her, his demeanor calm but somewhat surprised by her fright. He studied her for a moment, and then dismissed her jitters, apparently putting it down to stress.

"You know," he began, in a hushed and solemn voice, "I'm not sure that he ever told you that the Marine Corps presented him with a Silver Star for bravery."

Claudine stared at Frank. How could he stand there talking to her so calmly? Was he really oblivious to what his son was going through or was she the only one who could see it? She wanted to point at the gravesite, force him to gaze at the atrocities that were committed against his son, but she knew it was futile. If it was meant to be, he would have seen what was occurring. The idea that she was being punished came to her. Frank continued to talk to her, taking no notice of her emotional state. His repeated mentions of the medal finally had an effect on her. For some reason it grounded her, distracting her from her husband's plight. She decided to listen to him, managing an occasional nod, encouraging him to continue with his story.

"To tell you the truth," Frank continued, "I was stunned when they contacted me and sent me a copy of the letter, more so when I found out he had refused to attend the ceremony. It didn't make much sense to them or to me. Why did he refuse to go to the ceremony? So

I tracked down those eight men he saved; I wanted to find out what happened firsthand. I did some research; it wasn't all that hard to find them all once I found the first one. Seven of the eight told me the same story, how he was out on point and rushed back to save them when they were ambushed. They said they owed him their lives. But one man, a soldier named Ben, told me a different tale.

"Ben said that he was with your husband on the day of the ambush. They were both snipers, sent out in advance of the company to check for Taliban. They had gone some distance when they came across a young woman, bound to a tree and beaten, probably taken from one of the local villages during a raid. She was still alive, but barely. Your husband decided to take advantage of the situation. Ben argued with him, told him to leave the woman alone, that it could be a ruse, but your husband wouldn't listen. Ben then said that your husband reached into his backpack, took out some white powder and sniffed it. After waiting a moment, he approached the woman.

"Wanting no part of it, Ben walked back to his company and was caught in the ambush. They were pinned down for almost twenty minutes, a lifetime for all of those men, and an end to their lives for some. Ben was badly wounded, unconscious when your husband finally came back and returned fire. At the hospital, Ben was told about how your husband came back from patrol and saved the rest of the men, but he never said a word to anyone about why your husband took so long."

Claudine found herself distancing her hand from the medal that sat in her pocket.

"His fellow servicemen, most of them his friends, were killed while he was high on coke and raping a helpless woman. That's why he didn't want to attend the medal ceremony, Claudine. It had nothing to do with grief or being humble. What little conscience he had made him realize how guilty he was for the ones who had died. That medal would always be a constant reminder of how repugnant he was."

Claudine turned from Frank and looked back at the gravesite. The ten men continued their assault on her husband. If anything, it looked as if the beating had intensified.

"After listening to Ben's story I debated whether to tell you," Frank went on, "but I decided against it. You wouldn't have believed me anyway. Spiritually, you're just like him. You've let him get away with his selfish and destructive acts ever since he returned from Afghanistan, and that makes you not only complicit with what he was, but just as reprehensible."

Claudine shifted, leaning back at his words, stunned, but unable to refute them.

"I prayed to God every night since he returned, Claudine. I prayed that he would pay for his acts, especially the one in Afghanistan. But God never answered those prayers—until now, I guess." Frank removed his hand from her shoulder and walked away slowly.

After following him with her eyes until he was out of sight, Claudine turned back to the gravesite. Though the men continued their attack on her husband, their shades were less substantial; they were fading. Unable to look away, she watched them maul her husband until all of their foggy substance had completely vanished. Then, with her head hanging low, she took small steps over to the gravesite.

Claudine looked down on the freshly packed soil not knowing what to expect. Would she see her husband's agonized face staring back at her? Would the ten servicemen who lost their lives due to her husband's destructive ways stare back at her in pity? Would they reach up and exact their vengeance on her as well? She folded her knees and bent low, extending a clenched hand until it touched the ground. She opened her hand and then pulled it back. A small, purple velvet box now rested on the flat stone.

"I'm sorry," she said, not knowing whom she was addressing, "I am so sorry."

T. T. ZUMA has had horror and crime stories published in various anthologies, including *Anthology:Year One*, and most recently in *Eulogies II*. He also writes reviews of dark fiction for *Horror World* and *Cemetery Dance Magazine*. T. T. Zuma lives in New Hampshire.

MICHELLE MIXELL

THE MORNING AFTER

I AWOKE TO THE SOUND OF BIRDS SINGING outside my bedroom window.

The cat was curled against my legs and I could feel her breathing through the sheet. The warm June breeze teased at the curtains, allowing a sunbeam to occasionally flash across her black-brown fur. She sensed my rising and blinked sleepy golden eyes at me.

I sat up, yawned and stretched my arms over my head. There was a slight twinge in my right shoulder, but not nearly as bad as I'd expected.

Glancing at the clock on the nightstand, I saw it was nearly ten thirty. I couldn't remember that last time I'd slept this late. I'd grown so used to spending the night barely managing to reach the edge of sleep, tossing and turning and tying myself up in the covers, that I'd stopped bothering to set the alarm. Fortunately, it was Saturday. I had nowhere to be for days.

I slipped from between the sheets, which were miraculously undisturbed. My sleep had been heavy and peaceful, dreamless even, for the first time ages. Dirty clothes were scattered about the floor, and I kicked them carelessly in the general direction of the hamper. I pulled a black T-shirt from the closet and slid it over my head. It was old and well-worn, one of many I had dropped from rotation after my recent bout of weight loss, as it was currently at least a size and a half too big.

As if prompted, my stomach gave a hungry growl. When was the last time I'd eaten a real meal, instead of just piecing on my ghostly way through the kitchen when my system was unclenched enough to accept food? Weeks, I was sure.

I pictured a plate of golden, syrup-drenched pancakes, and my stomach rumbled once more.

I laughed. Laughing again felt nice.

The summer wind rustled through the trees in the back yard as I pushed the curtains fully aside, letting in a flood of late morning sun. It splashed across my face, so pale and drawn lately, and I could swear I felt my skin sigh thankfully as it soaked it in.

The whole world felt ... lighter. Hopeful.

Renewed.

I looked down at my hands. The dark brownish stains under my nails reminded me I still had a lot of work to do yet today. I'd left too much unfinished last night, but the tiredness had hit hard and sudden, and the promise of my first real, decent night of sleep in six months had been too tempting to pass up.

The pancakes could wait a bit longer.

The stench of bleach assaulted my nose as I opened the bathroom door, but it was not entirely unpleasant. It was the scent of freshness, after all, and that was the theme for today. A fresh start.

A puddle had formed next to the bathtub that I hadn't gotten to before turning in, and I dabbed at it with my toe. I had expected it to dry overnight, but was pleasantly surprised to find it still damp, barely even sticky.

I wiped my toe with a tissue, which I tossed in the toilet, and then sat. We'd had quite a bit to drink the night before, and my bladder was thankful for the release.

As I went about my business, I reached over and pulled back the shower curtain.

His eyes were still open, and were staring straight at me. I wondered if he could see me now, the way he hadn't seen me in so long.

I smiled. Even now, they were beautiful eyes.

I finished, flushed, then knelt beside the tub. I brushed his hair back from his stone-white face. Ever since he'd started growing it long, I'd loved to run my fingers through it, and now I did so one last time.

I leaned forward and kissed his forehead, then gently closed his eyes.

Even over the bleach and blood and other, nastier things, I could smell a faint whiff of the Preferred Stock cologne he wore and the yellow dial soap he washed his hands with. I felt a slight pang in my heart, and sighed.

"I'll miss you so much," I whispered. "But this was really the right thing for us. I already feel a lot better."

And I reached back for the carving knife I'd left in the sink the night before.

MICHELE MIXELL is an author, photographer, artist, and dinosaur wrangler originally from Central Pennsylvania.

G. ELMER MUNSON

COOKING WITH KATE

As she stared out at the audience, Kate found she could not move. The lights were too bright, almost blinding; she should have gotten used to that years ago. The music stopped and the crowd leaned forward in anticipation. They were waiting for her to say it— her catch phrase that would trigger the "APPLAUSE" sign, sending the crowd roaring into the next commercial break.

She couldn't remember it. She'd said it hundreds of times, thousands maybe, but it just wasn't there.

"Your line, Kate," Scott whispered from his spot behind the oven. She didn't hear him. She barely saw the crowd. Her mind raced as she stared into the lights and waited. "Kate, wake up." He rapped his knuckles on the hardwood floor.

"What?" She blinked and looked around, seeing row upon row of confused faces among the crowd.

"Your *line*," Scott repeated.

"Oh!" she blurted out, donning the plastic smile everyone had come to love. "Don't go away, because when you're cooking with Kate, you're making things great!" The music started right up, the "APPLAUSE" signs blinked overhead and the crowd's confusion shifted to squeals of approval. *I hate that line*, she thought, breathing with relief as the "ON AIR" lights went dark.

Behind her, Scott stepped out from behind the oven, his headset cocked to the side exposing one ear. "What the heck was that?"

"What?" Kate asked. "So I forgot my line. Fucking sue me."

"Come on, Kate, you're the face of this network. We need you to be in the game, yeah?" He had done it again; he'd taken the fatherly tone she so hated. She crossed her arms and frowned.

"I said I'm sorry," she lied. "Can't that be enough for now? Don't worry, I'm not gonna fuck up your show."

"It's our show."

"Fine, I'm not gonna fuck up our show."

"That's my girl," he said.

I'm not your fucking girl, either. She hadn't been anyone's girl in longer than she cared to admit and she most certainly wouldn't be his. When tonight was finally over, she wouldn't miss Scott. Not one bit.

"We're on in ten, nine, eight," he said, his fingers silently counting down the rest as he ducked behind the oven.

"K," she responded, turning back to face the crowd. *Smile time*, she thought. *Big Smile.* As far as everyone else knew, it was just another show; another night, another dish. Tonight was cranberry roasted pork with wild grain rice and almond green beans. *A teenager could have come up with that one.*

What rested in front of her was not pork, nor was it drenched in cranberry, but it looked close enough that the audience would never know. At least she hoped they wouldn't, because it needed to be convincing. At least Scott didn't notice.

When the "ON AIR" sign lit up and the music came on, Kate saw him standing at the back of the room. He looked so out of place she couldn't believe no one else noticed him. With his long dark robe and scraggly hair hanging free to cover his face, he looked better suited for a cave than a studio. She'd held out hope that he might not show; so much for hope.

He moved his head, so slightly that no one else could have seen it. In that move, she saw the glint of crimson red, hidden behind his black hair, right where his eyes should be. She found that part the most disturbing of all. Not what he'd asked of her, not what would happen that night, but his lack of eyes.

She opened her mouth, fighting the urge to scream out at him, to say she could not go through with it, consequences be damned. She let out a squeak that could not be heard over the applause of the crowd or the brass of the band as they finished their overzealous theme song. She looked down, cleared her throat, fixed her smile, and continued the show.

Kate worked on the sides, putting off the meat until last. She didn't really know what would happen when the flesh finally reached her gas oven, but she knew it would change everything. Every few seconds she would glance up at him, partly to see what he was doing but also just to make sure he was still there.

She thought she'd find this distracting, maybe stumble a few lines, or worse, drop a dish on live television. She did none of that. She knew if she dropped everything and quit before finishing then she would go down with the rest of them. In truth, she would go down first. The night was not about the show; it was about saving skin...her own skin.

She chattered on about the rice and the way to slice and toast almonds at home without burning them. All the while he stared, waiting for the main course. She glanced down at the slab of meat sitting in front of her. The side dishes were all done. The crowd was ready. She looked at the clock and wondered if she could drag it out to the next commercial.

Not yet, she thought. *Don't do it yet. Not until the commercial.* From the back of the room he moved his head, a slight nod in her direction. He knew things; things no one could possibly know, things no one had seen, things that had never been spoken out loud. He knew everything, including what happened to her husband.

For years Kate knew the old bastard had been fucking every intern at the studio. She knew that, at fifty-three, she'd lost the body she once had and the sex drive to go along with it. Even with no kids, she looked and acted like a grandmother. She knew he only stayed married to her because of the show and the network's image. After all, he was the show's executive producer.

She knew that he didn't need her, and she *thought* she'd learned to live with that. Then she talked about quitting the show, and he turned on her. That changed things. He opened his mouth, said the things he'd said, insulted her the way he had. That's when she decided she'd had enough.

People sent flowers and sympathy cards, gave condolences and shed tears for the poor departed Carl. His funeral was quite a spectacle, with crowds lined up for hours just to watch the horse-drawn casket pass by. No one ever suspected Kate. No one would ever know.

But he knew. Somehow he knew everything. He even knew how much better she felt when it was over. He said that's why he picked her. He came to her while she sat alone in her enormous and empty house. He told her there would be a feast; they would provide and she would prepare. In the end, if everything went according to plan, she would be set free. If things did not go according to plan then she would pay. She didn't know if she believed him, but she did believe she had no choice.

Kate watched him at the back of the studio as he patiently waited for the feast. She had nothing left to do but prepare the main course. Once it went in the oven, it would begin. That's what he'd told her. Something would begin.

She forced her hands from her sides, reaching out to touch the adductor magnus that lay before her, drowning in a pool of blood that had begun to coagulate under the intensity of the overhead lights. She ran her hand along the length, ignoring the stink, admiring its sleek surface. Her thighs flexed unconsciously as her fingers slid to the tapered end. Her fingers came back coated in sticky red. She absently wiped it on her white apron. *I fuck this up,* she thought, *and this is gonna be me.*

She looked out to the crowd. People fidgeted in their seats and whispered back and forth. Gone were the laughter and smiles, replaced by confusion and discomfort. She turned around and Scott stood there, out from behind his oven and in full view of the audience. He knew that was a big no-no, but he stared at her without even trying to hide. The audience seemed oblivious to his presence.

"Kate?" he whispered, pulling his headset down. His fingers fumbled with it and it clattered to the floor, the noise echoing through the unusually silent stage. No one seemed to notice. "Kate, what are you talking about?"

"What do you mean?"

"What's an, uhh, an adductor magnus?" he asked, eyes wide, face pale. "You said—"

"Inner thigh, Scott. Fucking Google it—" she interrupted before stopping. Sometimes she thought out loud, but then couldn't remember what she'd said. She thought she'd been talking about pork, how to keep it from drying out, ways to keep the glaze from burning. *What did I say?* She looked up and saw that "ON AIR" was still lit.

In a panic, she looked towards the back of the room. He was no longer there; he'd walked up the aisle, through row upon row of confused guests, past the band and towards the kitchen. He stepped past the security fence, around the monitors, and up onto the stage.

He stopped just across the island from Kate and opened his mouth. "Finish it," he said.

"No," she whispered. "I can't do it."

"Don't," he said as a crooked smile of blackened teeth appeared across his chin, "and you will replace Carl." She looked down at the roasting pan already in her waiting hands. Behind her the oven door opened, gas flames reaching up to lick the steel shelf as she slid the pan in and slammed the door.

"Good," he said, turning away from her. He walked back down the way he came, into the crowd that had stopped whispering amongst themselves and now sat slack-jawed and staring straight ahead. He walked among them, reaching out a single bony finger to touch each one. None reacted; none moved.

Kate stared as everyone he touched grew dark and swollen, each audience member sitting immobile as their bodies blackened. Their bloated flesh shimmered as something crawled underneath, growing as it moved around their bodies. Soon he had touched every one of them, even the band who had dropped their instruments and the cameramen who sat behind the lens, continuing to broadcast everything.

Behind Kate, the oven bell went off. She didn't remember setting the timer; she *never* set the timer, but it chimed away, announcing to the studio that the meat was done. *How long has it been cooking?* Against her will, she opened the oven door and grasped the pan. Her flesh sizzled, skin melting to the four hundred twenty-five degree metal. The stink made her gag but she swallowed it down.

She felt the pain but could not drop the pan. Movement was no longer her own. She turned towards the island, searing fat from her hand dripping to the floor. She set the meat in front of the close-up camera. She couldn't remove her melting hand, but that didn't matter. It had been done. Kate looked up and the room exploded.

All at once, the audience burst like overfilled ticks. From every person burst a wave of fluid and organs, their guts flowing down the aisle on a flow of blood to collect in puddles by the stage. What remained of their bodies slid to the floor, jagged holes in their chests open wide. From each husk crawled a black shape, dripping with gore and growing near man-sized right before Kate's eyes.

They stood on four legs, hair sprouting from their backs and spreading across their bodies. Their eyes opened to reveal cloudy, deep yellow pupils swirling in a vortex of pulsing red veins. Their jaws shot out in front with dripping teeth protruding past black gums that snapped together like a bear trap.

Nearly in unison their mouths opened wide to unleash a ferocious growl as terrifying as it was loud. From behind her, she heard a thump as something heavy fell down. She turned and saw Scott on the floor, wide eyed, hands over his ears, and teeth clenched in pain.

"He's the one," the stranger said, somehow standing next to her, his rotting breath licking at her ear. "We eat him." Scott looked up and shook his head from side to side. A whimpering sound escaped as he backpedaled away, his ass sliding on the smooth wood floor until he reached a set of stairs.

He didn't even see them. He fell backwards over the edge and wailed the whole the way down. He went silent when his body landed with a wet slap on the concrete below. From beside Kate, a strange staccato grunting came from the back of the stranger's throat; it took her a moment to recognize it as laughter. He followed it with a sound like a high pitched choking, and the animals behind him howled once more.

Kate turned in time to see them running together across the stage, their shaggy bodies jumping past her like a herd. They came so close she could feel the wind on her body and smell the sour stench of death passing by. Again she swallowed back her bile, afraid to show any of the weakness she felt. They headed down the steps with a furious growling and snapping of jaws.

Eat him there, she thought. *Keep him down there.* Although she never cared for Scott, she certainly didn't want to watch. The noises that echoed up the stairs made her stomach churn. She turned away, but the stranger stood close by, keeping her in place.

"You'll have to cook him," he said. She tried to step away but her hand had melted to the roasting pan. Her skin crackled but would not come away from the slowly cooling metal. She could go no further without pulling it along, and when she moved the roasted flesh slid to the side with a disgusting sloppy sound. A bit of juice splashed on her arm. She tried to ignore it.

"I can't do it."

"You can do it." He brought his arm down to her hand and ripped it away from the pan, a chunk of seared skin still stuck to the edge. Her fingers had fused together like webbing. She choked back a scream and yanked her hand back, hugging her deformed arm to her chest as if squeezing it would take away the hurt.

"Fire it up," he said. The flames inside the oven grew, rising so high they slipped through the cracks around the door before settling down to their normal burn. She heard claws tapping up the stairs and turned around. The things came into view, the ones in front carrying Scott clamped in their jaws. He was either unconscious or dead. Kate couldn't tell.

He bled everywhere. So much of his body had been mauled that she could barely tell that he was human. They moved towards her, walking slowly with their heads down. When they dropped him at her feet they sat down like dogs, mad yellow eyes staring up at her.

"They're waiting," the stranger said.

"For what?"

"For you to feed them. They're yours now."

"No, not mine."

"Well," he said with a snicker, "we'll see." He held out a single finger. The nail had turned black, the jagged edge both sharp and disgusting. He sliced it down towards the island and returned with a chunk of Carl's thigh, the warm bloody sauce running down his arm and dripping on the floor. The stranger took a bite and licked his lips. With a smile, he held the rest out to her.

"Eat," he said through a dripping mouthful.

"No."

"Eat." He pushed it closer to her face. She could smell the flesh of her husband, so different now than when she'd removed it from the grave. It smelled sweet from the brown sugar in the glaze and the bourbon she'd slipped in while the cameras were off. It smelled enchanting. It smelled luxurious. It smelled … good.

"Last chance," he said. Without thinking she opened her mouth and closed her eyes. When the meat entered her mouth she bit down slowly, the warm juices dripping slightly down her chin. It reminded her of good pork, the sauce just sweet enough to offset the salty meat. She hadn't had well aged meat in a long time. She chewed it to a paste, savoring every bite until there was nothing left to do but swallow.

When she opened her eyes, his hair moved back. It went to the sides, individual strands slithering from his face and collecting in a knotted ponytail as if they had a life of their own. Blazing red sockets stared at her, his mouth set in a wicked grin. Dark sinewy things hung from his gums. Something crawled from beneath his robe and onto his face, stopping to eat a scrap of meat from between his teeth.

She felt it coming and could not stop it; she leaned against the island and vomited on her shoes. As the meat came up she found herself wanting more. The animals behind her whimpered and stirred but remained where they were. At their feet, Scott made a noise, a pathetic sound like a child's whine. His hand moved across the floor and clutched Kate's ankle. She squealed and kicked it away in horror.

One of the animals sniffed the air and snapped its jaws, front paws padding the floor next to Scott. "They're hungry," the stranger said, reaching down and stroking the meat she had pulled out of the oven. "There's not enough here for us all. You'll need to cook some more."

"I can't cook Scott," Kate said. "I wouldn't know where to begin."

"We start with the tender bits," he said. "Watch." He made the choking sound again, and the animals pounced, ripping Scott to pieces before her very eyes. He opened his mouth as if to scream, but his throat was ripped away before he could make a sound. His jaw continued to move, blood pouring from between his lips and spurting through his open neck. His hand came up as if to stop the flow of blood, but he could only clutch at the air.

Kate stared mute as they tore pieces away, one by one moving forward to drop them at her feet. The stranger bent down to pick one up. "I think you'll find more than enough to work with," he said, admiring the small curved piece he held. It looked like Scott's tongue. It moved in his hands, the final spasm of a dying muscle.

She looked at the animals, once again seated and staring at her. Some sat still while others fidgeted. She smelled the tempting meat behind her and felt a pang of sympathy for the beasts. *They just want to eat*, she thought. Kate looked over at Scott's remains before turning to the muscle and fat piled at her feet.

With her one good hand, she reached down and picked up his calf, the flesh barely clinging to the bone. *Fresh meat this time.* A recipe came to mind, one she had not made in years. It would be perfect. She looked back towards the seats, nothing but puddles of filth where the audience once sat. Above her head, the "ON AIR" sign remained lit. The cameras stared at her in mute witness to the show. She cleared her throat and turned to the stranger.

"I'll need a few things," she said.

"Good," he replied. "Then let's begin."

G. ELMER MUNSON is a New England writer of the strange and unusual as well as the horrors of everyday life. His first novel, *Stripped*, is available from Post Mortem Press. Find him on Facebook, Twitter, and at *gElmerMunson.com*.

SCOTT T. GOUDSWARD

EVENING COMMUTE

I DROVE HOME THAT NIGHT AFTER WORK and saw my neighbors on their lawn. Raising my arm to wave, I caught myself. I'd often seen them, a retired couple, trimming and mowing the grass. They did subtle "country cute" decorations for the various holidays, no flashing lights or inflatable snow globes. There'd been more than one occasion when I'd seen them leaf blowing their driveway clean after a hard rain or light snow. Tonight it was different.

I pulled the SUV over to the side of the road and flipped on the hazards. Darting out the door, I got tangled in the seat belt while the door alarm chimed and echoed through the dark. Mr. Anderson was face down on the lawn; I imagined his nose and mouth choked with trimmed grass. His wife was a little further up on the driveway lying on her side, head resting on an outstretched arm like she stopped for a quick nap. Was it a dual stroke? Maybe one of them had a heart attack? When the other ran to their aid, they keeled over? I reached for my phone, and dialed 9.

One sticky rivulet of blood oozed down the driveway from Mrs. Anderson. I hadn't noticed it until a passing car lit up the scene. Mrs. Anderson's throat was torn out. Had her husband of over fifty years lost it and taken a garden rake to her? Anderson lay before me. I didn't want to disturb the scene, but I had to know.

Using the light on my phone, I saw the grass beneath his head was dark and discolored. The stain crept from underneath him onto my shoe. I stepped back and pressed 1. It never occurred to me to look around, check the bushes, and look behind the trees or in the shadows. I pressed the second 1 and held the phone to my ear, hands shaking. Dogs barked in the distance, at a passing car, at someone coming home from work, or maybe a killer with the flap of ragged flesh from Mrs. Anderson's throat.

The only relevant sounds were my car idling, the electronic chime of my door alarm, and the hiss of breath escaping from Mr. Anderson. I never checked to see if they were alive; I assumed both dead. I bent down and rolled him over, his white hair stained red from his own blood.

"*911 What is your emergency?*" All I could do was scream. Anderson's lower jaw was gone. His tongue flopped against his neck leaving bloody snake trails on the wrinkled skin. "*911 What is your emergency?*" In the blinking red of my flashers I saw the fear and pleading in his eyes and then Anderson breathed his last. His hand clutched feebly at his abdomen; the content of the cavity slopped over and trailed off on the lawn; as if something had hold of it and ran off until the flesh tore away. I fought the reflex to vomit and covered my mouth.

Strong hands grabbed my shoulder. I looked up into the eyes of a cop, screamed and passed out as the vomit exploded from my mouth. The last thing I remember seeing before the blackness took over was that tongue hanging limp and my cell phone lying in Anderson's cooling blood.

I woke up on my own lawn; someone pulled me over to my own yard. My car was still blinking on the street in front of the Andersons' house. My hazard lights seemed ineffectual against the glare of police cruisers, ambulances and fire trucks. I sat up groaning as the blanket someone wrapped me in slid down. The back doors of both ambulances were open. In one sat a police officer wrapped up like me, drinking a bottle of water. Two covered lumps lay on the Andersons' driveway.

"He's awake," I heard as a paramedic and a cop came towards me. I stood up and stepped over the blanket. The cop grabbed my arm, fearing I was going to pitch over into the grass. It was a good grab.

"You okay, buddy?" The cop asked. He let go of my arm, salt and pepper hair visible beneath the rim on his hat.

"Well as can be, given the circumstances." The paramedic took the blanket and draped it over my shoulders. I tried focusing on his name badge.

"Feel strong enough to answer some questions?" The cop asked.

I licked my lips with a dry tongue. "Can I get some water? I think a desert shit in my mouth." They led me over to the ambulance and sat me down on the bumper. The cop handed me a bottle of water. "Can you turn off my car before it's out of gas and battery?" The cop nodded and headed over towards it. The paramedic, a young kid, twenty-five if he was a day, put on rubber gloves and took my blood pressure.

"Sir, I need you to calm down and breathe deep." His name tag read Johnny s. "Are you diabetic, sir? Have you eaten recently?" I knew what he was asking I must have been whiter than white.

"Reilly. My name is Peter Reilly." I pointed my thumb over my shoulder. "I live at 895 West Caverty Farm Road." He took out a small light and looked into my eyes. The kid was keeping his game face; I wondered if he'd seen what was under the tarps on the driveway, leaking gory trails down the asphalt. He listened to my heart while I took deep breaths and ruled me "okay." The cop came back and the paramedic nodded.

"Want to tell me what happened?" The cop asked. I looked up at the sky. The full moon hung high, shrouded by clouds.

"I was coming home from work. I saw the Andersons lying on the lawn," I drained half the water.

"What about the old man? Forensics says he was moved. They said he was rolled onto his back by the blood." The cop took notes into a small notebook.

"I heard something, thought he was breathing. I rolled him over to see if he was still alive. It was the death rattle." I cringed and the cop caught me again as I lurched forward.

The vision of Anderson's tongue flopping around filled my mind and the bloody trails across his throat. I felt myself blanch and drank greedily from the water and set it down on the bumper. "What could do that?" Despite the safety around me, my breaths came hard and fast. The cop motioned for the paramedic to come back.

"This guy is going into shock." The cop stood and stepped back. The paramedic slid an oxygen mask over my mouth and nose.

"Breathe deep, sir." I watched the strobing flashes on the lawn cut through the night as pictures were snapped of the scene. After what seemed an hour or longer with the oxygen mask on, they 208 | finally removed it and let me walk around. The picture taking had stopped and yellow police tape was stretched across the driveway, tied tree to mailbox. Investigators walked in and out of the house chatting idly with each other; cussing when they walked through the blood on the driveway.

"Think you can ID those two slabs?" One of them said approaching me. He wore a sport jacket over jeans and a concert T-shirt. I didn't see a gun, and wondered if it was tucked under his belt or under the coat.

"As long as I don't have to look at them again, Mr. and Mrs. James Anderson." I said and rubbed my eyes trying to erase the vision from earlier.

"How long have you lived next door?"

"Since I was a kid. I inherited the house after my folks passed."

"They have any enemies?" I felt the gorge rising in the back of my throat and held it back with several quick swallows. His badge was hung around his neck on a chain. Something he'd seen in the movies, no doubt.

"We're talking about two retirees, not Nazis in hiding. What could do that?" I walked over to the bodies and pointed down at them. "Her throat was ripped out. And Mr. Anderson ..." The detective led me by the arm back to the ambulance for a seat.

"Did they have any kids?" I had to stop to think for a minute. I'd gone to school with their youngest son until he enlisted in the marines.

"Four sons and one daughter, none of them are local, a lot of grandkids." I looked over at my own house, all the dark windows. The auto timer in the living room should have snapped on. No one was investigating my yard; my shed was still intact. No bloody smears on the door. None of Mr. Anderson's intestines were hanging from the roof.

"You know any of their kids' names?"

"This is fucking horrific! We live in the woods, it's always quiet, and people actually wave to each other. What if it's a psycho is working his way up and down the street?" Spittle flew from my lips as I ranted. "Are you letting other people know about this?"

"How do you know it's a he?" Detective suit-coat raised an eyebrow.

"Anderson was gutted, his jaw ripped off. Just seems unlikely a 'she' would do that." The detective fished a business card out of his coat pocket and handed it to me.

"We're keeping your cell phone and your shoe." I looked down and noticed one of my sneakers was missing. "It has blood on it. We took it off when you blacked out."

They let me drive my car home and told me to call out the rest of the week. I left the car in the driveway. Standing on the small side porch I looked out into the back yard, expecting the shadows to rush me and rip out my guts and toss them in the mailbox. I rubbed my stomach and opened the storm door.

I barely got the alarm code into the keypad before the thing went off. Would something come for me tonight, or tomorrow? I'd been assured of a police presence on the street. But what did that mean? One car driving up and down once an hour or squad cars parked outside my house all night?

Cops or not; I locked the door and wedged a chair in front of it. I checked for my cell before remembering it was in custody. The land line was gone so if shit went south, I'd have to trigger the house alarm. Or just open the window and yell til' the boys in blue showed up.

Flopping on the couch I tried to watch television, the news had no mention of the attack. I scrolled through the stations for any mention of the slaughter, there was nothing, and I wondered how they kept it out of the mainstream. It had to have leaked from a chatty cop or paramedic.

I turned off the TV, disrobing as I walked to my bedroom, checking on the way that the front door was locked. The stairway to the second floor was dark and I thought about getting my laptop. In the bedroom I checked the other alarm pad and collapsed into my blankets. I never figured out the "night / sleep" settings on the alarm so it wasn't set when I was asleep. There was piercing electric chime that sounded out each time a door was opened, that could wake anyone from a dead sleep.

Around 3 A.M. the alarm blared. Panicked I flailed at the blankets to get free. I sat on the bed and looked at the panel. *Zone 1 kitchen faulted.* I listened, trying to calm my heart and breathing, thinking *I was making too much noise.* No footsteps, no creaking floor, no clicking of a round being chambered. I reached under the bed for my baseball bat and headed toward the kitchen.

I flipped the light switch for the stairwell and it was empty. Dust swirled in the light from what I guessed to be one of the many drafts. I bolted to the end table and switched on the lamp. The hazy glow of the street lamp filtered through the thin closed curtains and beyond that the added shimmer from the moon. The living room was clear.

Through the dining room or kitchen, which way? I charged through the doorway into the kitchen, baseball bat ready to smash anything in my way. I took great heaving breaths. The door was ajar, it had hit the chair. A loud crash sounded and I dove under the table. The refrigerator hummed, the sink dripped, and outside the storm door slammed into the side of the house, again. I sat for a moment on the floor in my underwear feeling like an idiot, and set the bat down.

Catching my breath I crawled out from under the table. I moved the chair, opened the door and reached out into the dark for the handle of the storm door and locked it. I slammed the kitchen door then locked and barricaded it again. When the kitchen was secure, I crawled back under the table, reached for my bat and sat there until the sun rose.

I woke to frantic pounding against the kitchen door. I rolled out from under the table and squinted against the morning sun streaming through the windows. A uniformed officer was at the door, looking like he was about to the break the glass. Shoving the chair aside, I unlocked the door and stepped back.

"Morning, sir." He said way too cheery. I grabbed the bat from the floor and sat down at the table and offered him a seat. "Hope you don't mind me saying, you look like hell."

"I slept under a table." I grumbled in response. "What can I do for you, officer ..."

"Officer Mills," I shook his hand. "Just checking in and making sure you're alright. Is there anything I can get you? I'll be on duty here for the next several hours." I tried staring at his face, but the sunlight was too strong. Cobwebs were clouding my brain.

"Coffee?" He shook his head and took out a small notebook and pen while I made the brew. I kept my back turned to him while the coffee brewed and then realized I was in my boxers. "Help yourself when that's ready, I seem to have forgotten my pants."

Mills read me back my statement from last night. Ride home, dead neighbors and special time in ambulances. My boss verified that I was at work all day.

"Did you hear or see anything last night Mr. Reilly?" He took off his hat exposing short cropped dark hair, and tucked it under his arm. He had a military build, looked like he worked out often.

"Before or after I saw my neighbors eviscerated on their lawn?"

"After." He said matter of factly.

"No, my door blew open from the wind last night, that's all."

"Why were you under the table this morning?"

"When the wind blew the storm door open, it slammed against the side of the house. Then the side door blew open and door alarm woke me up. Freaked me out. So I locked it up tight and crawled under the table." He jotted some notes on the pad. "Do you really need that bat?" He tucked the pad back in his pocket and got up to leave.

"Is there anything new? Any leads?" Shaking his head he left. I closed both doors and poured a large mug of coffee, then waited.

The police presence was noticeable. When the press tried to invade my home, a cruiser parked in the driveway. I felt trapped. By ten a.m. and two pots of coffee later, I'd been photographed peeking out of the curtains more times than I could count. News vans lined the street, cameras rolled to talking heads interspersed with interviews with my living neighbors looking for their fifteen minutes. Apparently word had gotten out.

By noon there was a different cruiser in the driveway and different cops on my front and side porches. I flopped on the couch jittery from too much coffee, waiting to crash. I replayed the night's events. Nothing seemed out of whack, except for the murders. I lowered the television volume and listened to the senseless babble from the news outside. I'm sure if I had a phone it would be ringing nonstop.

Where's the spare? I bolted up the stairs. In the hallway I opened the blinds and peeked out of the slats into my neighbor's yard, half expecting to see a reporter or worse on my roof. Their driveway was empty, I saw the stain of Mrs. Anderson's blood. By now all of their children had to have been notified. Why weren't they here? It was going to be a closed casket funeral that much was certain. Mrs. Anderson's wounds they could hide with a high collared shirt or a scarf, but not her husband.

The hallway was gloomy and little clouds of dust kicked up with each step. I barely used the upstairs; it was storage for my junk and what my parents left. The first room was all of my books, DVDs and CDs, in tubs, boxes, random piles on the floor. On the small built in shelves, I found my old flip phone which was dead. I carried it and a couple books downstairs. I plugged the phone in and started to read. Despite all the coffee I fell dead asleep on the couch.

Again, I was awakened by pounding on the door, this time the front. Blinking red and blue lights poured in through the closed curtain. I pulled one aside to see another uniformed cop. I unlocked the door and cracked it.

"What?"

"Are you alright, Mr. Reilly?"

"Yeah. Why?" I looked through the cracked door. The sun had fallen and a full moon hovered in the night sky.

"No one's been able to get a hold of you all day."

"I've been asleep on my couch and my phone is in evidence. What's happened?" Some of the news vans were gone and I felt a draft coming down the stairs. Did I leave the window open? Did I open the window? I looked around the room. The TV was on and muted, the cell phone was sitting unplugged on the floor. *That was supposed to be charging.* A cold shiver raced down my spine.

"Am I in danger here?" I heard my voice rise and the cop pushed past me into the house.

"Mind if I look around?" I shook my head, closed the door and collapsed on the couch. My hands were shaking. Did someone get in? I heard the cop walking around the kitchen, then the bathroom back to the dining room and finally return to the living room.

"What's downstairs?" He asked.

"Cellar." I stammered

"Access from the outside?"

"Bulkhead doors around the side, couple windows."

"Upstairs?"

"Just windows, no doors." I stopped to think. "And my bedroom," I motioned at the doorway with my hand.

"Is there someone I can call? A relative or friend?"

"No. I moved home when my parents passed." I counted the number of friends I had on one hand. He headed toward the cellar door and unclipped the latch on his gun.

"You stay here and don't move." I nodded in response watching as he disappeared through the doorway. My legs felt rubbery and made of lead. The cop re-appeared moments later.

"Doors and windows are locked. The bulkhead is bolted and that door is so swollen from the damp weather I don't think anyone can get in. I barely moved it." He looked at my face and shaking hands. "Do you want me to have you moved? I can get you to police safe house."

"Where's detective suit-coat? And what happened?" The cop walked towards the front door and unlocked it.

"Detective Barnes will be camped out in your driveway all night." He took a step outside and looked at me again. "Your neighbors across the street were murdered at the dinner table less than two hours ago."

"But they had a kid," I whispered horrified.

"The key word Mr. Reilly is had. My name is Griffin, I'll be out front and Officer Henry is at the side door." He closed the door and tapped on the other side until I got the strength to get up and lock it. I leaned against the door; my legs were weak and threatened to give way. Then it struck me why didn't the door chime go off? The same chime that had annoyed me each and every time any of the doors were opened. If the cop opened the cellar, it should have shrieked. It also should have cried out when the front door opened

---

I looked out the front window. Griffin was perched on the railing of my porch texting on his phone. I looked over at the floor and again at the phone that should have been plugged in recharging. The clock on the cable box said it was eight. I'd slept for almost seven hours while my neighbors were killed.

Even though he couldn't see me, I nodded at Detective Barnes across the street as he staggered outside, wearing the same suit coat from last night. He covered his mouth and ran to the side of the garage and threw up. The paramedics were next, leading wheeled gurneys out the front door, each one laden with the grizzly cargo of a sealed black body bag. The night was strobed in the flash of cameras. This time the press had settled in and was out for blood and stories. I felt the gorge rise in my throat when they wheeled out the last gurney with a child sized body bag on it.

I spent the rest of the night perched on a chair, head resting on crossed arms, curtains trailing down my back staring out of the bay window. Most of the police eventually left. The media-whores and lookie-loos skulked back to their houses and news vans and sped off into the darkness. Not me; I didn't want to miss a thing. One pot of coffee in a thermos was next to me in the bay window, four peanut butter and fluff sandwiches on a plate and an empty gallon jug on the floor for bathroom issues. Fox news played on the TV in back of me, volume muted.

I had no guns, no rifles or machetes. What I did have was an impressive collection of cutlery and a fireplace poker in easy reach. My secret weapon for the killer, should he be that fucking stupid to return, was the "battle ready" katana I bought off of HSN, kept on a neat lacquered stand on the mantle. I checked the time on the old fully charged flip phone and sighed. Not even midnight.

Officer Griffin nervously waved at me and I returned the wave. I cranked open the window and moved a little closer so I wouldn't have to shout.

"You want some coffee?" I shook the Thermos at him.

"No thanks. I'm off duty in fifteen."

"Fifteen? Then what?" The panic that had been replaced by exhaustion and coffee jitters returned.

I'm going home." I got up from the chair and grabbed the carving knife. "You have one unmarked car three houses down on the left," he said. I relaxed my grip on the handle. "You have one cop in the attic window across the street with a rifle." I set the knife back on the bay. "And up around the curve in the road there's another cruiser." I felt like a fool. I sat back down on the chair. "And my replacement should be here soon." I cranked the window shut as the cop shot me a placating smile and a finger wave. At exactly midnight he walked down the front stairs and was joined in the driveway by the cop on the back porch.

At around One A.M. the new cop on the porch near my window walked to the stone wall that separated my yard from the *living* neighbor and pissed on it; like he was marking his territory. All he had to do was ask to use the bathroom, knock on the door or the window glass. What was I expecting to happen? The killer waltzing up the street, and yell *"Hey, I killed five people in two days. I'm a bad man, come arrest me."* Then I'd run out with my katana that might or might not break, and claim vengeance for my fallen neighbors

Seriously what the fuck was I doing? There were cops, lots of them. But no matter how many times I willed myself to take the ten steps to my bedroom and pass out, my body refused to move.

The Andersons had been taken fast, one on the lawn the other in the driveway. Mr. Anderson's blood was still steaming when I found him. The Killer did his wife and then Anderson, and ran off guts in hand. It was the only scenario that made sense. But where was he? The neighbors across the street were at the table for dinner? No noise, no screaming or fight? He must have been in the house waiting for them to be all together. Had he been watching them, watching me?

At Two A.M. the cop walked around the house. I cracked the window and heard the officers talking on my back porch. I couldn't make out any of the words. I turned back to across the street. I saw the silver glow of light reflected from the rifle scopes. It gave me a warm fuzzy feeling for about eight seconds.

Did the cop say one sniper or two? For a brief second I could have sworn I saw light reflected off two scopes ... or was it eyes? Massive unblinking eyes watching me. Then the streetlight refracted light of shattering glass that tumbled rained onto the lawn. It was almost calming like a tortuous ice storm. Then I heard the cry, and a fierce growl. I reached for the window crank to yell for help. I saw the arm fly out of the window, still in the police uniform sleeve and bounce off the street. The skidding limb left a trail of blood and bone fragments.

Then the eyes, he was watching. But who, or better, what? Another arm flew out the window, then a leg. I stood slowly; knowing he could see me from across the street with my plate full of fluffernutters and battle ready katana. I took the ten steps to my bedroom, opened the door. Something wet slapped against the window. I mashed the buttons on the alarm pad, police, fire, ambulance, silent mode, and instant alarm, all of them. And nothing happened, just silence. He'd been in my house. The display across the alarm read *BATTERY*.

I closed the door and went back to my chair. There was a long red smear down the glass. Whatever had slid down the pane was gone. I imagined it was part of the cop across the street, which part I didn't know. The deepest roots of my mind not consumed by fear, told me to get my ass off the chair and warn the other cops. Get more cops.

I picked up the katana, listened to the comforting metal hiss as 216 I slid the blade from the scabbard and walked to the kitchen. The chair I used to barricade the door had been moved. The door was closed, both locks engaged. Ready to scream and I opened the door.

The storm door was open, both panes broken. Shattered glass was littered across the porch and down the stairs. The two cops were dead and gutted. Their bodies twisted and mangled. A hiss escaped my lips. Was there more than one *he*? I backed into the kitchen. The only smart thing I had ever done since I got the house was putting flashlights in every room. I grabbed the light and flashed it at the road, hoping the cops around the bend saw it, assuming they were still alive. There were foot prints on the deck leading away towards the back yard, huge and bloody and not human. No fucking way. "I will not become another horror movie cliché."

I locked the door set down the katana, and piled every chair I could find in front of the door. Not that it would do any good. With sword down my side, I prepared for the killing blow.

I opened the curtains. Silhouetted against the moon like a bad cartoon was a bi-pedal creature. The horrible thing standing on my dead neighbor's roof was looking across the street towards my house. At me. Its eyes glowed silver in the moonlight. Thick fur covered what I could see of the body. A panicky laugh escaped my lips as I saw the fully charged flip phone sitting on the bay. Before the cover was open, the thing on the roof was in my yard, backlit by the streetlights.

The monstrous beast stood there on my lawn, muscled chest heaving with each breath. It was covered in blood; I assumed not its own. Then another creature loped up the street and stood next to it. In its fang laden mouth was what looked like a chewed on arm. It dropped from the muzzle onto the grass. Blood and foam glistened from the mouth.

The phone slipped out of my fingers and I screamed, like a girl lost at the mall. One of them howled in response, in victory. It knew I was in denial and then I was pissing myself while running up the stairs. *I was that horror movie cliché.* I looked down the hallway. Spare room, other spare room or hall closet? There was a trail of piss behind me, leading a trail right to me.

I grabbed the flashlight off the wall charger and clambered into the crawlspace. It was a small cramped space, with no escape. Where else could I go? Out on the roof was out of the question, they could get on to roofs. The cellar? They, may have been down there. At least if the alarm worked I could have called more good guys for 217 them to devour as a distraction while I escaped. Why the fuck did it want me?

I crawled deeper into the darkness pulling whatever I could find over, boxes of books, old clothes and blankets. I kicked a box of old cassettes and the cardboard tore apart, it helped me burrow deeper in. And then I stopped as I heard the front door explode in. I heard growling and heavy breaths. The creak of a stair followed by more I tried to hold my breath and failed. Snot and tears rolled down my face.

Then I heard them in the hallway two or less short steps from where I lay buried; soft growls, steps as they circled sniffing trying to locate my scent. I tried to back up further. There was nowhere to go, I felt hot breath on my neck and turned the light around just in time to see the silver eyes reflected in the flashlight's beam.

"Fuck me sideways, there's three of them ..."

SCOTT T. GOUDSWARD is from New England. His anthology *Once Upon An Apocalypse* will be coming out from Chaosium. *www.goudsward.com/scott.*

JULIE STIPES

SKINNY GIRL

FEBRUARY—184 POUNDS

LISA STEPS ON THE SCALE, her first time since high school. She is alone in her dorm room and allows the tears to fall, dripping onto the driver's license in her hand that reads five foot four, a hundred fifteen pounds. Never did she suspect one-eighty-four, sixteen pounds shy of the double century mark. Maybe one-thirty-five, but never—

Time for a diet. Almost seventy pounds to lose. Seventy!

Lisa steps off the scale and faces her reflection, a sad image, her eyes dark and leaking like an old faucet. She slaps herself hard across the face. Red fingers stay behind.

She was pretty and petite once, a time when she could eat fast food for every meal and not gain an ounce, back when metabolism was on her side. Now everything turns to fat as she troughs down the food.

She removes her clothes and re-weighs herself naked, and she is disgusted by her image: rolls, cellulite, cottage cheese thighs.

Two lousy pounds. Sixty-eight to go.

She weighed that when she was ten years old.

This time next month the scale will be ten less, she tells herself. Ten pounds a month, not a bad goal. Exercise, eat right, and in no time the fat will shed away and you'll be skinny again.

MARCH—188 POUNDS

A pound of fat is roughly the size of a softball. Lisa imagines four of them smashed around her belly. She grabs her stomach with both hands.

Pregnant?

There was that time with Brayson Mills a couple months ago, but her last—

She tries to remember her last period, checks under the sink to count her feminine products and returns with one of the home pregnancy tests she bought the last time she had missed her period.

Her hands shake as she reads the instructions on the box for the second time in her life. It says to pee on the strip and she does. It says to wait the allotted time for results and she does. It's the longest sixty seconds of her life. As soon as the time expires, she peeks between her fingers. A pink line materializes, confirming her pregnancy.

No, no, no!

She imagines a future as a young mother in college trying to juggle a newborn. She'd lose her friends and would probably have to drop out, maybe move back in with her parents, work three jobs to buy diapers and whatever else babies needed.

Lisa reads the instructions on the box again to be sure. 1) Remove pregnancy test from package; 2) Remove plastic strip illustrated by figure A; 3) Urinate in designated area; 4) Wait one minute for results (60 seconds, it states in parentheses); and a conjured 5) Pray to the gods. Underneath the five-step plan is a diagram that dumbs it down further:

+	Pregnancy Plausible
–	Pregnancy Implausible

Pregnancy Implausible!

She looks at the results window to the pink dash, the pink hyphen, the pink minus symbol, whatever one would choose to call such a great symbol of relief. She slaps herself again for reading it wrong. That single pink line symbolizes many things for Lisa, such as never having unprotected sex again—vetoing it altogether while in college—or never having to worry about gaining baby weight.

Lisa smiles at her reflection. For once in these last few months, she is able to find happiness in something, even something as unfortunate as a pregnancy scare. Her smile fades as she realizes her weight gain is still a mystery.

APRIL—188 POUNDS

No loss; no gain.

Lisa allotted herself three fast food trips per week, four less (maybe more) than the norm, and stayed away from up-sizing her greasy meals. She drank soda, but that would soon change to cut the carbohydrates out of her diet; that was the trend, counting them, writing them down like sacred text and working the implausible equation to reach a sum of zero.

Next month will be salads instead of burgers, apple slices instead of fries, diet sodas instead of regular. The pounds will drop.

MAY—180 POUNDS

Eight pounds!

Lisa shrills at the lighter person in the reflection. There is no difference in appearance, but the digital meter is never wrong. Technically, she had started her diet at one eighty-four, but eight pounds lost was eight pounds lost. Best of all, she had followed the stricter diet of cutting back the carbohydrates, and stayed cautious over her food intake in general.

Sixty-five pounds remaining to reach her high school weight.

She'll lose that next month, she tells herself.

Lose?

To lose something one must first misplace something. What she was trying to lose was something she had created: fat. She hadn't misplaced anything.

After the weigh-in, Lisa hits the school library and flips through a book about the Atkins diet. She learns not to cut some of her carbohydrates, but to cut them all. Meats, cheeses, fats—good to go; pastas, sweets, breads, starches—those are the mortal sins. This is how she interprets the book, at least. There were people "just like her" losing ten, twenty, even forty pounds a month by eliminating carbohydrates from their diets and not worrying about the other crap.

Lisa closes the book and puts it back with the others on the shelf.

It's worth a shot.

On her walk home, she sees a poster advertising Herbalife tacked to a bulletin board. It proclaims LOSE WEIGHT NOW, ASK ME HOW, followed by a toll free number. She writes it down.

JUNE—161 POUNDS

Lisa imagines a basket filled with nineteen softball sized chunks of her fatty tissue—what she had lost this last month—and it makes her sick.

So hungry ...

Cutting carbohydrates from her diet had worked wonders. She now sees the difference: her stomach slimming, legs thinning, bra unfortunately less snug. Her neck has thinned out, her cheeks a little less plump. It has also created a yearning hunger in her belly that talks to her often. She would like nothing more than a double cheeseburger with bacon and a large order of salty-crispy-oily-delicious fries and a gallon-sized chocolate shake.

Her stomach churns.

She cheats this once—to celebrate—by imagining towers of Chinese takeout boxes around her. She attacks the cartons, barely taking time to breathe. Ghost smells haunt her nose: egg rolls, chow mien, fried rice, beef and broccoli, kung pao anything.

Suddenly she's nauseated. She leans to the garbage can and purges the virtual food, as well as some green mucus.

She weighs herself again: an even one-sixty.

The smiling woman in the mirror lifts Lisa's shirt and tells her she's fat.

Bulimia, she decides. The thought of throwing up makes her queasy again.

Nineteen pounds: nearly two-thirds of a pound lost per day.

She'd be down to a hundred forty-something by this time next month.

JULY—152 POUNDS

Nine more.

She wonders what happened to the hundred forty-something she had promised herself, and weighs herself again in case the scale is wrong. It reads the same. She buys a new one from the market and it, too, tells her she's fat.

She cries most of the night.

Next month her reflection will be thinner.

AUGUST—148 POUNDS

Six months. Thirty-six pounds. Not bad.

Is that how the diet works, a big chunk of weight-loss before a gradual slow-down? If only she had checked out the book instead of skimming through it.

She'd give it another month and try another diet if the pounds stopped dropping.

SEPTEMBER—145 POUNDS

Lisa calls the toll free number for Herbalife. LOSE WEIGHT NOW, ASK ME HOW. An outlandishly hyperactive lady spiels for an hour about herbs being the healthy way to go, how she and her husband had been with the program for almost two years. Her husband lost sixty-two pounds, and she lost twenty. Completely natural, she says. The weight will come off fast at first, and then gradually slow until a healthy weight is achieved.

Lisa orders two hundred dollars' worth of pills, snack bars, shakes, protein powders ... the complete package deal. There is even a powder to mix in with her drinks to help speed her metabolism and give her energy.

For the next month, she has a shake for breakfast (strawberry, chocolate, or vanilla), half a snack bar (to settle her stomach), a handful pills for lunch, followed by the second half of the snack bar, and a protein shake for dinner. And that special powder— a legal form of speed when broken down chemically—mixed in her drinks. It fills her body with go-go-go power.

She does this for thirty days.

OCTOBER—133 POUNDS

Twelve more pounds have fallen and Lisa has never felt so alive. She forgets about the promised 30-day money back guarantee and places another order with her rep for another two-month supply.

NOVEMBER—124 POUNDS

The diet is not as triumphant as the previous month, but Lisa has lost another nine of those unwanted pounds. Nine pounds shy of her original goal weight.

People approach her now to tell her how great she looks. *Have you lost weight? You look amazing. What's your secret?* A cute guy in biology class asked her out on a date, her first in a while. Finally, her life was changing.

Lisa undresses in front of the mirror, amazed at the sight. Skinny again. Almost as skinny as she was in high school. Her breast size is down a cup (at least), but she can see her ribs now and it makes her smile. Her hips and thighs are emaciated and beautiful, stomach flat, her face carved like a starving model. None of her clothes fit, but that's a good thing. Her waist is no longer a *waste*, her reflection tells her.

In seven months she's lost sixty-one pounds, a gym bag full of softballs. The thought makes her queasy; she had weighed sixty-one pounds in third grade. As if she had lost her entire childhood.

DECEMBER—120 POUNDS

Four pounds.

She cries for the first time in months.

JANUARY—119 POUNDS

A single fucking pound.

Lisa steps off the scale and meets herself at the mirror. She slaps her face as hard as she can, enough that it will bruise. The woman in front of her bears no emotion. She circles around and sees fat: hips too broad, thighs too thick, a backside hanging too far out, rolls in her sides, a plump stomach and her "waste."

This woman has become an evil little liar.

There are other diets out there.

Whichever is fastest, she tells her bony/obese reflection.

The underweight/overweight image tells her that fasting will be quickest, that she should starve herself. When her body wants food, she'll give it protein only, absolutely no starches or carbohydrates. Drowning herself in water will clench the appetite.

She can't gain weight if she doesn't eat.

Lisa fasts for the entire next month.

Her body eats what it can to survive.

FEBRUARY—110 POUNDS

Her stomach has been in wild knots for days, her midsection cramping and twisting into pretzel shapes. She is already on her tenth glass of water for the day and it is only noon. She's peed five times and needs to go again. Lisa has surpassed her goal weight by five pounds and doesn't care. Five pounds of unnecessary fat, enough to fill a purse.

She has another date with the guy from biology class. They'd dated on and off for the last fourteen pounds. She gauges everything by her weight now, even time. Every day he lies. *You're beautiful. You don't need to lose weight.*

What does he know?

He tries to fatten her up by taking her out for dinner and to the movies—typical dates—but Lisa finds excuses for not eating. She passes on the popcorn at the theatres, as well as the candy and soda. I'll have some of yours, she tells him, but she never does.

Others worry. Her mother, her roommate ... what do they know about health? Every last one of them is overweight. Half the planet is overweight. More people die from obesity-related issues than from most diseases combined.

MARCH—102 POUNDS

It's been a year since first stepping on the scale. Lisa admires the beautiful young woman in the mirror and laughs at the thought of desiring to weigh one-fifteen. Jawbones accentuate her face. She hides her deep socket eyes with mascara and eye shadow. She's gone from a size twenty to a size two, and her fellow students gawk.

It's all part of being beautiful, the woman in her reflection tells her.

She removes her clothes, revealing a malnourished figure composed of skin and bone, a rib cage, a visible bulimic stomach. dwindling muscles, hips and kneecaps jutting in awkward points, anorexic arms and twig legs. A figure with many shadows.

Anyone would die to have her body.

APRIL—96 POUNDS

She'd slap herself if she knew her face wouldn't bruise.

The world is suddenly against her.

Her boyfriend broke up with her. *You have to stop with the diets or it's over between us.* And so he ended it.

Her roommate, behind Lisa's back, scheduled an appointment for her with one of the school counselors. *I'm worried about Lisa's health, and that she's going to shrink down to nothing. Starving herself,* she had said.

Even her clothes want nothing to do with her now. Her jeans no longer fit without belts and she constantly shops for new clothes to fit the new Lisa. Down to an A-cup, she practically swims in her tops. Soon she'll no longer have use for a bra.

Lastly, her body's turned against her, constantly fighting with hunger. She stops counting the glasses of water. She forces herself to eat, usually a small salad chased with supplements and energy drinks.

MAY—92 POUNDS

Lisa cries into her pillow and it hurts because she's so fragile. She is exactly half the weight at which she originally started: one eighty-four.

Half.

She remembers the softball-sized pounds of fatty tissue and visualizes ninety-two of them collected in a bathtub. She imagines her old self, split directly down the middle.

It took her roommate storming out, her boyfriend leaving, and eventual meetings with the counselor for her to realize she had a problem. *You are going to die, Lisa!* That was the last thing her roommate said to her before leaving. And she was right.

Wiping the tears from her eyes, Lisa drives to a place she has avoided for over a year—a fast food joint. She orders the biggest burger on the menu with everything on it, with an order of fries and a large chocolate shake. She forces the food down and reads the nutritional information on the tray mat. Her entire meal is 1,840 calories, mostly from fat, with seventy-two grams of carbohydrates and over three grams of sodium. The numbers are listed for her on the placemat.

More calories than she's had the entire month.

And then her stomach lurches and the meal exorcises like a food demon. Her head falls into the mess and again she cries.

JUNE—84 POUNDS

Lisa tries to eat. The best she can manage is two "normal size" meals per day, one of which is usually rejected by her body. She rejoins Herbalife, this time to try gaining weight and to utilize the protein and energy, but finds she can rarely finish a shake or a measly bite of a snack bar.

Her body's no longer hungry, ever, her appetite gone. Acclimated to malnourishment. The pills go down, but they make her sick like the food. Everything makes her sick. Water sometimes decides to come back up. She drinks gallons a day to ease the pain.

JULY—81 POUNDS

When she finds sleep, she dreams of someday learning to eat again. She dreams of gaining a hundred and four pounds to be where she had started, but realizes each morning when she wakes that such a task is impossible. She wishes she could stand in front of the mirror and tell her skeleton reflection that she was wrong, but she can no longer stand to look at that woman. She's repulsive.

She weighs herself daily, by the ounce, for any signs of gain. She hopes others with her condition find the courage to stand up, as she is unable to do even that now, to rise out of bed, to get help. Hope is a mirage. Every ounce …

AUGUST—79 POUNDS, 2 OUNCES

SEPTEMBER—78 POUNDS, 6 OUNCES

OCTOBER—78 POUNDS …

MICHAEL BAILEY

STICK AND BONES

A log head
Knots for eyes
Nimble hands
Puny thighs

Should be fed
Stomach lies
No demands
Only ties

Bark skin shed
Bad disguise
Shaking hands
Despite tries

Sap is bled
Wooden cries
Hope withstands
Stick girl dies

MICHAEL BAILEY is the multi-award-winning author of *Palindrome Hannah*, *Phoenix Rose* and *Psychotropic Dragon* (novels), *Scales and Petals* and *Inkblots and Blood Spots* (short story / poetry collections), and the editor of *Pellucid Lunacy* and *Chiral Mad* (anthologies).

MARIANNE HALBERT

MURDER CONFIT

EVANGELINE'S LONG-DRIED BLOODSTAIN lay a few feet from me, permeated into the plywood, caked and dark. Dull compared to the glossy sheen of the duck confit sauce that was now splattered and soaking into the floor.

"You're positively *mad*," Lester breathed. He said it to Keither, but then his eyes roamed the room, looking for confirmation. I knew 'mad' could mean angry. Really, *really* pissed off. I knew it could also mean insane. Out-of-touch. Delusional. When Lester used it to describe Keither, I think he meant bat-shit-crazy. But when I looked at the revolver trembling in Keither's hand, looked in his smoky eyes, to me, it definitely applied in every possible way.

"Keither," Lester said, "you called us all out here today under the pretense of a celebration. You were going to start painting again," and he looked at me. I'd almost felt invisible for a few minutes, and even that small gesture made me self-conscious of the stains across my white shirt, the Crème Brûlée clinging to the short spiral curls of my dark blond hair. "Christ," Lester continued, "you even ordered all your favorite foods, the ones you and Evie used to get." He looked at me again. "Scared the poor delivery girl to death when you pulled that gun out. And this turns out to be a fishing expedition? To garner a confession from one of us? I may be your agent, but I'm not a fool." Keither's gaze was fixed on him.

Erbie was at the bar, silver forked tongs dropping ice cubes, clunk, *clink*, into his tumbler. He'd brought his own supplies, ice and booze. Perhaps as a house-warming gift, or just insurance that he'd be able to numb himself. Standing this close to his sister's portrait, to that stain, couldn't have been easy.

Arthur took a small step toward Keither. Besides Keither, he was the only artist in the room, and as he stretched out his hand, I could imagine him molding his metals, bending them at will. Arthur towered over the rest of us, and the word *Gumby* flitted through my mind. His face seemed to have turned a shade greener ever since the gun had made its appearance. He was lanky, but had a broad forehead, and his shiny silver hair was pulled taut in a long ponytail. It seemed as though each hair might just pop out of that broad forehead, straining his long neck the way he was, Adam's apple bobbing up and down before he found his voice. Arthur spoke then, his voice just a pitch too high to convey confidence, but steady enough for sincerity.

"Look, chap, we're all broken up over Evangeline. We all loved her." Then remembering I was in the room, he glanced at me. *All of us except, of course, the girl who delivered the duck confit*, was what that look said. Almost as an afterthought he added, "In our own way."

"Some of us more than others," Hector snickered. He was studying the painting of Evangeline, tracing the birthmark on the small of her back with a lover's caress more than the art critic's eye he was known for. He still seemed to be taking all of this as a joke, in spite of the gun. Not like Erbie, Evangeline's brother, whose slender, delicate hand was pouring black label bourbon over the ice, merely disinterested in the drama unfolding. Ignoring us the way he might ignore a couple arguing on the train home, or several ants underfoot, fighting over a crumb.

Arthur, on the other hand, Keither's oldest competitor in the art-world, was taking it seriously, but only in the therapeutic, *let me help you through it* sort of way, instead of the, *barrel the guy down, cuff him, ask questions later* sort of way. Except I couldn't picture a therapist's Adam's apple bobbing while his soothing tone hypnotized his patient. In fairness to Gumby, I don't suppose many patients point pistols at the good doctor during their sessions.

Lester, Keither's agent, was the only one losing it. Lester may have been the only one to know sometimes if you cuff 'em too late, well then, it's just Too Late. He brushed his hand up over his forehead, probably a life-long gesture from when he'd actually had hair to sweep off his face, and I was thankful that he didn't have a comb-over. He was the least attractive man in the room, so it didn't really matter. With the stains, with a man holding a loaded gun, a mad man at that, and probably a murderer among us, a comb-over shouldn't have mattered at all right then. But I was nineteen. So in spite of a slight pot-belly, legs a bit too short to aesthetically support his torso, and a mostly bald head, Lester never gave in to the comb-over and I was grateful. Lester, who had known Keither longer than anyone in the room. Longer even than Evangeline, who in her own way, was in the room with us. Yes, Lester, the only one, besides me, who knew Keither wasn't only angry, wasn't just bluffing, he was Mary-mother-fucking out of his mind with grief.

"She wouldn't have left me," Keither insisted. "She wouldn't have committed—" and there was a moment, five seconds, maybe ten, when someone could have overtaken him. He was trying to spit out the word. Suicide. His eyes squeezed shut, his knees buckled. His arm, the one holding the gun, drooped. But Erbie was too busy pouring his liquid bronze over the ice, Hector too busy trying to come up with a witty retort. Lester, Arthur and I, well we weren't busy or ignorant, but for our own reasons, we didn't overtake him. Then the moment passed.

Keither circled the room.

"For months, for the last five friggin' months, I didn't question what they said. She'd written it in her own blood." His voice sounded so anguished. "*Poison. Pain.* Only we all know she wasn't poisoned. Her wrist was slit on glass shards. So what the *fuck* did she mean." It wasn't a question. I mean it was, but not really. More of a challenge. He was desperate to believe someone in this room knew what Evangeline had meant when she'd written it.

Hector stood near the painting hanging on the half-finished wall behind him. Exposed two-by-fours, no drywall, just the large gray outer stones for a portion of the wall, then nothing but the two-by-fours, and the open air beyond. I wasn't standing close enough to know if a breeze caused his goosebumps, but his muscles flexed, stretching his evergreen polo tight over his chest and tan biceps. Ever the critic, he proceeded to criticize. "Well, there's the obvious. She knew you'd be the one to find her. Your love was poison, you caused her *pain*." Sandy blond curls almost fell across one eye. His eyes never seemed entirely open, squinting, glaring, maybe genetically that's just how they were, but I didn't like looking at them, in spite of how blue they were. The little bit I could see that is, with him glaring that way. "Guess, bleeding out the way she did, she wouldn't have had the time for an essay on the subject, or even complete sentences."

The bottle almost caught poor Lester's bald head. Maybe it was fate that his legs were so short, but it soared just over him and made straight for Hector's blond curls. Hector must've caught sight of it, squinty eyes and all, and lucky for him his reflexes were quick. He ducked and it shattered against the stone wall, little shards of glass showering his curls. The liquid bronze didn't look so bronze on the stone. It just looked dark, and where some had sprayed in little droplets, it gave the illusion that it had rained, on the inside of the stone wall. Evangeline continued to look away on the canvas above. Everyone turned toward Erbie, who was already kneeling, looking for another bottle of booze, to replace the one he'd thrown.

Lester ran his hand over his head again. This time it appeared he was making sure it was all still there. "Jesus. Keither, enough's enough. You start building this mansion on the mountain for Evangeline, now it's become some kind of half-built shrine to her. I thought after five months it would be finished, but it hasn't changed since the day...since that day. There are still builder's tools scattered around here, like they dropped 'em and ran." He was stating what we all had to be thinking. It was surreal. The front gate, the long driveway, the façade of the mansion. Then to enter it and see tile floor that suddenly stopped, a wall completely open to the elements. There was even a staircase in the corner that went up and ended mid-air, leading to nothing. Lester's voice was trembling, but I could see him struggling with it, struggling not to lose it, and I was pulling for him.

I was gaining some respect for pot-bellied Lester. He didn't back down. Maybe he had known Keither so long he didn't think Keither would actually kill him, or maybe he realized if this wasn't resolved soon, it might be resolved badly. But Lester didn't back down. "You don't even have working utilities. No phone, no plumbing."

For the first time, Keither seemed genuinely apologetic, at least toward Lester. "I found something today. You know, I'd proposed to her the night before she died. She was giddy. Not at the thought of us being engaged, rings and paper didn't bind us, we both knew we'd be eternal. She thought of the fun the critics would have with it," and he tilted his head, dark waves spilling over his shoulders and rested his gaze on Hector. "Artist and artist's model wed. 'What fun it would be,' she'd said. And she wanted to commission a piece, a wedding present for her. She knew how I liked to use a variety of elements in my work, not just the paint, but tangible, three-dimensional objects, of personal meaning. A collage. I didn't realize until today that she'd gotten started so quickly on finding the items for this new piece. Not exactly something old, something new. But something from everyone in this room. Everyone who had an impact on our lives in that moment of time."

I hadn't noticed the box until then. There were a number of boxes throughout the entryway, the foyer, the studio. They'd all struck me as so benign, holding drop cloths or wood screws. But he shoved one near his feet, pushing it like an accusation toward us.

He pointed the gun at Hector. "I found a list in there. Her handwriting. Your name's on it and crossed off, so I figure something of yours is in the box. Take it out."

Hector moved away from the stone wall, a few delicate splinters of glass dropping from his curls. He seemed a little relieved. "That's it? You and your sleuthing skills couldn't figure out my contribution?" He approached the cardboard box, and pulled back the lid. He reached in and retrieved a newspaper clipping. "My rave review of 'The Eve of Waning'. I should have titled it 'Folderol and Gimcrackery.' Why the public raves for your collage of worthless trinkets escapes me. You know," he chuckled, "she offered to sleep with me if I gave you a good review in the *London Times*. And here it is. Although the little tease never did make good."

"There's motive," Erbie slurred. "Might not be just the duck cooked in its own fat today. Right Hector? Or should I say Critic Confit?"

"Francophile," Hector spat.

"Philistine," Erbie mumbled.

Erbie shuffled in Hector's direction. His loafers were soft, almost silent on the floor as he moved away from the bar. "You may be one of the most well-respected art critics in the Western Hemisphere, but my sister," it came out *sisser* thanks to the bourbon, "was too smart to pimp herself out to a guy like you."

Arthur offered to go next. He knelt down, his silver ponytail streaming down his back like a river between his mountainous shoulder blades. He sifted through the box, carefully. For a moment I thought he wouldn't find anything, but then he pulled out two small black wire circles, hooked together. He palmed them, then opened his hand, held his arm out toward Keither.

"What is it?" Lester asked. Keither hadn't moved, but he was studying it, no recognition showing on his face.

"Rings of course." Arthur smiled. "Critics compared us, art-houses wanted us to be rivals, but our work is completely different. I work in metals. You never have. I used a wire-cutter to snap this small bit off a hanger used in one of my earliest pieces—"

Now recognition dawned on Keither's face. Recognition, and disbelief. "It's not from the hangers—"

"The ones that held her wedding dress and his navy uniform. The ones I used in 'Parental Ascent.' I only used part of the wire for that piece, saved some for me, and some for, shall we say a special occasion."

"It could be him," Hector said, brushing more glass from his hair. Maybe Hector was beginning to take this seriously after all, now that he'd been tagged with a motive. "You two were rivals, different styles, sure, but we compared you all the time, and let's face it, the rich can only put so much art work in their homes. Your profit was his loss, and everyone knew Evangeline was your muse. Without her you'd fall apart. You *have* fallen apart. How much art have you sold since her death, Arthur?"

"This is no time to be pointing fingers at each other," Lester said. "Keither, the fact that this box exists doesn't prove anything, she still may very well have—"

"It's him," Hector said. He'd switched suspects pretty fast.

"What?" Lester said. Trying to act dismissive, but some worry over any possible suspicion was obvious.

"She was going to have Keither fire you," Erbie mumbled. "You knew it, and having a grieving artist as a client, an artist who might make a comeback is better 'an having no client at all. He was so successful, you put all your million dollar eggs in one basket-case."

"That's ridiculous. She wasn't going to have Keither fire me."

I felt sorry for Lester. At first, because of how his voice had changed, stuttering on the words *ridiculous*, and *me*, begging for confirmation, but mostly, because of how his eyebrows went up when he looked at Keither's face. Keither's expression said it all, but Lester pressed him, "*Was* she?"

Keither seemed uncomfortable. "She thought you were pushing too hard for me to do what was commercially profitable—"

"And that's a *bad* thing?" His stout arms raised above his bald head. "It paid for this house. It paid for her *ring*—"

"She knew I wanted to pursue some of my own projects. I had creative needs that wouldn't have made much money."

"So suddenly you want to be the starving artist? Die broke and let our grandkids appreciate your genius?" Lester was so hurt, I don't think he even realized he'd quashed Hector's possible theory regarding motive. Lester hadn't known he was on the way out.

"Lester, it was just talk, nothing definite," Keither said.

"Just talk," he huffed, his short legs marching toward the box. "No wonder she was able to fool Einstein over here into writing a good review, she sure fooled me that morning into thinking this really meant something to her." He rummaged, more roughly than the others had, and a faint tinking of glass emanated from the box. "Here, here, happy engagement." He crumpled the paper and threw it at Keither's chest, where it bounced off harmlessly and landed at his feet. Lester walked away, bellied up to the bar and sat there, too hurt to even bother making a drink.

Keither retrieved and unfolded the paper. "The bill of sale. From the first piece you sold for me." His eyes narrowed as he tried to make out something on the paper. "Twelve years ago. Has it really been that long?" he whispered.

"How many more names on the list?" Hector asked. "Are we all there?"

"Two," Keither said.

"Two? Then who's missing?" Arthur said. "Erbie, let's get this over with."

I also wanted this night to end.

"No one is missing," I said. They all turned to me, all with surprise, except for Keither, who of course knew my name was on the list.

"But you're just the delivery girl," Hector said.

And he was right. Just the girl who worked at a restaurant, delivering fine food to customers who could afford it. Sashimi grade ahi with ginger wasabi, and Crepes Suchard the day they broke ground on the mansion. I recalled how they had spread a blanket, and were half-way through a bottle of Dom when I arrived, sunlight shimmering off of their golden-stemmed champagne glasses. Knowing that she would disrobe before he painted her. Watching how his arm draped her waist, and how she laughed and pushed him off so she could pay me.

The following week, the foundation was coming along, and he wanted to paint her in the open field, windflowers and mountains as the backdrop. That afternoon I brought them grilled Portobellos in a garlic vinaigrette, salmon Caesar, and espresso mousse. I hesitated when I saw her posing, her skin so exposed. So perfect. Keither, oblivious of the paint covering his hands, some swiped on his brow, so focused. They didn't even notice me. I left the food and sent a bill.

At least once a week it went like that, for nine months. And each time I would linger an extra moment or two, watching them, their passion for the art, for each other. I stepped forward now, toward the cardboard box. That put me closer to a breeze coming through the open wall, and I caught a whiff of the duck sauce from my shirt, and vanilla from my hair. I knelt down by the box. Only a champagne glass, a tube of paint, and a small piece of paper remained. I took the paper out.

"A receipt from the night you proposed. She called me that morning, asked if I still had a copy." I'd kept a copy of all their receipts. A memory lane of stolen moments. "Duck confit. Broccolini. Crème brûlée. For two."

Understanding dawned on the men in the room. Understanding about why Evangeline would want the receipt, but they couldn't have understood how much I belonged in this studio. How intimately I'd known her. When Arthur had said we all loved her, he was right. Each of us, in our own way.

Keither seemed agitated. All of us were done except Erbie, and it didn't seem we were any nearer to a motive, or a killer. I'm sure Hector resented her for using him, Arthur may have realized that without her, Keither would no longer be a competitor, and Lester could be feigning surprise over her suggestion that he be fired, but it was clear Keither hadn't zeroed in on any of them. He was trembling with frustration."Erbie, come over here," Keither demanded.

Erbie was leaning up against the half-built wall. His eyes looked tired."What's the point Keith? The cops ruled it suicide. I can tell now you don't really believe any of us could have hurt her.""Erbie, what did you bring her?"Erbie shrugged his slender shoulders, and shuffled in his soft loafers toward the box. "Alright, alright." His feet stood still once he got there, but his head wobbled gently from side to side as he tried to focus. "Paint and a glass left. A glass, from my mother's collection." There was a note of melancholy in his slurred words. "I brought two glasses to Evangeline, to use how she wanted. To celebrate, to put in the painting, wha'ever."

Keither narrowed his eyes. "You brought her the glasses?"

We all knew there was only one in the box. The other had broken five months ago, and a large, sharp piece of it had slit the artery of Evangeline's wrist. In the serious, vertical kind of way.

Erbie nodded, and a sob escaped his throat.

"What about the paint?" Keither asked, waving the gun in Erbie's direction.

"What about it? She wanted you to do a painting, she got paint. Not exactly shocking."

For the first time that evening, I heard a certainty creep into Keither's voice. "Evangeline would never have bought that paint for me."

Erbie looked offended. "It's the same kind you always used, she knew that—"

"It's the wrong size." Something changed in the air just then, and I could sense everyone bracing for a revelation. "I only bought Titanium white in the large tube, and she knew that." I couldn't tell if Keither was more excited that he may be onto something, or more horrified that it may have been her own brother, her blood, who killed her. I knew Erbie was lying about bringing her the gold stemmed glasses. I'd seen her and Keither use them before. I looked at the stain on the floor, the large dark dried pool, and the words beside it. Poison Pain. I imagined an artist adding oil to pigment, and longed to interpret Evangeline's desperate message. To go back to the moment when the letters flowed. There had to be more she was trying to say, but what? The words ran through my head again and again. *What was she trying to say?* I looked at Evangeline's scrawls, written in her own blood, and couldn't help notice the confit sauce in the shape of a cross, or, a letter...

"Not poison pain," I whispered. Keither looked at me, looked down to the words on the floor. He didn't understand and flew toward me, gripping my arm.

"Poison *paint*," I said. "She died before she could finish. No time." *For an essay, or even complete sentences.* Erbie would have known how Keither worked. He wasn't a neat artist. The art was always brilliant, but during the process, Keither was covered in paint. His hands, forearms, face. Terre verde, raw sienna, titanium white. Keither must have been making the same connections I was, and he grabbed the tube out of the box and opened the cap. He approached Erbie with the gun in one hand, paint in the other.

"Why don't you paint a picture, Erbie?"

Erbie waved a drunken arm at Keither.

"Why did you do it?" Keither demanded, the gun inches from Erbie's face. "Why Evangeline?"

"It wasn't supposed to happen like that," Erbie slurred. He seemed to be talking to Evangeline, looking at the portrait. She refused to look him in the eye. "I haven't managed my share of our inheritance very well." Then he turned to Keither, as though it were all his fault. "If you two got married, then I was out of the picture if anything 'appened to her. As her husband, all of her inheritance would go to you." He raised his glass, "so you had to go." He drained the glass, and his head drooped. His voice trembled when he spoke again, feeling sorry for her, and for himself. "She wasn't supposed to know, or get hurt, but she figured it out and we argued. She had already set those glasses in the box, and when I'm angry, I have a tendency to break things."

Keither looked like he was going to be sick, but he steadied himself. He kept his eyes on Erbie. "Lester, do me a favor. Use your cell phone to dial the police. We have a confessed murderer."

Erbie shoved Keither, and ran toward a door at the end of the room. Keither looked horrified, and shouted, "Erbie, no! Stop!" but it was too late. Erbie had already flung the door open and was stumbling through it, arms flailing, and I saw him disappear. His scream carried through the open doorway, faded, then cut to silence.

We all stood there looking at each other, stunned. Arthur's voice had gone back to its normal, low pitch.

"He had way too much to drink tonight." I think when Arthur said that, he didn't realize what he'd put in motion, but Lester's wheels were turning and we all followed his momentum.

"Yes, *way* too much," Lester said. "Toxicology will confirm that. And he was distraught over his sister's death." He looked at Hector who realized what they were thinking, and he hesitated, deciding whether to play along.

"Keither *did* tell him to stop," Hector said, "but he was at the precipice before any of us could reach him." Then they all looked at me. I looked down at my shirt, at the food I'd spilled when Keither had pulled the gun.

"He ran past me," I said. I hesitated, waiting for approval. Lester nodded slightly and his eyes told me to go on. I felt slightly more confident when I said, "Knocking the tray right out of my hands."

We all looked at each other, a look of understanding, conspiracy. Keither hadn't deserved Evangeline's death, and he didn't deserve to be blamed for Erbie's.

It was about a month later when he called me to come to the house. But he didn't want any food. Just me.

I walked up the cobblestone drive, and stepped around to the back side of the house. Scaffolding climbed to the doorway where Erbie had exited this world, and I could see an elaborate balcony under construction. I turned and saw two headstones under a black cherry tree, and I walked toward them. One said merely, *Evangeline.* The other had no name, only a prayer:

Confiteor Deo omnipotenti,
mea culpa,
mea culpa,
mea maxima culpa.

I turned back toward the mansion, walked around front, and entered the foyer. I saw men working. Keither had installed utilities. I walked into the studio, and was relieved the wall hadn't been completed yet. The breeze felt good on my face. I looked down and saw that tile flooring covered the entire room. He had his canvas ready, brushes and paints. All he needed he said, was a model.

He watched as I shed my clothes. I stood near the opening in the wall as he got the angle and lighting just right. I wondered about the stains buried under the tile, and wondered if Evangeline was at peace. A mourning dove flitted in and landed briefly on a support beam, cooing, almost purring, before departing.

Keither approached me, putting his hands on my waist and arm to position me. He moved one hand to my face to tilt it. One moment he was the artist, and I was the model. No different to him than his brushes, the canvas, the paint. A means to an end. His eyes studied my skin tone. He remarked that I was a shade darker than her. His fingers moved up my ribs. Then spontaneously his lips brushed mine. His hand wrapped behind my neck and he kissed me. I relented and our tongues teased each other, hungry and searching. But when he pulled back, I knew he'd kissed someone else.

"I can't love you," he grumbled, as though I had asked something of him. He became somber and retreated back to his canvas. I felt even more naked than before.

I looked out across the exposed vista. Past the gravestones, the lazy field of tilting windflowers, and beyond the lavender ridges in the distance. Keither's words ran through my head, and I realized I didn't need him to love me. For today, I just needed him to paint me.

MARIANNE HALBERT is from central Indiana. She has had dozens of her dark short stories traditionally published in various magazines and anthologies. Her collection, *Wake Up and Smell the Creepy*, is available on line and in print. Follow her at *www.halbertfiction.webs.com.*

HOLLY NEWSTEIN

EIGHT MINUTES

In July of 1944, the Ringling Brothers, Barnum and Bailey Circus big top burst into flame during a matinee performance in Hartford, Connecticut. It took eight minutes for the fire to utterly destroy the huge, three-ring tent. One hundred and sixty-eight people died in the fire. Here are three of their stories.

THE PRETTY LION-TAMER LADY, CLAD IN BOOTS AND JODHPURS with a red scarf at her throat, flicked her whip at the big lion. He snarled and swatted a paw at her, but she smiled, unafraid. She flicked it again, and the lion jumped onto the tall stool. Charlotte stared, her eyes round and amazed. Then the lady made the big cat sit up and beg. Charlotte wished she could do that.

She took a sip of her lemonade. It was stifling hot in the tent and smelled of dirt and dung and canvas. People were crammed into the bleachers, watching eagerly as the lions and tigers moved gracefully and unwillingly around the ring. In the center ring, another lion tamer—a man—was making a jaguar jump through hoops of fire. Charlotte fidgeted in her seat. Her cotton dress was sticking to her back and her curls to her neck.

Mum handed her her fan. "Here, Lottie." Charlotte waved the fan energetically, accidentally hitting the fat man sitting next to her.

"Sorry, mister," she whispered. The fat man glared at her and took another mouthful of popcorn from the big tub he had balanced on his lap.

The pretty lady made the big cats bow to the audience, and then she bowed, and everyone clapped. The band played a fanfare.

Some people thumped the bleachers with their feet. Charlotte tried to do it too, but her sequined red silk shoes were too soft to thump.

Mum had not wanted her to wear them to the circus. "Put on your other shoes, Lottie. If you wear your ruby slippers, you'll only get them all dirty." Charlotte had pleaded with Mum.

"If Dorothy went to the circus, she'd wear her ruby slippers. Pleeease!"

Finally Mum had given in, declaring it was too hot a day to argue.

"But don't come crying to me when they get ruined," she warned.

Charlotte practically danced the six blocks to the circus grounds with her Mum and Auntie Helen and her little brother, Joe, enjoying the way the sequins on her shoes twinkled in the sun. Her Auntie Helen had taken her to see *The Wizard of Oz* last year. It was Charlotte's first time at the movies, and she had been enthralled. After that, she enjoyed nothing better than playacting scenes from the movie. Her dolls were Munchkins, and she took turns being Glinda and Dorothy. Auntie Helen had made her a pair of ruby slippers from red satin for a Christmas gift, and they were Charlotte's prize possession.

Auntie Helen wanted to see the sideshow first, so they paid their nickels and entered the small, stuffy tent with the big scary-looking posters outside. Charlotte clung to Mum's skirts, fascinated and terrified, as they watched the man who swallowed swords slide them down his throat and pull them out, as easily as if they were lollipops. The Fat Lady sat on a wooden chair and looked miserable in the heat, fanning herself with a folded-up program. Her rolls of flesh drooped into her lap and down her legs and arms, straining the seams of her shiny circus dress, which was splotched with dark sweat stains.

Auntie Helen whispered to Mum that the lady weighed five hundred pounds.

"That's what too many sweets will do to you," Mum answered. Charlotte shuddered.

The worst was the armless and legless woman. She lay on her stomach on a platform, surrounded by pillows. She was painting a picture on a little easel, with a paintbrush held in her teeth. Charlotte felt sick to her stomach, watching the grotesque lady move her head and neck like a turtle. Several boys were pointing and snickering, saying what a great third base she would make.

The woman kept painting, as if she didn't hear them. Auntie Helen told them to hush up or she would tell their parents.

Charlotte was happy to get out of there. Mum bought everyone lemonade, which was cool and sweet and washed away the sweaty sour smell of the sideshow tent.

Now the big top went quiet. The high-wire acrobats were climbing up the ladder to the tightrope. Mum said they were a family who lived with the circus and traveled everywhere. The acrobats in their sparkly costumes made it up to the little platform at the very top of the tent. The spotlights were shining on them. Charlotte looked away for a moment and noticed the roustabouts taking apart the lion cage. The pretty lady was shooing the big cats into a chute that led out of the tent.

Her eyes went back to the high wire. The band stopped playing except for the drum roll. The acrobats made a pyramid, balanced on a bicycle, and a young lady in a feathered headdress took the top spot. Charlotte gazed at her. She was even more beautiful than Glinda. She was going to stand atop the pyramid as the bicycle crossed the whole big top, and not fall.

Just as they started rolling along the bright wire, something flickered in the corner of Charlotte's eye. She looked over and saw a tongue of white flame eating its way up the canvas, streaking along the dark wall as it rose and widened. People began scuffling and pushing out of their seats, and ladies screamed. She watched the flames, mesmerized, as the band began playing and people began moving around her. It was beautiful, and it moved so fast.

She did not see the people practically tumbling out of the bleachers. She did not see the fat man fall out of his seat, raining popcorn everywhere. The screams of panic melded with the pounding sound of the band playing *The Stars and Stripes Forever* as hard as they could. She saw nothing but the flames, spreading and widening up the sides and the roof of the big top.

Suddenly a hand closed on her heel, and she came back to herself.

"Lottie! Lottie! Come down! We have to get out!" Mum was screaming in a voice Charlotte had never heard before. She took her mother's outstretched hand and jumped down, landing on the fat man still sprawled on the ground. Mum pulled her up and they were immediately caught in the crush of bodies, pushing and shoving to escape.

Auntie Helen had baby Joe clasped tight to her, and Mum kept a grip on Charlotte's hand. The heat was intense as the fire overspread the top of the tent. Charlotte couldn't see anything. People kept pressing up against her, running over her feet. She followed close to Mum, whimpering in fear.

Someone lost their footing and fell against Charlotte, and her wrist slid out of Mum's sweaty grip. Charlotte shrieked and stumbled under the surging tide of feet and legs, pressing to get out. Feet tromped all over her, hurting her back and legs, even stepping on her head and grinding her face into the dirt. She struggled wildly to get up but could only roll, fending off the feet with her hands as best she could. Finally, bruised and bleeding and dirty, she crawled under the bleachers and hid in a jumble of fallen chairs.

It was hard to breathe, the air was too hot. The entire tent was aflame now, illuminating the inside with an intense smoky glow. Charlotte felt her skin prickling, like hundreds of tiny needles were poking her.

"Mummy! Auntie Helen!" Charlotte cried, her voice raw from the smoke and fumes. The few people who were still in the tent didn't hear her. They were running and pushing as flames dripped from the roof of the tent. The flames sizzled as they landed on the ground and on people. She was lost, and she was scared to leave her spot, lest she get stepped on again. Mum had always said to stay put if she ever got lost, and someone would find her. But what if nobody was looking for her?

Suddenly she had an idea. She had her ruby slippers on, didn't she? She could click her heels together, like Dorothy, and she would go home. Excited by her cleverness, she scrambled to her feet and stood, fragments of flaming canvas spiraling wildly around her like shooting stars.

She looked down at her feet. Her slippers were torn and dirty, like Mum had said they would be, but she was sure they were magic. They had to be.

She stretched out her arms and closed her eyes.

"There's no place like home. There's no place like home," she whispered into the searing air. She clicked her heels together, once, twice, three times. Her blonde curls burst into flame. Her cotton dress too, burning white as Glinda's gown. For a moment she was transfigured, like Glinda in her bubble, a white pillar of light in the smoky darkness.

A piece of flaming canvas, twisting in the superheated air like a slow tornado, fell on Charlotte in a bright, murderous embrace, and she disappeared in a puff of black smoke.

The two boys stood in front of the lemonade stand. "Hurry up, Iz," Doug said impatiently. "I want a good seat."

Izzy fumbled in his pocket for change. "It's too hot for popcorn. I want something to drink." He pulled a nickel out of his pocket and handed it to the sweaty man behind the counter.

"Yah, it's a scorcher all right. Here ya go, kid." He gave Izzy a paper cup of cool lemonade.

"Lemme have a sip," Doug said.

"Get your own."

Doug pushed Izzy with his shoulder, slopping the lemonade in the cup and out over Izzy's hand.

"Thanks, you wiener," Izzy muttered.

"Anytime," Doug said with a smirk.

They pushed their way through the crowd, past the sideshow tent where the Fat Lady and the Sword Swallower were advertised on posters. Everyone smelled like sweat. The men smelled of Ammens Medicated Powder, and the ladies like perfumed talcum. Babies fussed in the heat. Inside, the tent was even hotter, without a hint of a breeze. The brass band played a march, moving the crowds along to their seats.

"Let's sit here," said Doug, stopping at the animal chute that rain into the tent from outside. "We can see the lions come into the ring."

"Front row, yeah," said Izzy.

Izzy Rosen and Doug Gibson had been friends ever since they could remember. Growing up in the North End of Hartford, they were inseparable. They walked to school together, played Little League on the same team, joined the Boy Scouts, and planned to join the Army together if the war was still on six years from now. Once, when some Irish toughs had picked on Izzy, calling him "kike" and "dirty Jewboy," Doug had chased them down and beat the crap out of the one he caught. After that, nobody messed with them.

For his fourteenth birthday, Doug's Grampy had given him two brand new dollar bills. The posters advertising the circus had already gone up all over town, so Doug ran down to McCoy's music store and bought two tickets for the July 6th show. There was never any question that he and Izzy would go together.

———

"How does he *do* that?" exclaimed Izzy, as the lion tamer made the snarling cat jump through a ring of fire with just a flick of his whip. In the second ring to their left, a lady lion tamer was making her cats roll over and beg.

"She's better than him," Doug said, pointing with his chin at the other ring. "But do you know what would make it even better?"

"What?" Izzy took the last gulp of his lemonade.

"If she was naked," whispered Doug.

Izzy choked with laughter and sprayed lemonade out of his nose.

"Good thing nobody's sitting in front of us," said Doug.

They had watched the lions, tigers and jaguars enter the ring through the chute, each animal one at a time, so close they could smell them. Even as the cast of performers paraded around the rings on ponies, elephants, and in clown cars, Doug could not take his eyes off the cats with their teeth and claws, their magnificent coats and shining, pitiless eyes.

When the big cat acts ended, the ringmaster announced the Flying Wallendas were up next. The spotlights were trained on the platform at the top of the tent and the high wire.

"No net," breathed Doug.

"They don't need it. They never fall," Izzy said.

"Ah, I bet they do sometimes."

A commotion erupted in the stands to their left, right by where the lady lion tamer was leading her cats into the chute. Screams of "Fire!" echoed through the tent. Doug and Izzy saw the white, smoky line eating its way up the tent, toward the platform where the Wallendas were assembling.

"You think it's part of the act?" asked Izzy.

"I don't know," said Doug. But people in the stands were getting up and leaving in a big hurry, so much so that they were knocking their chairs over.

"Maybe we better go," said Izzy.

A wave of people crowded in front of them, rushing for the exit.

Doug looked up and saw the fire spreading above them in a blazing wave. The people in back of them stumbled down the bleachers, joining the melee of folks surging for the exit.

"Come on, Iz. I know a better way." Doug grabbed Izzy's arm and they climbed up the bleachers toward the back of the tent.

"I got my Scout knife," said Doug. "I'll cut a hole in the canvas, and we can get out that way."

Izzy's eyes were big with fear. They reached the top of the bleachers, and the fire was heading toward them. The tent was filling up with black, oily smoke.

"C'mon, we gotta jump," Doug said

"I can't," Izzy said. They looked down at the crush of people below them, pressing up against the animal chute. People on the other side were helping others over the top of the chute and pushing them out the gap between the chute and the tent.

"Look, Iz. That's how we get out. Come on!" He shoved Izzy in the back and jumped himself, knocking a man over as he fell.

"Sorry, mister," Doug said, but the man got to his feet and pushed on, not even noticing Doug.

"Doug! Doug! Where are you?" Izzy yelled.

"Here!"

Doug wormed his way over to where Izzy stood, hanging on to a bleacher support.

"My ankle," groaned Izzy. "Told you I couldn't jump."

"C'mon, let's get the heck out of here."

They pushed their way into the river of people piling up by the animal chute. The fire was close now. Doug's neck was blistering in the inferno. They stepped up to the chute, and Doug hauled Izzy up to the top. Hands on the other side grabbed Izzy and pulled him away, but as they did so, Doug realized that the pile they had climbed over was a mass of squirming people. Hands clawed at his legs and he lost his balance, falling backwards. The next wave of humanity buried him and pulled him deep into the pile, like an undertow.

Doug was kicked, stomped and clawed as he sank into the seething mass of bodies. His ribs hurt, and the air was squeezed out of him. He rolled and wiggled, pushing up against the thrashing tide, trying to turn himself face down so he could crawl out. A mighty thrust of weight pushed him to the bottom of the pile and mashed his face into the dirt and trampled grass. He brought his hand up and scratched madly at the dirt, clearing a small depression where he could get air. His rib cage was so compressed by the shifting mass above him that deep breaths were impossible. Still, the air was slightly cooler and not smoky, and he inhaled it gratefully.

He was completely pinned down, flat on his belly. It was impossible to move, except for his arms and hands. He drew his arms under him, trying to make a little room for his rib cage.

It occurred to him that he was going to die. Burned to a crisp by the fire.

Would you rather die by fire or by drowning? He remembered how he and Izzy had weighed the pros and cons of each during a long-ago conversation. Tears burned in his eyes, but he did not have enough breath to cry.

The screams changed in intensity, blending from panic to agony. The stack of humanity above Doug began to thrash ever more wildly. A searing rush of agonizing pain blazed up along his feet and the backs of his legs.

Oh God! Take my soul to keep!

I'm not dead.

Doug opened his eyes. He could breathe a little better. His clothes were wet and sticky in places, and he couldn't feel his feet. But he was alive. The pile above him was still and oddly lighter.

There came voices, not panicked voices but anxious ones. In the distance he could hear sirens, and people calling other people, and cries of grief.

I'm not dead. Get me out of here, he thought, but he lay still, feeling it wasn't safe yet. An acrid smell of burnt flesh and leather, of urine and feces and scorched clothing surrounded him.

After a few minutes, he heard footsteps. Men were walking right by him. He heard the creak of wheelbarrows.

"OK, here we go," said a voice. Something shifted in the pile far above him, relieving the crushing weight a little. A couple of more shifts, and then someone staggered right by where he was and retched violently. Doug's own stomach heaved at the smell of fresh vomit. Groans and grunts kept sounding above him as the pile got lighter and lighter. And then, suddenly, he could move.

He lifted his head. "Help," he croaked.

"Jesus, Mary and Joseph! Someone's alive in here! Alive!" a man yelled.

Footsteps hurried over and hands yanked at the mass holding him flat to the ground. Thunks sounded as things from the pile were tossed in the wheelbarrows. Then hands were touching him, shaking him.

"Kid! Kid! You alive?"

"Yes sir. Get me out of here, please." Doug's voice rose. "Help me!" He tried to struggle to his feet, but the hands held him down.

"No, kid, hold still. Your legs. We got to get you a stretcher."

"What about my legs?"

"Never mind right now. OK, here's the doc. We gotcha, kid. Close your eyes for a minute while we lift you. OK fellows, one, two, three!"

Doug was hoisted in the air by eight pairs of hands and gently placed facedown on a stretcher. With his first deep breath of air, his ribs stabbed with agony. He opened his eyes.

Less than a foot away, stacked haphazardly in a wheelbarrow, was a charred black-and-brown tangle of bodies, their arms and legs bent like giant crabs. Their hair and clothes were burned away, their mouths opened in silenced screams, their teeth blackened in their gaping maws, their eyes melted into shiny gray jelly on their cheeks. The stench was stupefying.

Now, finally, he was terrified. A wet stain spread across the front of his pants.

They carried Doug out to wait for the ambulance. The hot sunshine burned through the still-smoky air. Doug felt light-headed and unfocused. He had no feeling below his knees, but his backside itched and prickled like he'd spent too long at the beach. Then he heard Izzy screaming.

"Doug! Dougie! "

"S'OK, Iz," he mumbled. Then Izzy was beside him.

"Doug, you saved me. Then I lost you. Oh God, I thought you were dead. Oh God, oh God!" Izzy was sobbing.

"Cool it, Iz. I'm OK." Doug felt as if he were far away.

"No, you're not. Your legs are burnt up. You saved me, and you got burnt." Izzy's voice scaled high with grief and guilt.

"All right, young man, your friend's going to the hospital now," said a calm, professional voice. A cool hand stroked his hair, which was just about the only thing that didn't hurt. Doug turned his head to look at Izzy.

"Iz, come see me in the hospital?"

"You got it, Doug." Izzy wiped his eyes with the backs of his hands, making black soot smears on his cheeks.

"You look like a raccoon, you wiener," Doug said, with a ghost of his wiseguy grin.

Izzy grinned back.

Lieutenant Keene of the Connecticut National Guard was numb. All his senses, including his sense of smell, had shut down long ago. He had been one of the first to heed the emergency call and arrive for the grim duty of cataloguing, sorting, and arranging the charred corpses in the Armory, where the bodies were laid out for identification,. He helped set up cots to hold the bodies, and he carefully placed blankets over the twisted bodies. Many of them had their arms and legs thrust out, as if they had kicked and punched the flames that engulfed them. He helped bring in fans to dissipate the overwhelming odors. He followed the doctors through the rows of bodies, peeling back watches from arms to find unburned skin in order to determine the race of the victims, helping detail scraps of clothing, shoes, and anything else that might identify the unrecognizable. There were women and children welded into one mass by the fire, bodies with hands, feet, hair and noses gone. There were children smothered by the smoke and trampling feet, nearly untouched by flame, who seemed to be sleeping peacefully in this charnel house.

He had thought he had himself under control until one of the doctors came in with a small bundle in his arms. The doctor took it back to the far corner of the Armory, where body parts, burned away from their owners, were being stacked. He gently unwrapped the bundle to reveal an infant, crushed and dismembered by many trampling feet, tiny fingers curled like scorched rosebuds.

Lieutenant Keene bolted from the Armory. Once outside, he vomited against the side of the building, the roiling contents of his stomach splashing on his feet. He took deep gulps of the hot, humid air, still tainted by the stench of burned flesh from the gruesome parade of bodies still arriving at the Armory.

He leaned up against the building, eyes closed. Someone pressed a bottle into his hand. He opened his eyes to see a young, sad-eyed woman. The pity in her face broke his heart.

"It's Coca-Cola. It'll settle your stomach," she said.

"Thanks," he muttered and took a swig. It felt wonderful going down his gullet, fizzy and icy cold.

"Here," said the woman. She rummaged in her purse and brought out a handkerchief. "My mother always said a lady carries a scented hankie with her. It might help with the ..." her voice trailed off and she lowered her gaze.

The handkerchief was embroidered with violets and smelled like Yardley's English Lavender. Lieutenant Keene put it in his pocket.

"I really appreciate this, ma'am. Sorry about this." He gestured at the puddle of vomit, already drying on the sidewalk.

"Thank you, soldier. It's a tough job you have." She sighed deeply. "Now I have to get back in line. I can't find my niece anywhere." Her voice hitched a little.

Lieutenant Keene stared at the woman. "Ma'am, for all our sakes, I pray she's not here."

People filed among the rows of bodies, lifting up blankets to stare into the faces of the dead. To spare folks, the less damaged bodies were laid out closer to the entrance for quicker identification. The featureless, charcoaled ones, with their bellies split open by the heat, were in the back.

To the lieutenant's surprise, the people were polite and calm. Very few went into hysterics, and only one woman fainted. But that could just as easily have been from the heat and humidity.

Maybe they're just numb too, he thought. *In shock, like farm animals waiting for slaughter.*

He made good use of the handkerchief, holding it to his nose and inhaling the lavender scent. It made him think of his own mother, and Saturday night baths, and bright spring days in Milford, where he had grown up. It kept his stomach quiet and his mind clear.

As the day wore on into night, people kept coming. Some came through two or three times, and left without going to see the nurses at the checkout table, where relatives signed the bodies out. Lieutenant Keene patiently escorted people through the rows of cots, over and over. He began to be familiar with the details of the dead, able to describe each one. He developed a sense of which body was likely to belong to a family simply by looking at the survivor's faces and tracing a resemblance to one of the corpses.

But there was one unclaimed one that baffled him. Her face was almost untouched, sweet in its repose. Her flowered sundress was still pink and white against her shoulders, while further down her body, it been burned away. Lieutenant Keene knew that clothing was key in identification. The sad-eyed lady had identified her niece by the only unburned thing on her body—a pair of tattered, red sequined shoes.

The doctors had estimated this little one to be about four or five years old. Her light brown hair was streaked by the sun, and her long eyelashes brushed her cheeks. Still, people looked and walked past her. She didn't belong to them.

The lieutenant found himself drawn to the girl. *Probably her first circus. She must have been so thrilled.* He pictured the still, waxen face alive with anticipation and excitement, holing a balloon and screaming in fear and delight at the clowns.

She's a little angel in Heaven now.

He brushed back a lock of soft hair from her cheek, so her face could be more clearly seen.

I guess that's what I'll call you until you have a name. Angel.

Around eleven that night, the Mayor announced that the Armory would close at midnight and reopen tomorrow at nine. There were still seventy or eighty bodies left unclaimed, mostly the charred ones. The queue of people had thinned a little, so Lieutenant Keene helped himself to a doughnut and coffee that the Red Cross had provided. He chatted with the nurses on duty, and watched the dentist examine the corpses in the back, making careful notes of each one's teeth to aid identification. The dentist had a cold, professional air, but Lieutenant Keene suspected he'd have nightmares later.

We all will, he thought. He pulled up a chair near the little angel and wiped his face with the handkerchief, trying not to think.

A young man, pale and drawn, came in. "I'm looking for my daughter," he said to one of the nurses. She was five years old. Brown hair. No, he didn't know what she was wearing. She had gone to the circus with her mother, who was in Municipal Hospital right now with burns all over her body. His wife and child had been pushed apart by the panicked crowd, and his wife had run back into the inferno to look for her. It took three men to forcibly drag her out before she perished. He had checked all over the city, with neighbors and relatives, looking for his daughter, and now he was here.

Lieutenant Keene took him to the area where the children were. Again, blankets were lifted, faces studied, scraps of fabric examined. Finally they came to the angel.

He studied the man's face, comparing it to the angel's face. The angel's hair was lighter, but they both had long, dark eyelashes. He thought the shape of the faces was similar too.

The man looked down at the angel. His eyes widened slightly, and he swayed on his feet.

"How old is this one?" he asked.

"The doctor says four or five." The lieutenant pulled the blanket down a little, to show the pink-and-white sundress on her untouched shoulders. "See the dress?"

The man stared, and his face contracted. Ever so subtly, he shook his head.

Lieutenant Keene watched him closely, wondering if the man was going to break down.

"No," he said softly.

"Beg your pardon?"

"No. No, that's not her. Certainly not." The man squared his shoulders and walked away. Lieutenant Keene silently watched him leave.

Wonder what he'll tell his wife, he thought. *Will he tell her it's easier to believe their daughter is missing than dead?*

"Angel, I'm sorry," he whispered to the little corpse. "So, so sorry."

He never returned. No one claimed the girl, and days later Lieutenant Keene put a bouquet of pink roses on her small white casket as she was lowered into an unmarked grave.

"Sleep well, angel," he said. But no one heard him.

HOLLY NEWSTEIN's short fiction has appeared in *Cemetery Dance Magazine* and the anthologies *Borderlands 5*, *The New Dead*, *In Laymon's Terms*, and *Epitaphs: The Journal of the New England Horror Writers*. Her recent story "Kristall Tag" is featured in *Evil Jester Digest* vol. 2.

SCOTT CHRISTIAN CARR

ATLHEA:
AN OPEN LETTER FROM HIRAM GRANGE TO HIS CHILDE LOST ...

Dearest, little Atlhea ...

Your mommy—
—she loved you so very much. Wanted you so very, very much ...
And your daddy ...

(Hitler!)

Your Daddy is in Old San Juan,
Drinking the monsters away ...

Your Daddy is in Peru, fighting the monsters, keeping them at bay ...

Now your Daddy is in Chernobyl,
Staring into the abyss ...
(the confluence)
... and realizing that the wasteland you left in his soul
dwarfs every other wasteland on the planet ...

Futilely wishing to undecide the worst decision
any father ever made ...

The monsters ... Oh, Atlhea. The monsters are memories.

True fact:
In my imagination, you have bows in your hair.

The absinthe doesn't wash away the weight on my shoulders,
the heaviness in my heart, the emptiness of my soul ...

The opium won't erase the questions that will never be asked,
Why is the sky blue, Daddy?

True fact:
In my dreams, in my imagination, in some alternate,
abyssal, other-reality ...
Daddy dares enough to hope, to believe,
That his little girl is alive and well, prepping for her prom ...
And Daddy is bracing himself to not hate her date ...

But here and now, Daddy is filling the void with memories
and monsters, absinthe and anger ... And you are not here.
Never were ...

Daddy is doomed—ever fighting the battle that he already lost,
all those years ago ...

Sitting in a *Hooters Bar & Grill* on Easter Sunday ...
This is my penance, my self-flagellation, my cross to bear,
My sacrilege, my shame—
Breasts and booze and self-loathing,
Traded for baskets and Easter grass ...
My undoing ...

True fact:
In my dreams you smile and kiss me on the cheek before
I give you away at your wedding ...

Daddy loves his little girl.
And in my memory,
Forever,
The letters of your name ...
A T L H E A ...

and they lived happily ever after ...
—H. G.

WWW.ANTHOCON.COM